Juneau Black

Mockingbird Court

Juneau Black is the pen name of authors Jocelyn Cole and Sharon Nagel. They share a love of excellent bookshops, fine cheeses, and a good murder (in fictional form only). Though they are two separate people, if you ask either one a question about her childhood, you are likely to get the same answer. This is a little unnerving for any number of reasons.

ALSO BY JUNEAU BLACK

THE SHADY HOLLOW MYSTERY SERIES
Shady Hollow
Cold Clay
Mirror Lake
Twilight Falls
Summers End

SHADY HOLLOW HOLIDAY SHORT STORIES
Evergreen Chase (eBook only)
Phantom Pond (eBook only)

Mockingbird Court

Mockingbird Court

A SHADY HOLLOW MYSTERY

Juneau Black

VINTAGE BOOKS

A Division of Penguin Random House LLC

New York

Published by Vintage Books, a division of Penguin Random House LLC, 1745 Broadway, New York, NY 10019.

Vintage and colophon are registered trademarks of Penguin Random House LLC.

Library of Congress Cataloging-in-Publication Data
Names: Black, Juneau, author.
Title: Mockingbird Court / Juneau Black.
Description: First Vintage Books edition. | New York : Vintage Books, a division of Penguin Random House, 2025. | Series: A Shady Hollow mystery; [6]. | Summary: "In the latest installment in the beloved Shady Hollow series, everyone's favorite vulpine investigator Vera Vixen must contend with a cold-hearted killer—and the ghost of her own past"—Provided by publisher.
Identifiers: LCCN 2025005871 | ISBN 9780593470558 (trade paperback) | ISBN 9780593470565 (ebook)
Subjects: LCGFT: Cozy mysteries. | Animal fiction. | Novels.
Classification: LCC PS3602.L293 M63 2025 | DDC 813/.6—dc23/eng/20250313
LC record available at https://lccn.loc.gov/2025005871

Vintage Books Trade Paperback ISBN: 978-0-593-47055-8
eBook ISBN: 978-0-593-47056-5

Book design by Christopher Zucker

penguinrandomhouse.com | vintagebooks.com

Printed in the United States of America
2nd Printing

The authorized representative in the EU for product safety and compliance is Penguin Random House Ireland, Morrison Chambers, 32 Nassau Street, Dublin D02 YH68, Ireland, https://eu-contact.penguin.ie.

For everyone who packs an extra book, just in case

Author's Note

You are about to travel into a world not like our own, which is, of course, one of the most wonderful aspects of books. If you have not visited Shady Hollow before, we must advise you that you may marvel at some of what you discover. Is it possible that so many animals could live next to each other, paw to paw, wing to wing, and yet find it all harmonious and fruitful? Is it possible that a wolf walks among sheep in a civilized manner? Is it possible for a shrew to share a meal with a buck without considerable awkwardness involving silverware? It is possible, and what's more, it is happening now, in the pages ahead. Leave your questions, bring your curiosity, and be welcomed to Shady Hollow.

Cast of Characters

Vera Vixen: A cunning, foxy reporter with a nose for trouble and a desire to find out the truth, no matter where the path leads.

Lenore Lee: This dark-as-night raven runs the town's bookshop, Nevermore Books, and has a penchant for mysteries.

Lefty: A masked raccoon who prefers to be the only criminal of note in Shady Hollow.

Chief Orville Braun: This large brown bear is the Shady Hollow constabulary. He works by the book. But his book has half the pages ripped out.

Bradley Marvel: A famous, fedora-wearing author of thrillers. The wolf's sudden arrival in Shady Hollow hints of twists and turns to come.

Darcy Montrose: The lynx is Bradley's coolly competent assistant, though that title hardly scratches the surface of all that she does for her boss.

Richard Renard: This fox considered himself a mover and shaker in the city. Unfortunately, he never considered what would happen when he made the wrong move and shook the wrong creature.

Priscilla Renard: Richard's elegant and wealthy wife, who proves difficult to find when officials want to question her.

Geoffrey and Ben Eastwood: This hospitable chipmunk couple operate the local bed-and-breakfast, a boon for city-dwellers arriving in haste.

Walter Fallow: Mirror Lake's beloved local lawyer has a proprietary interest in any legal cases in his domain.

Wendell Knox: This bison is a detective with the metropolitan police, and he follows the trail of suspects to Shady Hollow. But he has his own theories about who's responsible.

Chloe McKibben: An old friend from Vera's school days, this cat is now a respected attorney in the city whom Vera calls upon for aid.

BW Stone: The cigar-chomping skunk is the editor in chief of the Shady Hollow *Herald*, and he believes that bad news makes for good sales.

Joe Elkin: A genial giant of a moose who runs the town coffee shop, the local gathering spot. If news is happening, Joe has heard it.

Gladys Honeysuckle: The hummingbird is the queen of gossip in Shady Hollow, and she'll flit her way into everybody's secrets to get the juiciest bits.

Sun Li: This panda is a former surgeon and current chef. He runs the Bamboo Patch, serving mouthwatering meals and exquisite tea.

Barry Greenfield: A senior reporter at the *Herald*. The old hare has the cynicism of long experience, and he never misses a trick.

Ambrosius Heidegger: This owl is a professor of philosophy and a bit of a know-it-all, but he's always got snacks.

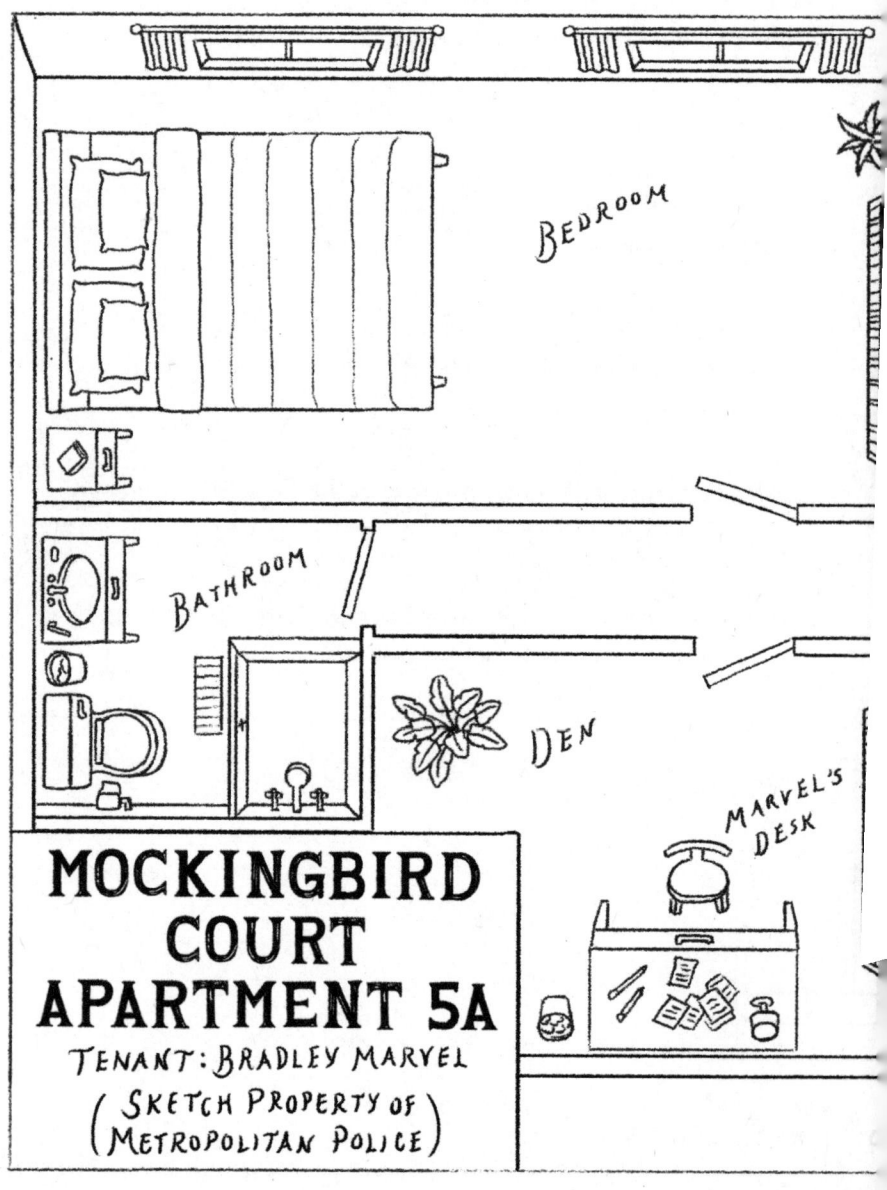

BEDROOM

BATHROOM

DEN

MARVEL'S DESK

MOCKINGBIRD
COURT
APARTMENT 5A
TENANT: BRADLEY MARVEL
(SKETCH PROPERTY OF)
(METROPOLITAN POLICE)

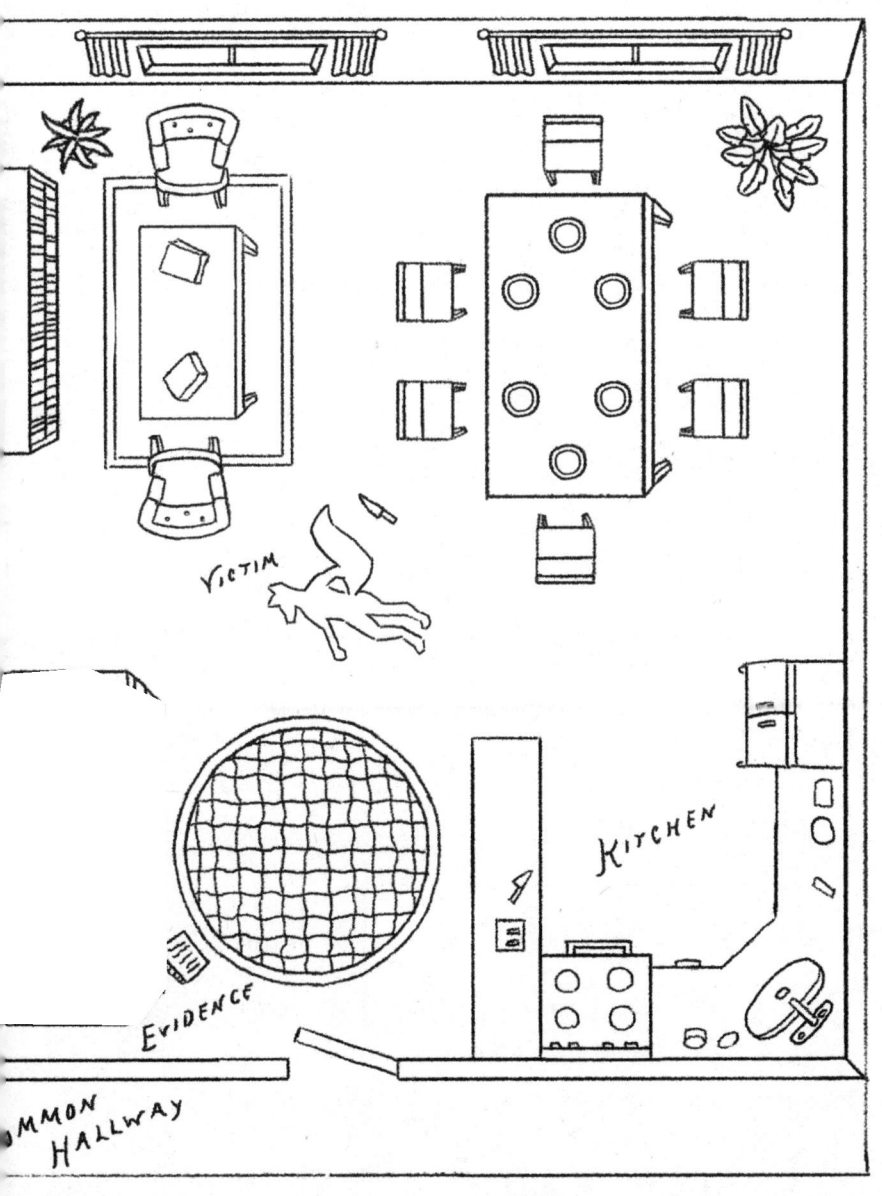

Mockingbird Court

Chapter 1

The ferry steamed upriver, cutting through the blue waves at a steady pace. Vera Vixen stood along the side rail, gazing at the trees passing by. Most were still the deep green of summer, but some had started to change colors, revealing their autumn glory. A few leaves dropped from a maple branch overhanging the river, bright spots of gold swirling in the ripples, carried into the ferry's wake. The fox smiled to see it, thinking that the leaves were almost like coins scattered over the blue silk of the water.

The woodlands were beautiful at any time of year, but fall was her favorite season. There was just something special about the cool, crisp breezes and the brilliance of the sky, and the way that the ever-shortening days seemed so precious and fleeting.

It inspired a creature to enjoy them to the fullest and not think too much about the coming cold.

The gentle scenery was such a change from the city, where she'd boarded the ferry. The city was all clash and hustle, with boats moving every which way on the busy bay where this river met with two others. The confluence brought together creatures from north, west, and south at a point along the eastern sea. It was a natural gathering spot and thus no surprise that creatures settled there and built it from a tiny village to the thriving metropolis it was today. The sheer numbers of inhabitants meant that buildings stretched taller than anywhere else, with birds nesting on the top floors, many mammals and others occupying the lower parts, and basements and subbasements dug for those who preferred to dwell underground.

It was invigorating and inspiring . . . until it was exhausting. On the ferry ride home, Vera watched with relief as the city's skyline shrank in the distance. She greeted each larger patch of farmland and forest with glee, knowing that the woodlands awaited her.

Under her paws, Vera felt a shift in momentum. The ferry slowed to a stop at Elm Grove, just downriver from Shady Hollow. Vera sighed, filled with that particular impatience of one who is near the end of a long journey.

Luckily, the stop would not take long. Several passengers disembarked, carrying traveling cases and knapsacks. Two rabbits hopped excitedly upon greeting each other on the dock, ears flapping. Some of those departing called cheerful farewells to creatures still on the ferry—a testament to those rare and fleeting friendships that arose when good folks traveled together, however briefly. The workers on the ferry, mostly otters and river rats, gently encouraged everyone to clear the dock so that they could cast off the lines and proceed upriver.

Just as the boat was pushing away, a gray shape rushed along the dock, aiming for the ferry.

"Wait for meeeeee!" the figure called in a frantic tone.

Vera knew that voice, and almost instinctively she looked to where the creature had come from. Sure enough, a small group of townsfolk were already giving chase, yelling, "Stop, thief!"

But it was too late. The thief in question leaped aboard, skidding to a halt only a short distance from Vera.

"Lefty," she said, offering a paw to help the raccoon up.

"Oh, hey, Vera," he replied. Then he turned anxiously to check the progress of his pursuers. They'd halted at the edge of the dock, exchanging tense words with the otter who'd cast off the last line.

"Sorry, we can't back up," the otter shouted over the increasing distance. "We're on a schedule!"

"You've got a thief on board!"

"You mean Lefty? I'll make sure he pays for a ticket!"

The sheep who'd been the lead pursuer bleated, "I don't care about the ticket. I care about my laundry!"

"I didn't take your silly sheets!" Lefty shouted, joining the argument. "It was a misunderstanding! Go back home and I'm sure you'll find the sheets . . . unless someone stole them!"

The sheep stomped angry hooves on the ground, then wheeled about and retreated to the scene of the crime (*alleged* crime). The two remaining pursuers, a stoat and a rabbit, just looked at each other and shrugged.

"Okay, I guess that's it," the rabbit called, conceding defeat in the chase.

"You can always send word to the police in Shady Hollow!" the otter called back.

"But also, don't bother!" Lefty added helpfully, peeking over the rail, his paws clutching the sturdy wooden side.

The dock shrank in the distance as the ferry chugged onward. Vera turned to Lefty. "So, did you steal those sheets?"

"Of course not!" The raccoon sounded appalled at the very notion. "I stole some high-grade honey and used the sheets to hide the loot!" He lifted a bag, clanking from the glass jars of illicit stickiness within.

Vera shook her head, not surprised at the petty thief's antics but still a little shocked by the cheek of him denying one theft only to announce another.

"Aw, come on," said Lefty. "Do you even know how much of this stuff Mr. Bell hoards? He won't miss it, and there's plenty of folks who appreciate a fine sweetener and are willing to pay for it. I say let the market decide. I facilitate transactions, that's all."

Vera sighed. "If I wasn't so tired from my trip, I would argue this point, Lefty. But I just can't."

"Aw, sorry, Vera. You do look a bit tuckered out." To his credit, Lefty did seem legitimately concerned. "What happened?"

"Oh, nothing in particular," the fox replied. "I had some business in the city, and I spent time with an old school friend. Do you happen to remember years ago, how there was a proposal to build a bridge across the river at Crooked Neck?"

"Yep. It was supposed to make it easier to access the western shore over there and get all the lumber and ore and crops to the city ports more quickly. But then it didn't happen. Wasn't there something about the span being too dangerous?"

"That's exactly what I want to find out," she said. "All the reasons for the project's failure were contradictory and very mysterious. Anyway, I spoke to the architect, who's living in the city. I had other research to do, too . . . and you know how chaotic it can be down there. The ferry ride back is always longer than you think."

This was not just a weary traveler's lament. The return trip to Shady Hollow actually did take longer than the ride downriver since the ferry had to compete against the current.

"That's true," the raccoon agreed. "But at least you didn't have half the city police force on your tail! Happened to me once, and whew! There's a reason they hire cheetahs as beat cops, you know?"

Not being in the same line of work as Lefty, Vera hadn't thought about it until now, but she conceded it would make running away difficult.

Lefty added, "It pays to know about the tunnels, is all I'm saying."

Vera decided to steer the conversation in a different direction. "What's this week's pie at Joe's?" she asked, going with the first thing that popped into her head.

"Candied apple pecan," Lefty replied instantly. "Real, real good."

Maybe she'd stop at Joe's before she even went to her own home. A slice of pie and a cup of hot coffee sounded like just the thing. Though the trip hadn't been terribly long, she had been hurrying from the moment she woke to the time she curled up in bed. That was city life, and when she was younger, it had all felt incredibly exciting and fun. But after living in the sedate woodlands up north for a while, she couldn't imagine ever moving back to the hustle of the city. She'd come to prefer the slower pace and the friendliness of the small towns along the river, especially Shady Hollow . . . which should be coming into view any moment now.

River traffic was heavier than usual, and Vera remembered that the Harvest Festival must be imminent. Or had it already started?

"Lefty, did I miss any of the Harvest Festival?"

"Oh, no, it doesn't officially begin for a few days. But folks are getting ready for it. Lots of visitors . . . who should want to buy *honey*," he added, rubbing his paws together in anticipation.

"Assuming you're still at large and able to peddle your ill-gotten gains," she warned him. "But I'm glad I made it back in time. I love the Harvest Festival." Who wouldn't? It was a week-long event that celebrated the very best aspects of the season, often in edible form.

Her belly growling at the mere thought, Vera remained at the rail for the rest of the trip. She could scarcely keep her paws still on the deck planks.

It was hard to say where the wilderness ended and civilization began. Vera watched the parade of trees—green, green, yellow, orange, green again, and a shock of scarlet—go by without a break. But then a small building poked out amid the colors, no more than a modest cabin. And then another building, and then two, and then she was no longer looking at a few outposts within the forest; she was looking at scattered trees within a growing town. *Her* town.

Docks and jetties poked into the water, and the buildings drew closer together, nestling along the shoreline. She saw familiar signs for boat repair shops, the local pub, and more. Each one felt like a friendly greeting. Funny how even a short time away could make one feel so strongly about returning home!

At last, the ferry approached the main dock in Shady Hollow. Creatures gathered near to greet relatives and friends. The otter crew guided the boat to its slip with the ease of long practice, and Vera gathered her traveling case and satchel, lining up with the other passengers to disembark.

On the dock, Lefty waved goodbye to Vera and dashed off with his bulky sack. Vera walked at a slower pace, enjoying the autumnal touches that were beginning to appear everywhere she looked. Wreaths made of wheat sheaves adorned with fabric ribbon had been hung on windows, bright gourds were tucked away in doorways, and (quite frequently) little wooden crates perched on stoops, all holding beautiful displays made from excess crops from backyard gardens. She saw bunches of herbs, long green and yellow squashes, windfall apples, and piles of chestnuts. Most of these boxes also bore a sign with some variation of GREW TOO MUCH! PLEASE TAKE! At one stoop, Vera secured a late tomato and a small bunch of basil, excellent sandwich components for later.

However, a snack would have to wait. She had a duty as a citizen to report what she had seen of Lefty, so she headed for the police station on Main Street—a small but handsome, red-brick building under a stand of oaks that were turning golden, branch by branch. She knew the place well, so she opened the unlocked door herself, calling out, "Orville? You here?"

All was quiet.

"Are you here if I call you Chief Braun?" she added with a laugh. Ever since Vera and Orville had become—in the words of the gossip column—an *item*, she found it fun to tease him about his title.

However, Chief Orville Braun wasn't there, no matter what name she called him. He must have been out on some errand.

She refused to believe that he was responding to a crime, because Shady Hollow generally didn't have any of that . . . especially when Lefty was out of town.

Vera ripped a page from her notebook and scrawled: *Lefty liberated honey from Mr. Bell (sheep) in Elm Grove. Pursue case?—Vera*

She placed it carefully on the top center of Orville's desk. Orville would understand the note, and if the sheep ever did discover the missing honey and decide to press charges, at least Orville knew the score.

Then she got an idea and wrote a second note: *Dinner soon? I missed you!* That one she didn't sign, only drawing a little heart at the bottom (like any good reporter, Vera believed in protecting her sources, especially when her source was herself).

After putting the second note by the first, she left the station and paused on the sidewalk. She could stop by Joe's Mug and avail herself of pie—her larder was never overflowing, and she wouldn't have much to eat at home until she managed to pick up more food at Brocket's Foods.

Drawn by the sounds of several voices, Vera walked toward the park in front of Shady Hollow's town hall. Always a pretty little spot, it was in the process of being dressed up for the festival. A pair of pigeons grasped a large canvas banner with their feet as they rose into the air, timing their wingbeats to keep the banner untangled. Vera read the words on it as the pigeons worked quickly to tie each corner to a sturdy branch of maple.

SHADY HOLLOW HARVEST FESTIVAL

COME ONE—COME ALL

TALENT SHOW—SOUP CONTEST—LIVE THEATER—SACK RACES

PUMPKIN-CARVING CONTEST—SAWMILL SOIREE

"Plenty of activities to cover for the newspaper, eh, Vera?"

She turned to see Mayor Windthrow fluttering down beside her. The ptarmigan looked harried at the best of times, but now his feathers seemed especially ruffled. He went on, "I hope we didn't overdo it with the schedule this year, but I couldn't abide turning any idea down!"

"The live theater is new, right?" Vera asked. "I don't remember seeing a play last fall."

"It is new! The Shady Hollow Players are doing a single scene from each play of the upcoming season. I hear Callie's soliloquy from *Across the Pond* is going to leave everyone in stitches."

Vera smiled thinking of her friend Callie Standish, the director of the Players and a talented actor. The vole was tiny in stature, but Vera had no doubt she'd command the attention of the whole audience the moment she set her paw on the stage.

"I'll have to be sure to come early to get a good seat for that," she said.

"I do hope the *Herald* plans to cover the festival! You know how much the events mean for the town," Mayor Windthrow said, swiveling his head left and right to survey the preparations. He raised a wing to catch the attention of the pigeons. "You there! The banner is too low on the right side! Pull it up! *Up!* Thank you!"

"I should let you get back to work," Vera said, edging away from the distraught ptarmigan. She figured if she stuck around, she'd be volunteered to hang garland or polish apples. Thinking of the mayor's words, Vera knew she ought to drop by the newspaper office and find out if she'd been assigned to any festival events in particular. BW Stone, the editor in chief, had surely discussed the matter with the mayor since both creatures were

firmly committed to success in all its forms. In BW's case, success was defined by the number of newspapers sold, so there
was no doubt the skunk would be calling for stories from all his
reporters.

Yes, it would be prudent to speak with BW.

But not till tomorrow!

Vera made her way to her own little house, a comfy den
made for exactly one professional journalist. She loved it so, for
it was hers. Opening the door (residents did not typically lock
them), Vera smiled to see all her familiar things. The teakettle
on the stovetop, the slightly saggy upholstered reading chair by
the fireplace, the books carefully lined up on the shelves. She
dropped her bags near the foyer and looked over the main room.

The shorter days and the lower sun meant less warmth filling the home, and there was also that ineffable chill of "empty
house" . . . which can be fully dispelled by the glow of firelight
or a friendly voice.

Thinking that perhaps Orville might stop by later, Vera
decided that a quick visit to the grocery was in order. She would
need to offer more than basil and tomato!

She switched out her travel-worn coat for her favorite green-
felt jacket and left once more. On the way, she met with several
friends and townsfolk who remarked on her absence. She gave
them the glossy version of her trip to the city (many Shady Hollow residents had never even been there, and it remained a sort
of distant, abstract idea for them).

Just as the sun was dropping below the mountaintop to the
west, Vera returned to her home, burdened with two bags
chock-full of groceries. The Brockets always carried the fresh-
est produce and the finest snacks and cheeses—it was difficult to
stop in without buying a little more than expected.

Back at home, Vera got a fire going, and the glow soon per-meated the front room, which had grown dusky and dim. She set about unpacking the food, then turned to her suitcase.

"Always unpack first. Do you want wrinkled clothes to be your souvenir?" Vera said under her breath, mimicking her mother's tone. But habits are habits, so unpack she did.

After her outfits and her toiletries were put away, she retrieved the signed copy of a chapbook of poetry and read the inscription once more: *To Vera—You're a lifesaver. Keats Loring.*

She smiled to herself, thinking of the eccentric poet she'd only recently met. Seeing him in the city had been a nice diversion from her errands there. She was glad to know that he was doing well, and he'd been quite happy to offer her the poems, which were so new that few other creatures had even read them.

"Put this in a safe place, Vera," the peacock had told her as he signed the book. "I really think it's going to be big, and that's a first edition, first printing, you know."

She slid the chapbook onto a shelf, where it would remain undisturbed. "Good luck, Keats," she murmured.

Next, she pulled out a small, framed photograph of two creatures: a distinctly younger Vera standing beside a gray-and-white feline. Both were smiling like fools. Vera put the frame on a shelf as well, regarding the image. "Seems so long ago, Chloe," she said to the cat in the picture.

Chloe was an old friend whom Vera had also visited while in the city. In fact, it had been Chloe who gave her the picture. The two friends had reminisced about their glory days well into the wee hours. Chloe had been a busy law student while Vera pursued journalism, but the two had always gotten along and found endless topics to discuss while they lived together as room-mates. Vera hadn't seen her friend in years, but knowing that she would be in the city to conduct some interviews, she found Chloe's name in the directory and sent a letter. She wasn't sure if the cat would respond, considering how long it had been.

Vera was touched when she received a reply only a few days later. Chloe's prose was like a warm blanket: full of reminiscences *and* a demand that the two get together for dinner, Chloe's treat. Much like she did in their school days, Chloe had supplied a full page complete with a schedule for Vera, including notes on the changes in transportation up- and downtown, and the best coffee on the way.

Settling down in her comfy chair, Vera smiled at the picture. Chloe had been overjoyed to reconnect, despite the fact that it had been Vera who abruptly left the city one day, without an explanation or excuse to Chloe (or indeed, anyone). It hadn't been Vera's finest hour, so she was glad to learn her friend had not been too put out.

Vera yawned. Maybe sitting had been a mistake, for she was exhausted! She ought to get up . . . but the fire was warm and the chair so soft. Her eyes slid closed for just a moment.

When a log in the fireplace snapped, the fox's eyes flew open. The sky beyond the windows was almost totally dark now and the interior full of thick shadows. The fire had burned low, and she hadn't lit any lamps.

She heard another snapping sound. But wait, that hadn't come from the fireplace.

Suddenly alert, Vera stood up, peering toward the door. "Orville? Is that you?" she asked, knowing it wasn't since her beau wasn't known for his subtlety. "Is someone there?"

Then a deep, ragged voice issued from somewhere in the darkness.

"Vixen, I've been looking for you."

Chapter 2

Vera yelped in shock and leaped up from her comfy chair.
"Who's there?" she demanded, moving fast. "Why are you in my house?"

Vera got to the door and flung it open. The last of the day's light flowed in, illuminating the inside and lightening the darkest corners. A large creature stepped forward, clad in a trench coat and fedora.

The wolf grinned wide, showing sharp white teeth. "It's me! Your old friend Bradley!"

Shock was replaced with confusion. "Bradley Marvel?" she said, trying to fathom why this creature of all the potential creatures in the world should be here in her living room.

"The one and only!" he said, with overly forced cheer. "I

thought, hey, it's been a while since I've been to that cute lit-tle Shady Hollow and visited that cute little Vera Vixen. So, surprise!"

Vera didn't loosen her hold on the doorknob—she might have to flee at any moment. It had been well over a year since Bradley Marvel had last visited town as part of a book tour (a tour that unfortunately coincided with a local murder). Marvel had made such a pest of himself during Vera's investigation that she had more or less forced him to leave under cover of darkness.

She never expected to see the blowhard thriller author again, and certainly not here. She said, "First, we aren't friends. Sec-ond, last time you were here, you were told to leave Shady Hol-low and never come back. And third, never call me cute. Not if you want to live long."

"Well, about that," he said, holding up his forepaws in a con-ciliatory manner. "It's just that . . . things have kind of changed. I mean . . . some stuff has happened. To me."

"So?" Vera held the door open with her hind paw and crossed her upper limbs. She wanted to lash her tail but knew that it would reveal how much he'd frightened her a moment ago. "I cannot imagine caring even a little bit what happens to you."

"Aw, come on, after all we've been through together?"

"I met you *once,* and you were in town for a grand total of a week."

He looked wounded. "But I helped you solve a murder!"

"You just got in the way," she corrected. "So, what's your real reason for bothering me again?"

"Well, uh, I've got a little problem."

"More than one, but that's a matter for your therapist. Of which there are many in the city, so again . . . Why—are—you—here?"

"I need your help!" Bradley burst out. "It's bad, Vera. It's a total misunderstanding, but it looks bad, and no one's going to let me tell my side of the story! I need a real reporter, see? A crack journalist with an eye for the truth, a nose for clues, a sense of justice!"

Vera knew desperation when she heard it, but dang it if she wasn't also just a little bit curious now. "What did you do?"

"Nothing! I swear I'm completely innocent!"

"Innocent of what?"

"Murder! Just because a body shows up in my apartment, everyone just assumes *I'm* the killer! I barely even knew the poor sap!" Bradley shrugged as if this were a common conundrum everybody could relate to, yet she could see the nervous pacing, the way he sniffed the air, as if scenting for danger.

"You've been accused of murder?" she asked.

"Well, not officially." He got a sheepish expression (which is particularly disconcerting to see on a wolf). "I sort of left the city before I could be accused. Or at least arrested."

Vera groaned, closing her eyes as if that could make Bradley disappear. Alas, when she opened them again, he was still there. She said, "You need to go to the police, and then you need to get a lawyer. I'm neither of those things, so please just leave my house right now." She stepped aside and made a sweeping gesture to encourage him to get out.

But Bradley stood there, fidgeting. "If I do that, I'll just get thrown in jail. I can't let that happen! I'm meant to *live free*, Vera."

"Well, if you didn't kill anyone, then I'm sure you'll be fine. Besides, what else could you do? Hide out for the rest of your life?"

"I could live here!"

"No."

"Not in your house," he said. "I meant I could live in Shady Hollow. Folks would probably be really impressed to run into me all the time."

"Bradley, do you not understand what it means to be on the run from the law? You can't tell anyone who you are. Not *anyone*," Vera added bleakly.

He frowned. "That is sort of a drawback. From a publicity perspective."

"You can't be serious."

"No, I can't, because when I think about it all, it's so serious I get heart palpitations." Bradley had never looked so miserable. "Please, Vera, I need help. I will pay you to investigate the crime. Prove me innocent!"

"I'm a reporter, not a private detective. Leave the investigation to the cops."

"Yeah, because that always works out so well," Bradley said with a snort.

"Look, I'll walk you to the police station, and we'll ask Chief Braun to send word to the city cops. Maybe you can convince them that you didn't deliberately flee justice."

He followed her out of the house, apparently content to be herded. "I think you're really being unreasonable about this, Vera. You can be a reporter, but in a freelance way . . . just this once. Think of how famous you'll become once you write the exposé piece about how I was unjustly accused of murder, a hapless victim of a broken and corrupt system. A noble hero! Do you think we should use the same photo that's on my books, or should I pose for a new one, maybe in profile? How's this?" He tilted his snout up as if he were about to howl at the moon.

Vera didn't answer, grimly counting the steps to the station and wondering just how one creature could talk so much with such a lack of audience.

"Look, sorry," he said, trailing after her again. "I take refuge in humor. A lot of rugged, solitary, heroic types do."

"Why is this happening to me?" Vera muttered to herself. She *really* hoped Orville would be back by the time they got there. Of course, she could probably trick Bradley into a cell just to keep him in one spot. She had no idea if he'd actually committed a crime, but she definitely didn't want to set him loose on her little town.

As they walked, Vera noticed more signs for the upcoming Harvest Festival and realized that the large number of attendees meant lots of folks would potentially see Bradley Marvel. Goodness, was it the worst possible time for a creature to choose to "hide out" in Shady Hollow?

Luckily, this time the police station door was wide open. She hurried inside, pulling Bradley along.

"Orville! Got someone very important to see you!" she announced.

"Vera, I got your notes . . . bad and good!" The big brown bear looked up with a warm smile . . . which quickly evaporated when he saw who was with her. "Who let *him* back into town?" he growled.

"I chartered a private boat," Bradley said, which was interesting information, though not actually what Orville was asking.

"Huh. Why don't you charter one right back to where you came from, then." Orville stood up from his desk, displaying his formidable size, nearly double the wolf's stature.

"Mr. Marvel here made a rather silly mistake," explained Vera. "Can you send word to the city police headquarters that he's here, but not at all because he was an idiot trying to flee from law enforcement and, oh yes, he really would be so happy to answer any questions the investigating officer might have regarding a possible murder in Marvel's apartment?"

Orville's eyes widened. "I know you write thrillers, but that seems a bit extreme for research."

"I didn't do it!" Bradley protested once more. "It's all a big mistake. I think someone's trying to frame me."

"Well, it's out of my jurisdiction," the bear replied, with relief. "But I'll send a wingmail. Let's see," he muttered, scrawling on a sheet of paper. "Be advised: Bradley Marvel of . . . what's your address in the city?"

The wolf said, "47 Mockingbird Court, unit 5A. It's the penthouse," he added proudly and puffed out his chest.

Orville made a rude noise, filling out the rest of the paper with the information the city police would need. Then he put the pen down. "I'll send this right now, and an officer should be here in a day or two to take your statement and see you back to your penthouse . . . or the big house. In the meantime, I strongly advise you to stay in town and make yourself quite easy to find."

"Yes, Chief," Bradley agreed, looking a bit calmer now, perhaps because Orville hadn't arrested him on sight. "Is that little hotel still around?"

"Bramblebriar Bed and Breakfast? Yes, it is," Vera said. She hoped that the inn's proprietors, Geoffrey and Ben, had rooms available—but considering what a pill Marvel had been the last time he was in town, they might not want him as a guest.

"Good. My assistant will be here soon, too, probably sometime tomorrow," Bradley said. "She'll need a room as well."

"You didn't tell the cops you were coming here, but you told your assistant?" Orville asked, incredulous.

"Well, somebody had to pack my bags, didn't they?" Bradley said. "She's probably on the next ferry."

Vera knew the schedule since her work often required her to travel to towns up- and downriver. "That'll arrive tomorrow morning then. Anyone else that you've got showing up in our town?"

"Er, no. Darcy's the only one I told. She was with me when I found the body. Completely ruined the carpet in my living room. The body did, I mean. Not Darcy. She's very tidy. *Excellent* assistant."

"So, there was a lot of blood?" Vera asked, focusing on that rather upsetting detail.

"Whoever killed him was thorough about it. I don't know why they chose my apartment though. Or how. Mockingbird Court has security. You'd think they would have kept the riffraff out of the lobby, let alone the rest of the building."

"Could have been a bungled robbery," Orville guessed, obviously still interested despite the crime not being in his territory. "One thief could have gotten angry at their partner, and it got violent. Though in that case, I don't know why you wouldn't have just notified the police."

"The police were already on their way," Bradley said. "My neighbors heard a ruckus and told the building supervisor. Plus, the door was left open, apparently, so everyone who came by could see the crime scene for themselves. Very bad for my image, you know. I just couldn't stick around."

Vera frowned. "I still don't understand. If it was just a random robbery or whatever, why would it reflect badly on you?

Everyone who's lived in the city could tell you a story of some crime that they experienced. At most, there would be an article in the paper because you're a well-known author. But it's just a coincidence."

"Well . . ." Bradley looked away.

Orville put his paws on the desk, anticipating the worst. "Oh, no."

"He was my editor at the publishing house. But he still had no business being in my place when I wasn't there!"

Vera groaned. "You ran away from a murder scene where you *knew* the victim? What were you thinking?"

"He wasn't thinking," Orville said flatly. He glared at Bradley. "I ought to keep you in a jail cell till they come to collect you! You neglected to explain that you're not only a witness; you're a suspect."

"But I shouldn't be! I wasn't even there! Darcy can confirm it. She was with me all evening."

"If that's true, why didn't you just tell that to the cops in the city?" The big bear's voice had grown louder with each word.

The wolf fidgeted in his seat, his paws crumpling the brim of his fedora. "Er, well, it's awkward, because I did have a bit of a fight with him the day before. Some folks might get the wrong idea. But I didn't kill him!"

Orville took a deep breath. "Listen. I'm going to send this wingmail. And Vera is going to walk Mr. Marvel over to the bed-and-breakfast to get a room, where he will stay until I order him otherwise."

"Um, can I eat first?" Bradley asked. "The boat didn't have meal service."

"Fine," Orville snapped. "Go to Joe's on the way. I'll join you there after I'm done at the message service, so don't try anything funny."

"Don't take too long, *darling*," Vera told Orville, with a pleading glance. The last thing she wanted was to be alone with Bradley for any amount of time longer than necessary.

She marched out of the station and down the street, Bradley Marvel in her wake. Residents took notice of the wolf, who'd snapped back into the confident attitude he used as a "world-famous thriller writer." He grinned at everyone, showing off sparkling white canines. When a squirrel excitedly called his name from across the street, he waved as though he were a one-wolf parade. Only Vera knew how false the facade really was.

Thankfully, Joe's Mug wasn't far, and Vera hustled her charge inside. The diner was cozy at any time of day, but in the evening, it was almost magical. Warm light spilled from the lamps hanging above every booth and table. The wooden surfaces of the pine tables and chairs glowed gold thanks to dutiful oiling and the many paws that had eaten there over the years. By the long wooden counter, a glass case displayed the daily desserts on offer, and a couple of young mice were squeaking excitedly as they pointed out the items they wanted most.

And the smells, oh the smells. Vera inhaled and caught the friendly aroma of coffee, and then the delicious scents of baked bread, the oil of the fryer, and the sharp, fresh tang of autumn fruits. Yes, she could endure Bradley's presence, as long as she was at Joe's!

It was fairly crowded with early dinner guests, so she deliberately chose a booth in the far corner, away from the windows. With luck, Bradley could resist the limelight for a half hour.

Moments later, a beaver waddled up to the table in a checked dress with a white apron. It was Esme, the harder-working half of the von Beaverpelt twins.

"What can I get for you, Vera?" Esme asked brightly, taking out her order pad.

"I'll take a coffee for sure," Vera said. "What's the dinner special?"

"It's a root vegetable stew with a side of rosemary rolls."

"Yes, that's fine, thanks, Esme."

"And for you, sir?" Esme's tone was polite but not deferential, and Vera couldn't tell if the beaver even knew who Bradley was.

Bradley perused the menu and proceeded to order the harvest loaf sandwich with a side of mashed potatoes and glazed carrots, plus lentil soup and an extra roll. "And coffee too. And maybe just a couple of doughnuts? Great."

Esme left to put in their order.

"It might be one of my last meals as a free beast," he said defensively to Vera. "Besides, I really am hungry."

"All right, Bradley," Vera said while they were waiting for their food to arrive. "Tell me what's going on."

The wolf sighed dramatically. "It's the curse of being famous, Vera. You're a small-town reporter; you wouldn't understand."

"Bradley, I lived in the city for years before I moved here. I was *born* there."

"But you aren't a big name like me! Folks just lose their heads around celebrities. It's a fact!"

"Cut the publicity hound act."

"Well, the truth is I don't know why someone would want to frame me. Maybe some obsessed fan wanted to make an impression, or they thought it would be a good start to my next Percy Bannon book. Or maybe they didn't like the way the last book was edited. I mean, that would be totally understandable. You know, we had a whole extra subplot where Percy meets a cougar and they nearly get married, but then the cougar is kidnapped by Percy's archnemesis, and then Percy goes to rescue her, but then it's revealed that she was working for the archnemesis the whole time, and Percy's heart is broken—of course he still battles all the minions and wins—but the entire time he's fighting, he's really fighting his own sense of betrayal and sadness, and it's tragic really. Fantastic subplot. But my editor said it slowed the pacing and the readers don't care if Percy Bannon is sad, so he cut it. Plus, it saved on paper costs. But I was so upset. And when I told him I wanted to do the same plotline for the next book, he said no, he already worked out everything with Darcy—" Bradley suddenly broke off.

But before Vera could ask anything, Esme returned with coffee mugs and a plate of doughnuts. "First shipment! Two cups of mud with rafts," she declared cheerfully. "I'll bring the rest out as the kitchen gets it done."

"Thanks," Vera told her.

Bradley was already stuffing a doughnut into his mouth, but he nodded thanks as well.

The door opened again, bells jingling, and Orville walked in, heading directly for the back table. Vera was so happy to see her beau she almost yelped with joy.

"Sent it off," Orville said to Bradley, taking a seat next to Vera and putting one paw around her. He wasn't usually one to make any sort of possessive gesture, but then again, Marvel had a reputation. The bear said, "So it shouldn't be too long before the city police deal with you, one way or another. That murder is big news—it was the top item on the police bulletin at the message service office. All law enforcement officials have been asked to keep a lookout for anyone involved. The name Bradley Marvel was mentioned."

"In a good way or a bad way?" asked the wolf nervously.

"The police bulletin is generally not where you want to see your name show up," Orville replied dryly. "It means you're either a victim or a suspect. Considering how annoying you are, it was a bit of a shame no one tried to kill *you*."

Vera gasped. "What if someone did try exactly that? After all, it was your apartment."

"Could be," Orville said, newly interested in what had been an off-the-cuff comment. "In the dark, a large fox might be mistaken for a wolf."

"Wait, the victim was a fox?" Vera asked. Bradley hadn't mentioned the species, and she'd been hoping that she'd never have to learn much more about the crime, especially if Bradley would soon be leaving Shady Hollow.

"Yeah, Rick was my editor. But we weren't friends. He took a red pen to all my best words. Said he lived to turn pages red. Well, I guess he died the same way, huh?" Bradley sighed into his coffee mug.

Vera's stomach clenched. She said, very slowly, "Your editor was a fox named Rick who lived to turn pages red."

"Richard Renard. Bane of my professional existence. Don't tell anyone else this, but I'm not sorry he's dead. Just wish it wasn't on my floor."

If Bradley was expecting a laugh, he was disappointed. Orville just frowned, commenting that only an idiot would confess to hating the victim of a crime for which they were a suspect. But Vera said nothing. She was thrown by something Bradley had said, memories of the past suddenly rushing back at her.

I live to turn pages red, Vera. Yes, Rick had said that to her as well, a long time ago. When he was her editor at her first newspaper job.

She watched Bradley and Orville bicker over the last doughnut, the truth sticking in her throat.

She knew the victim, too. And like Bradley, she wasn't sorry he was dead.

Vera Vixen had grown up in the city, the only kit of parents who were both professors at the local university. They had expected Vera to follow in their academic paw prints, but she had dreams of becoming a reporter, and she never wavered. When Vera was ready for college, she sat down with her parents and informed them that she was going to study journalism. This came as a shock to them, and they never stopped mentioning how they hoped she would change her mind about devoting herself to "scribbling stories about the goings-on in the city." (And since Vera lived at home while she went to college, she got to hear these comments quite regularly.)

After graduation, Vera landed a job as a cub reporter at the *City Times*, the biggest paper in town, and the one where Vera had always imagined working. That also meant it was time to move out of her parents' home and into her own apartment downtown. Which would mean finding a roommate.

So, Vera answered an ad in the very same paper at which she worked: a creature by the name of Chloe McKibben was looking for another female to share a downtown apartment. The two potential roommates made an appointment to meet at a nearby coffee shop. Vera was always happy to drink coffee at any time of the day or night.

Vera was feeling both very grown-up and a little nervous. It was early afternoon on a Tuesday, and the place was almost empty. The fox looked around and spotted a gray-and-white cat with green eyes sitting at one of the tables. She was wearing a fuzzy cardigan in a pretty shade of dark pink. The well-dressed feline nodded, and Vera approached the table.

"Are you Chloe?" the fox asked, extending a paw. "I'm Vera Vixen."

The cat took Vera's paw and greeted her in return.

"Have a seat, Vera. Tell me about yourself."

Vera told her about her recent graduation from college and her new job at the *City Times*. Chloe shared that she was a second-year law student, and her grandparents were helping out with tuition so that she could concentrate on her studies. She explained that the apartment was a two-bedroom unit in a building right around the corner, and that she would be happy to show it to Vera. The fox agreed readily, and they left the coffee shop, already fast friends, and headed to their new place.

The apartment building was a handsome three-story stone building, and Chloe informed her that their unit was on the second floor. The fox followed the cat up the stairs and down a long, carpeted hallway. Chloe stopped in front of #206. She unlocked the door and stepped to the side so that Vera could enter first. Vera could hardly believe that she was going to be lucky enough to live here. The living room was furnished with a dark green, impossibly comfy-looking couch and a plush chair. There were bookcases lining the walls, and more books piled everywhere else. Vera felt immediately at home, and she hadn't even seen her room yet!

Vera and Chloe quickly agreed to become roommates. The cat gave her a set of keys and welcomed her to the neighborhood. Vera was only sorry that she would have to spend several more days back at home with her parents. She could sense their continuing disapproval of her new job and her decision to move out, even if they quit saying so out loud.

The days passed quickly as Vera packed her belongings and arranged to have a few pieces of furniture delivered to her new apartment. Chloe was rarely home since she was busy attending classes at the law school and studying in her off-hours at the library. So Vera had plenty of quiet time to unpack and organize her new space before she was due to start work at the newspaper the following week.

Finally, the time had arrived. Vera got up early and dressed carefully for her first day of work as a real reporter. (Chloe had already left for school but called out a "Good luck!" as she raced out the door.) Vera chose a dark green sweater and a blue-and-green plaid skirt. She wanted to appear professional but not too dressed up. She packed her messenger bag with her notebook and plenty of pens and pencils. She trotted quickly down the street and made her way to the *City Times*.

The newspaper office was large and bustling, with creatures of all types running back and forth and shouting to one another. The atmosphere was buzzing like a beehive. Vera stood in the doorway taking it all in. She heard a voice call out, "Are you Vixen?"

Vera glanced around to see where the voice was coming from. She spotted a handsome red fox in a blue button-down shirt and suspenders. He was waiting for her response.

"I'm, uh, Vera," she managed to get out. "This is my first day."

The other fox replied, with a smile, "I'm Richard Renard, and I'm your new boss. You can call me Rick. Let me show you around."

Vera desperately wanted to appear professional, but it took her a moment to react to the surprisingly handsome creature. He stared at her and waited as Vera gave herself a quick mental lecture about not being a cliché and succumbing to a good-looking boss.

As she followed Rick around the *Times* offices, Vera found herself fascinated by the energy of the newsroom and thrilled that she was now a part of it. Rick introduced her to countless creatures bustling about, whose names and job titles she could never hope to remember. Finally, Rick arrived at an empty desk in the warren of little spaces that made up the main newsroom.

"This is your desk, Vixen," he said. "Welcome to the *City Times.*"

Vera thanked him and put down her messenger bag. She was relieved to have a place that belonged to her, and she sat herself down in the battered chair. Her chair. The chair in which she'd sit while writing articles that would make a difference!

She glanced up to see Rick still standing there.

"Exciting, isn't it?" he asked. "I can already tell you've got the stuff, Vixen."

"Call me Vera," she replied.

Vera reminded herself to remain professional, but when she returned home to the apartment she shared with Chloe after that first day, she could not keep from gushing about Rick Renard. Chloe listened with an amused tolerance. Of course, Vera knew that she should focus on her work, but knowing that she would see Rick every day at the newspaper lent a spring to her step. She took extra care with her appearance and her wardrobe, sometimes borrowing outfits from the more stylish Chloe.

After Vera had been working at the paper for a few months, Rick stopped at her desk and asked her if she wanted to follow a lead with him. Of course, she said yes, and her boss took her to a small, dimly lit restaurant some distance from the office. Her stomach was in knots, as she tried to act as though she had secret business lunches with attractive colleagues all the time.

Rick ordered several dishes without asking Vera what she wanted, all while regaling her with amusing stories from his early days as a reporter. She listened in admiration to tales of his exploits and dreamed of the two of them breaking a story together. Then he did something that drove all rational thought from her brain.

Rick's eyes darted around the room, and he leaned forward over their small table. He placed his paw on top of one of hers and whispered, "I'm so glad we met, Vera. I know we're going to be very good friends. More than friends. I think you know it too."

The young fox's heart almost stopped beating. She couldn't believe that this was happening to her! She had read many romance books in her time, but nothing like this had ever occurred in real life. And yet, they were work colleagues. "Yes, but I'm not sure it's right . . . if we work together . . ."

"I won't tell if you don't," he said with a wink. His eyes practically sparkled with charm.

Before Vera could come up with a response, Rick removed his paw and sat back in his chair. The server had come by to drop off the check. The older fox pulled some money from his pocket and left it on the table, including a generous tip.

Vera hoped they would walk back to the newspaper office together. Rick, however, had other ideas. He said, "I'm meeting a source to get some background on a story. You head back to the office. There's still plenty of work to be done. We can talk about the rest later."

Her paws barely touched the sidewalk as Vera made her way back to work. She dreamed about having regular lunches with Rick, and then maybe even dinners. Perhaps he would take her to the theater, just like a real date. Yes, this was the beginning of the best years of her life!

———————

Vera blinked, yanking herself back to the present just as Bradley was wrapping up . . . well, some sort of tale. She hadn't been listening, after all.

Orville looked carefully at her. "You okay, Vera? You look upset."

"I'm fine, Orville. Really. Thanks for asking." She mustered a smile for the bear, wishing that life were much, much simpler.

Chapter 3

Vera didn't sleep well, lost in dreams that took her down city streets she hadn't trotted in years, only to find everyone she had ever known—friends, parents, co-workers—blocking a way out, anger apparent on each face. *Vera, you knew better. Vera, how could you. Vera, shame on you.*

She spent the better part of the night wide-eyed and sleepless, wondering why the past had come to pounce on her. She huddled under the comforter, curled into a near-perfect circle with her paw over her snout and her tail wrapped protectively around her, in a vain attempt to shut out the world.

It was a long time ago, Vera, she told herself. *It wasn't your fault, well, not really. And who would look back that far?*

Maybe someone investigating a murder would.

When the sun started to seep through the curtains, an energetic knock at the door got her out of bed.

"Message for Vera Vixen!" a voice chirped from the other side.

She opened the door to receive a folded note printed on paper that denoted a local delivery. It was from Orville, requesting that she come to the station as soon as possible.

Was there some other development? Vera tamped down the fear that Orville was somehow luring her there to be arrested. But for what? Her nightmares had really skewed her sense of proportion. Of course her own beau wouldn't arrest her . . . especially since she'd done nothing wrong!

Dressing quickly, Vera arrived at the police station less than a quarter hour later.

She found Bradley Marvel sitting in a chair across from Orville at the desk he used every day. Orville had a mug of coffee in front of him; Vera could tell even from the doorway that this was not coffee from Joe's Mug, but rather the office coffee produced by the hideous pot in the corner of the police station. She took it as a sign of Orville's distress and frustration that he didn't even have a chance to get the better stuff from Joe's. She also noticed that Bradley didn't have his own mug in front of him, suggesting that Orville was either too kind to inflict police station coffee on his guest, or (perhaps more likely) that he didn't want to extend any courtesy to the creature he'd found so incredibly annoying the last time he was in town, and who was now suspected of murder, and whom he would be very glad to see leaving Shady Hollow once again.

"Hello, I got here as soon as I could," she said as she walked in.

Orville looked up, relieved to see her there. "Oh, Vera. Thank goodness." His eyes looked a little wild. "Since Mr. Marvel's assistant is expected on the next ferry, I thought we could all walk over together and meet her. She may have some important information, more recent than what Bradley was able to share yesterday."

"More importantly, she has my things. I'm wearing the same thing as yesterday, you know! Thank goodness I'm not on a book tour." Bradley Marvel brushed an imaginary piece of lint off his trench coat.

Vera tried to smile, although she was not feeling particularly cheerful. She'd forgotten Bradley's assistant was meant to arrive today. Of course that was the reason Orville asked her to join them . . . not because he somehow uncovered Vera's shameful past. "That sounds like a good idea, Chief. I for one have a few questions that I'd love to ask someone who's just come from the city. And I'm sure that Mr. Marvel will be happy to know that his assistant is safe."

Bradley shrugged. "I'm sure she's fine. Darcy is nothing if not resourceful."

Orville glanced toward the wall, where a small, carved cuckoo clock hung. When it came time to chime the hour, it released the figures of two small bears in police uniforms out of the doors to bang the chime with their nightsticks. Vera didn't know when the clock had been given to the station, but it predated her own tenure in town. She reflected that the artist must have known either Chief Meade or his predecessor very well, considering how long it must've taken to carve.

"The ferry should be along any moment," said Vera. "Why don't we head there now, and perhaps stop at Joe's Mug along the way?"

Joe's was in the opposite direction of the ferry docks, but Vera could see Orville's expression brighten at the prospect of getting real coffee.

The three creatures left the station and turned onto the street in the direction of the diner. Bradley Marvel asked no questions about their route, which made Vera think that he had never bothered to notice where anything was in the town. Granted, his last visit to Shady Hollow hadn't been for very long, but then again, Shady Hollow was not a large town. As a journalist, Vera had deliberately developed the habit of mapping out her environment wherever she was. She wondered if Bradley ever did something similar as a novelist.

She asked, "Mr. Marvel, how do you use setting in your books? Are they inspired by real places, like Shady Hollow?"

Bradley looked surprised at this. "Setting? Oh, you mean like background, places for Percy to run through while he's on a mission." He looked around, as if seeing the village around him for the very first time. "I can't imagine using this as a setting. I prefer more exotic locales. My readership craves the excitement of the unknown."

Before Vera could ask a follow-up question, they arrived at Joe's Mug. Orville opened the door for Vera (he'd do that even if they weren't dating), but it was Bradley who went through first. Vera rolled her eyes and followed, thanking Orville for his courtesy.

Inside, Vera was drawn immediately to the case at the front counter, now filled with the daily selection of pastries and muffins. A young moose stood behind the counter and smiled at all of them. "Good morning! What can I get for you? We've got some apple cinnamon muffins, fresh out of the oven. And then there's this walnut pastry that I think you might like in particular, Chief. I tested the recipe so I could debut it at the Harvest Festival, but it was so good, I decided not to wait."

Orville nodded. "Thanks, that sounds perfect. And I'll take a large coffee, please."

Vera added, "I believe I'll try the muffin. And of course I'll take a coffee as well." She grinned at Joe Junior, who was quite aware of her affection for the beverage.

Bradley Marvel seemed captivated by the various treats inside the glass case. He pointed to three of them, which Joe Junior put in a bag for him.

"It's nice of you," said Vera, "to bring a snack for your assistant. She'll have not had an opportunity on the boat to enjoy a good meal, since the overnight options are limited. She'll appreciate something fresh."

"My assistant . . ." Bradley said, as if he'd never heard the word before. "Oh! Yes, I suppose she eats as well." He pointed to the apple cinnamon muffins in the case. "Put one of those in there, too," he ordered Joe Junior.

The transaction concluded, they left the diner, now moving at a slightly quicker pace because the ferry was indeed expected to arrive quite soon. Orville scarfed down his treat on the way, crisp flakes of pastry and powdered sugar falling like an early snow in his wake. As Vera walked the main street of Shady Hollow, she was all too aware of glances from the other residents and interested faces in windows of the businesses they passed. It wasn't every day that a celebrity like Bradley Marvel was in town, so Vera understood the curiosity. But she also had to wonder if news of what happened in the city had already started to spread here. Folks might have strong opinions about the notion of a potential murderer walking their streets, even if he was in the company of the chief of police.

Well, that was a problem for later. For now, Vera was extremely interested to meet this assistant. She wanted to know what type of creature could tolerate the wolf every day, and what that relationship might look like. It was clear already that Bradley depended on his assistant and trusted her to a great degree . . . even if he did forget that anyone besides himself ate food, too. Maybe she was new. Vera didn't remember the wolf mentioning an assistant the last time he was in town, and no one had accompanied him on that fateful book tour last year.

They reached the ferry docks, where a small number of other creatures had already gathered, waiting for friends or loved ones to disembark, or perhaps to receive a shipment of some product that they'd ordered from the city. The ferries were a vital link between the larger city and these smaller towns along the river.

Vera craned her neck to look downstream and saw the bow of the ferry coming toward them. It should be along the docks in a few minutes, based on the white froth of the wake it was creating as it cut through the water, pushing its way against the current. Bradley was also looking in the same direction, and he seemed quite anxious, to judge by how fiercely he nibbled a pastry.

"How is it?" Vera asked.

"Rrrlle gmmd." Bradley's words were muffled by his chewing, but he did have a genuinely happy expression on his face for a moment. He wiped his mouth with one paw, and his face fell again. "You know, I don't imagine that the food is this good in prison."

"Probably not," said Vera. "But you insist you're innocent. Do you really worry that a case could be made against you?"

"Well, it's difficult to have a lot of confidence when the body was found in my apartment."

"But you said that your assistant can provide you with an alibi," Vera noted. "So surely that's a point in your favor."

Bradley still looked nervous. "Yes, I'm sure it'll all be sorted out. That's what attorneys are for, isn't it?"

"You'd better hope it doesn't get that far," said Orville. "Believe me, you would not enjoy the experience of being arrested, even if it all ends well."

"Then again," said Vera, "it could provide you with some interesting background material for your new book. What's it about? Could you work in a scene in which Percy Bannon needs to spend some time in a prison?"

"Oh, I have no idea."

Vera thought that that was an odd response, because surely Bradley Marvel would know whether his own hero might find himself in such a place. From what Vera knew about fiction writers, they were always eager for new ideas and ways that they could expand their stories, if only because bigger books tended to have bigger price tags.

At that moment, the ferry pulled up to the dock, and a few otters jumped onto the wooden planks, holding lines that they cast over the posts to secure the ferry to solid land. The whole process of docking took only a few moments because this crew had been at it so long they could do it in their sleep. Within moments the gangplank had been pulled down, and passengers started to disembark. Most of them carried cases or bags or boxes, and in one unexpected case, a rather large pumpkin.

Vera waited until Bradley made a small sign of recognition, and then she turned to see a lynx walking down the plank. The lynx was quite burdened with items, including a suitcase, a knapsack, and a large, boxy leather case that Vera knew held a portable typewriter.

Vera stepped forward automatically, reaching to help the other creature with the load. "Hello there. You must be Mr. Marvel's assistant."

The lynx nodded, but it took a moment before she released her grip on the portable typewriter case and allowed Vera to grab it from her. "Yes, I'm Darcy Montrose." She blinked and drew a paw across her eyes. "Excuse me, I'm very tired. Turns out I can't sleep on boats."

She looked then at the wolf who was her boss. She offered him the larger of the two suitcases, almost thrusting it toward him. "That's yours," she said in a brusque tone.

"Everything is in there?" asked Bradley.

"Yes, of course. That's my job, isn't it? To make sure everything's done?" she added pointedly.

"I hope the journey upriver was smooth," Vera interjected, hoping to keep the tone light.

"Certainly smoother than the situation I just left." Darcy looked back at Vera. "How much do you know about it?"

"Only what Mr. Marvel told us yesterday. I am Vera Vixen, by the way. I'm a reporter with the Shady Hollow *Herald*. This is Orville Braun, Shady Hollow's chief of police."

"Police chief, huh?" Darcy looked over the large brown bear. "I'm surprised you haven't arrested Bradley yourself."

"I've thought about it. More than once." Orville reached forward to help her with another suitcase that one of the stewards had just brought forward. "I'll have some questions for you, too," Orville told Darcy, "But first let's get you settled where you'll be staying."

"Oh, thank you, sir. It's so nice to have the opportunity to relax for a moment before an interrogation." The hostility coming off Darcy was palpable, but Vera suspected that the brash attitude was a result of the extraordinary circumstances of the last day and a half, or even just learned behavior from living in the city. Either way, Vera was sure of one thing: this Darcy was a very capable creature who would not be caught off guard.

Chapter 4

They all made their way to Bramblebriar, and in the early morning sunlight, the streets of the town practically sparkled. Above them, the leaves were turned into stained-glass mosaics of greens and yellows and fiery oranges. Orville did his very best to discourage passing townsfolk from getting too chatty with the newcomers, a task that he accomplished quite well simply by growling whenever someone came too close.

However, there was no stopping Gladys Honeysuckle from zipping down in front of the group, her beating wings invisible but her small black eyes all too alert.

"Well, good morning to all!" she buzzed. "Do my eyes deceive me, or is this the famous author Bradley Marvel?"

"A discerning reader, I see!" Bradley returned, giving the hummingbird a courtly bow. Vera heard Darcy mutter something under her breath but couldn't catch the words.

"Have you got a new book coming out this week, and I missed it?" she demanded. Gladys was the gossip columnist, and she was over the moon about the prospect of a celebrity in town.

"He hasn't got one *this* week," Darcy responded. "But all of Marvel's loyal readers will get a new book soon! Isn't that right, boss?" She smiled at Bradley, but it was all teeth.

Bradley looked about to snap back, but then he—shockingly—did not. He simply gave a nod to Gladys, and said, "Percy Bannon will return in another adventure!"

"Oh, I can't wait to tell everyone!" Gladys gushed. "Bradley Marvel, here in Shady Hollow!" She darted off, disappearing among the multicolored leaves.

"Great," said Orville. "Now news of a fugitive is going to show up in tomorrow's paper."

Vera said, "I'll track Gladys down and tell her that she's legally required to hold off."

"Good luck with that," Orville said. "Okay, now turn here. Bramblebriar is on this little street."

It was a cul-de-sac, and the inn took full advantage of the serenity of its location. The tall, many-gabled house was surrounded by a garden, full of late-blooming flowers growing in pleasing disarray. Narrow gravel paths allowed a creature to stroll among the beds, and here and there, larger evergreen shrubs had been carefully pruned into whimsical shapes: pyramids, globes, and waves. It was a hint of the effort the owners put into every aspect of the business.

Darcy seemed skeptical of the sign outside the inn, which read:

BRAMBLEBRIAR BED & BREAKFAST

SHADY HOLLOW'S MOST CHARMING INN

But she was nonetheless very polite to Ben Eastwood when he greeted them at the door. Darcy was soon installed in a small but pretty room on the same floor as Bradley's. She had stared so longingly at the bed that Vera suggested she take a morning nap. "I'm sure a few hours won't matter, and you'll be better equipped to recall what happened when you're not yawning so much."

"As if I could forget!" Darcy muttered. "I blamed the boat, but the fact is that I don't think I would have slept at all no matter where I was."

"It must have been a terrible sight," Vera said.

"It's weird, you know. I write dramatic scenes all the time, but the moment I finally saw one, I couldn't even register what I was seeing."

"Oh, are you a writer as well? What do you write?"

The question had been meant to offer Darcy a more pleasant thread of conversation, but the lynx looked angry and didn't answer, instead saying, "I really have got to get some shut-eye. I'll let the chief know when I'm ready to talk later."

Vera nodded and left Darcy to settle in. Downstairs, she informed Orville of the slight change in plans. The bear took the news calmly.

"No problem. It's not as if it's my case, anyway. But I expect the city cops would appreciate having a statement that's a little closer to the event. Memories become unreliable rather quickly." (Over the past year or so, Orville had spent a lot more of his downtime at the station reading about police work and methodology.)

"No more word from the city yet?" she asked.

"Not yet, but I wouldn't be surprised if a wingmail arrives later today. Why don't you come back to the station with me, Vera? I expect you'll be writing a story about Bradley's unannounced visit, so you'll want some information, and I've got the police bulletins."

"Yeah, I suppose BW will want one," Vera said, for once not enthused about the prospect of writing an article.

"You okay?" Orville asked her, casting her a sideways glance as the two walked away from the B and B. "You seem a little distraught. Though that wolf showing up yesterday is enough to make anyone distraught." He offered his paw, and she took it, not sure she deserved the consideration. The two walked paw in paw for the rest of the way.

"It *was* an unpleasant surprise," Vera said. She wished that were the whole problem. She hated the fact that she was hiding anything from Orville. And while there was nothing wrong with knowing the victim of a murder, it just felt so awful to be reminded of her connection to Rick Renard after all these years. With any luck at all, a city cop would arrive, escort Bradley and Darcy back to the city, and Vera would never hear another word about the case.

But something told her she wouldn't be that lucky. No, her luck was liable to run the other way. Because anything associated with Renard was bad. Always had been. Why should his murder be any different?

She realized she'd not been listening to a word Orville was saying, and she asked him to repeat himself.

"I said, even in the city, murder stands out among crimes," Orville told her. "Fleeing the scene was the worst thing Marvel could have done for himself. *And* he dragged his assistant into the whole business. That seems unfair. She ought to have said no."

Vera shook her head. "It's not always easy to refuse an order from someone you work for."

"Miss Montrose might have thought she had a duty to help her boss, especially if he was the one signing her paycheck."

"Maybe. Though I think there's something strange about that relationship. Did you notice that when we were talking to Gladys, Bradley seemed to almost be intimidated by Darcy?"

"I guess I didn't," he admitted. "But in that case, he'd let her go and get another assistant, yes?"

"If he could. But she might be employed by the publisher, in which case she would be more likely to answer to . . . the victim, Mr. Renard." She found it slightly difficult to even say his name.

"Good point. I'll ask her later," Orville said. "It could help sort out possible motives."

At the police station, Orville shared the bulletins that he'd received, and Vera got a rapid update of the later years of Richard Renard.

According to the documents, Renard was an editor at the publishing house responsible for Bradley Marvel's popular series of books, as well as a number of others. And Renard wasn't just a regular editor; he was quite high up the ladder. His bio mentioned he had a seat on the board.

"He must have left journalism a while ago," she muttered. She only knew Renard as a street-level reporter, and she would never have pictured him hobnobbing with the elite of the city. He'd preferred to write scandalous things about them instead.

"Hmm? What's that?" Orville asked.

"Oh, I was just reading the info on the victim," Vera covered quickly. "Says he worked in journalism before making the leap to book publishing."

"Huh. Think of that. You might have worked at the same place as him, if you'd stayed in the city after school."

Vera made a noncommittal noise. When she'd first shared her life story with Orville, she'd glossed over that very awkward time in her life. She quickly scanned the rest of the reports.

"Only one victim, and no one actually saw the crime occur. Looks like the weapon was a knife, probably from the kitchen in the apartment. Maybe Renard was murdered on the spur of the moment . . . an argument gone too far?" Vera guessed.

Orville shrugged. "Who knows, since there are no witnesses. Not yet anyway. You're familiar with the city, Vera. Is it really that likely that no one saw anything? The city's so crowded, it seems impossible to achieve total secrecy."

She considered the bear's question. "There are a lot of creatures all living close together, true. But most folks are too busy with their own lives to pay much attention to what others are doing . . . unless they have a specific reason to do so. The police might find some witnesses, but I wouldn't count on it. What puzzles me most, though, is that if no one was home, how and why did Renard go there?"

"That's a question for the city cops to answer," Orville grunted. "I just want to be able to return Marvel to them without a fuss. Do you have whatever you need for your article?"

"Oh, yes. I'll head to the *Herald* office now to do the write-up. Let me know if there are any more developments?"

"Will do. Say, I was going to ask if you wanted to go for dinner tonight, but maybe we ought to put it off till Wolf & Co. are headed back downriver."

"Sure. Then we can make it a celebration dinner," she said, trying to sound cheerful.

"To celebrate what?"

"A murder occurring far, far away from here."

Orville chuckled, and Vera wished she could laugh too. But all she could think was how her friends would feel about her if they learned about her connection to Rick—and what she'd done because of him.

She arrived at the newspaper office, still preoccupied and upset. The Shady Hollow *Herald* building stood on Elm Street, and several workers greeted Vera as she trotted inside. The presses were quiet, and they wouldn't be cranked back up until it was time to print the next edition tonight, but creatures bustled here and there, all chattering and hooting questions and answers as they worked to assemble the day's news. Vera inhaled the air of the newsroom, a strangely soothing blend of ink, old coffee, and cigar smoke.

With her mind distracted by the murder in Marvel's apartment, it took a long time to be able to concentrate on her own work, but Vera eventually managed to take care of several small items on her to-do list, such as compiling the upcoming events for a column titled, yes, Upcoming Events.

She was startled when her colleague Barry Greenfield called her name.

The older hare waved a paw in front of her face. "Hellooo? Vera? If you were any more distracted, you'd trip over the rug. What's going on? Does it have anything to do with Marvel showing his snout here again?"

"You heard?" Vera asked. A glance at the clock on the wall told her a full three hours had passed since her arrival.

"Everyone's heard. Gladys is doubtless whipping up some copy about it right now."

"Ugh." Vera put her head in her paws. "I meant to tell her to hold off on that tidbit, but I forgot. And she's going to ask me for a quote. I know it."

"Well, you were seen with him. As was the chief," added Barry.

"Which makes me wonder why he's here at all." The hare gave Vera a significant look, clearly hoping for a scoop.

"Look, Barry. It's complicated." Vera gave him the briefest possible version of what she knew of the murder and Bradley's involvement. The hare took it all in stride, and Vera soon concluded, "And if things go as they should, Bradley Marvel will be going away soon anyway."

"Huh. And what if things don't go well?"

"Then I'll give you the full rundown so you can write the inevitable article."

He blinked in surprise. "Me? Why not you?"

"Er, conflict of interest, maybe. Marvel seems to think I'm his pal. Though he really just wants a friendly ear to pour his story out to."

Barry flicked his long ears and grinned. "Oh, don't worry. I'm good at *sounding* friendly."

Vera noted the qualification and smiled back. "When you talk to him, don't mention the crime at all, but can you subtly work in some questions about his reasons for being here? And also figure out about his situation with his publisher . . . I think there might be something there."

The hare nodded sharply. "No problem."

"Then let's pop over to the inn, and I'll introduce you."

"Oh, you go ahead and prepare him, won't you? I want to stop by my den and grab something first."

She wondered what he was so keen to retrieve (Was there such a thing as wolf repellent?), but she agreed and walked herself over to Bramblebriar. Though she was certain the interview would be tedious, at least it would take place in the lovely front parlor or perhaps even on the porch.

She waited at the corner, watching her colleague bounding down the street toward her. He must have made tracks to get to his place and back so fast!

"What'd you get?"

"A book," he said, somewhat unhelpfully. "Shall we go find our famous author?"

"Not much chance of avoiding it," Vera muttered.

They turned the corner and beheld the inn. The Eastwoods went all out to make their place as picturesque and welcoming as possible. With the advent of autumn, that meant bundles of flint corn hanging from the fence posts, the multicolored kernels on the cobs looking quite festive against the sun-bleached husks. More cornstalks were tied to the porch posts, and early autumn blooms like sunflowers and marigolds grew in the flower beds and pots. The rocking chairs on the porch all had cushions in bright red and orange, and a blanket was carefully folded over the back of each, should the air grow chilly unexpectedly.

Bradley was in one chair, dressed in his full regalia of trench coat and fedora. Darcy stood nearby. "The fourth estate!" he called in greeting from the rocking chair he'd claimed. "Come, come! Have a seat!"

Vera said formally, "Bradley, I'd like you to meet my colleague at the *Herald*, Barry Greenfield. Barry, this is Bradley Marvel."

The two creatures shook paws, and everyone sat down. The hare produced his notebook and pen.

Darcy had been leaning against one of the upright posts, a sheaf of papers in her paws. She quickly shoved them into a pasteboard accordion file. "So much for discussing the latest draft, huh, Mr. Marvel?"

He chuckled, shifting in his chair with an attitude that Vera thought seemed a bit cagey. "Darcy, this is what's called public relations, and it's extremely important."

"Oh, yeah? Got anything to relate to the public besides being wanted for murder?"

Vera and Barry exchanged glances. Apparently, they'd interrupted a business meeting. A rather tense one. The hare asked, "Is this a bad time?"

"Never!" Bradley replied with a practiced grin. "Make yourselves comfortable. I'll order some refreshments."

The lynx rolled her eyes. "You'll excuse me, won't you? Somebody's got to work around here." She flounced inside. Vera wondered what work Darcy could do without her boss available, then thought that she probably just wanted some peace and quiet.

Vera leaned back in her rocking chair, which was just as delightfully comfy as she remembered. It almost made it worth it to have to listen to Bradley drone on.

Then Ben Eastwood came outside, practically overloaded with a huge tray balancing a pot, a few cups, and a plate of ginger scones.

Okay, it is worth it, Vera decided, giving Ben a grateful smile.

The chipmunk poured a cup for all three creatures and told them to give a holler if they needed more of anything before bustling away again. Vera looked appreciatively at the steaming tea and the plate of ginger scones. She helped herself to a cup and a scone and settled herself back. She was looking forward to watching Barry interview a subject. The veteran reporter would surely have a few tricks that she hadn't seen, ways to get the subject to talk about uncomfortable topics, less-than-flattering scenes from their careers, and the like.

"Mr. Marvel," Barry said, with an eager tone that Vera had never heard from him before. "I'm so excited to meet you. *Weaver's Luck* changed my life."

Huh, don't lay it on too thick, Barry, Vera thought as she watched the hare butter up his interviewee.

"Please, call me Bradley," the wolf replied. "What a pleasure to meet a creature who remembers *Weaver's Luck*. That book changed my life as well. It was the first time I got published, and I could show the world I was a real writer."

Over the next few minutes, Vera was astounded to hear the wolf appear so modest and genuine. All the posturing and boasting had fallen away. The hare and the wolf were in their own world of two—chatting excitedly about the protagonist of *Weaver's Luck* and his various adventures. Vera had never read the book, so she busied herself with thinking about the details of Rick's murder and who might be responsible. From what she remembered of the creature's habits, there would be no shortage of potential motives!

It was a fine day, with a sky of perfect turquoise interrupted only by high, thin clouds that resembled delicate wisps of silk, and despite her intention to listen, Vera drifted. She became dimly aware of the distinctive clackity noise of a typewriter in use. Darcy must have opened her window and was now working away at something. Vera nibbled a ginger scone and wondered what the lynx might be writing.

Vera's ears perked up at one point while Bradley and Barry were yapping on about literature. The pair were *still* talking about *Weaver's Luck*.

"I put my heart and soul into that novel," the wolf said earnestly. "I worked on the voice of my character and the tone of the book for years. Writing it all in little notebooks, scratching out old ideas, jotting new ones down. I type my books now—efficiency matters. The Percy Bannon books are completely different. I could knock out one of those in six months."

Of course you can, Vera thought to herself.

"So, your publisher must be pleased with your efforts, right? Or do they demand too much?" Barry asked, slipping in the question and inviting Marvel to spill.

"Oh, hey, you know how it is. Everyone wants more, more, more. But I'm an artist. I can't rush things!"

Didn't you just say you rushed the Percy Bannon books? Vera thought but was wise enough to not say aloud. Barry was every bit as sharp as her, and he'd never let a contradiction slide for long.

"Do you ever find yourself at a loss for ideas?" Barry asked.

The wolf looked to the side for a moment and took a big gulp of his tea. "Whoo, talking makes me thirsty! What was the question? Ideas? Full of ideas. Too many ideas!" He laughed.

Barry was scribbling furiously in his notebook. "Remind me. How did you first get published, Bradley?" the hare asked.

The author sighed and then smiled, as if enjoying the memory of himself as a young, aspiring writer.

"It hasn't been *that* long, but it feels like forever ago. The publishing world wasn't all that different then from what it is today. It all hinged on who you knew. I was lucky enough to live in the same building as a junior editor at one of the big publishing companies in the city. Lew Zeidler was a boar who lived just down the hall from me. We had exchanged hellos at the mailboxes and in the laundry room. When I found out where he worked, I made a point of running into him more often. After a few months, we were friends who would meet for a drink after work or go to a concert on the weekend. He was a genuinely pleasant creature. I worked a series of crappy jobs back then, but I always wanted to be a writer, and I worked on my novel every chance I got. When I finished what would become *Weaver's Luck,* I asked Lew if he would consider showing it to his boss. He agreed, and the rest is history."

The fox poured herself another cup of tea while Barry and Bradley continued to discuss the state of the literary arts in the city and the wider world. Barry skillfully wove in a few more pointed questions about Bradley's recent work and his feelings for his late editor, but Vera would have to wait until later to collate all the responses and glean some information from them.

In spite of herself, she was curious how Bradley could have gone from being a serious author to pumping out the Percy Bannon books. Granted, they were bestsellers, but Marvel would never win a literary prize because of the series. Barry Greenfield had once told Vera (while sitting in the audience at a Bradley Marvel reading at Nevermore Books the previous fall) that he considered the Percy Bannon books to be little better than kindling. But he had read *Weaver's Luck* and was legitimately impressed by Marvel's craft. And Barry Greenfield was not easily impressed.

Vera mused over how one creature never really knew another creature fully. She hadn't known Rick fully either, she couldn't help but remember now. And that had ended in disaster.

One thing was certain. She had to keep herself clear of this whole situation. The sooner Bradley returned to the city, the sooner she could breathe easy.

Chapter 5

When all of the tea had been spilled and drunk, and the ginger scones eaten, Barry announced that he had everything he needed for his article. Bradley dutifully signed the hare's first edition of *Weaver's Luck*. The two creatures shook paws again.

Vera said, "Marvel, I believe you're expected at the bookstore next. I can show you the way."

"Great. Let me just pop inside and tell Darcy something." The wolf disappeared into the corn-shock-bedecked doorway.

Vera waited until he was out of earshot, then leaned closer to Barry.

"Well? What do you think?" she asked in a low tone. "Did you get any info besides the details of Marvel's rise to stardom?"

"Yeah, he said more than he meant to," Barry noted smugly. "I'll compile the notes and give you a copy later today. Plus, I'm going to get a great article out of the feel-good stuff. Folks love reading about that kind of thing, and Stone will be thrilled."

She nodded. "Sales do perk him up."

Waving goodbye, the hare went back to the *Herald* offices to write up his fawning article on Marvel. BW Stone would be clamoring for it before the ink was dry, if only so that he could print **EXCLUSIVE INTERVIEW** at the top of the next edition.

Shortly thereafter, Vera and Bradley moved on to Nevermore Books. When she learned Marvel was in town, Lenore had asked Vera to bring the author by to sign the sizable stock of Percy Bannon books that she kept at the ready. The series was popular with many Shady Hollow residents. Signed copies were sought after as gifts and keepsakes. Lenore was always conscious of what her customers wanted.

The wolf was somewhat subdued as they headed to the bookstore. Marvel walked quickly with his paws in his pockets, and Vera trotted after him, neither inclined to chat.

Nevermore Books was a restored granary building with a tall silo that stood on the corner of Walnut and Main. The silo had been cunningly repurposed with multiple floors wrapping around the interior, each one devoted to a different subject: fiction, history, poetry, science, and more. Labels hung on the railings so it was clear what books could be found on each floor. Earth-bound creatures used the stairs to go between the levels, but birds could fly up and down the open center.

The bookshop was one of the best parts of living in Shady Hollow, and Vera was proud that the owner was her friend.

As soon as she and Bradley entered the store, Vera breathed in the soothing atmosphere of book paper and cinnamon tea. She would spend the day here if she could.

Violet Chitters, a mouse who worked part-time for Lenore, greeted them from the front desk.

"Morning, Vera! Welcome back to Nevermore, Mr. Marvel." Violet smiled politely. Vera happened to know that Violet was rather overwhelmed by Bradley Marvel. When he last visited Shady Hollow, she had been so much in awe of him that she couldn't speak. She was a year older now and managed to maintain her composure this time around.

"Hi, Violet," Vera replied. "How's your family?"

"Oh, pretty much the same," Violet said. "Dad's been especially busy at the sawmill because of the festival—what with the final party being held on-site by the millpond."

"That's right, the Sawmill Soiree," Vera said. "I suppose I'll have to decide what to wear for it."

"Nothing too fancy," Violet warned. "Last year, that whole barrel of hard cider spilled on the dance floor, and my mother is still annoyed that it ruined her dress."

Vera remembered how the smaller dancers had been swept up in the cider-scented waves until they came to rest on dry ground like so much driftwood.

"Anyway," Violet went on, "I can't wait! Mom's been helping get ready. She contracted Thad, Moira, Quentin, Lillian, and June too. I escaped because I already have a job."

Vera chuckled, thinking of a small army of mice overseeing the preparations, though naturally the sawmill workers would pitch in too. "I'll see you there, I'm sure. But I believe it's time for Mr. Marvel to sign some books."

"Of course. This way." Violet led the wolf to the table where she had gathered all the stock that he was to sign. There was a pitcher of water and a glass, as well as an assortment of pens. Seeing that the author was in capable paws, Vera went in search of Lenore.

The fox found her friend in the tiny back room that served as the receiving area for the bookshop. When new books were delivered, they had to be uncrated and their titles entered in the large ledger that Lenore used for her inventory. At the end of the day, she went through the sales slips and removed the titles that had sold from her inventory. Then she had to decide whether to order a replacement copy if it was a popular book or simply be happy that it was gone if it had been gathering dust on the shelf. It was a balancing act to be sure.

The raven was happy to see her friend. She put down the new books that she was working with and greeted Vera.

"Well, Vera," the raven said. "How's it going with your good pal Bradley?"

Vera sighed in response.

"I left him with Violet. He's going to sign all your Percy Bannon stock."

"I wished I'd had some warning," Lenore said. "I could have ordered more."

"He wasn't exactly planning ahead when he fled the scene of a crime."

The raven cawed in appreciation, and then said, "Interesting that he came here, of all places. Then again, you do have a reputation for solving crimes."

"I really don't know what he expects me to do," Vera grumbled, unable to forget the present issue. "That is, I do know, because he outright asked me to investigate for him. I barely know him, and it's not as if he made a good impression the previous time we met. And even if we were pals, I'm a reporter, not a PI."

Lenore nodded in commiseration. "It's odd. You'd think he'd run to a good friend."

"I don't think he has any," Vera said, voicing a theory that she'd been harboring since his arrival.

"Hmmm. I don't have any suggestions for legal help, do you? Mr. Fallow doesn't deal in criminal law much at all, and anyway, Marvel would need an attorney based in the city. What about that lawyer from Castor & Castor? The one who came up to help Stacia with that whole mess?"

"Oh, you mean Flint Lennox. He'd be excellent, but Esme mentioned to me a while ago that he's tied up with some incredibly complex case. Trial's going to start very soon." Vera didn't add how sad Esme had looked when sharing the news. Though she resisted putting any label on their relationship, it was no secret that the attorney found lots of reasons to visit Shady Hollow when his caseload permitted.

"Too bad," Lenore said.

Vera perked up. "Wait, I do know someone who fits that description, actually! Where's my head? My old roommate, Chloe McKibben. I *just* saw her on my visit down there, and she mentioned that she'd recently joined a firm specializing in criminal law. I doubt she'd want to have anything to do with this case, but she'd be able to suggest a name of a colleague."

"Do you want to drag a friend into this?" Lenore asked.

"Well, it's just asking for some information, and Chloe can always say no. But honestly, the faster Bradley gets out of Shady Hollow, the happier we'll all be. And if he gets an attorney in the city, he'll surely return there."

"True. Okay, you should send her a wingmail as soon as you can."

"I'll stop at the messenger office on my way back to work," Vera said. "And, uh, Lenore? Maybe we could meet up soon, just us? I have something I want to talk to you about."

The raven bobbed her glossy black head. "Of course. Is it serious?"

"I hope not."

"Intriguing. I'll find you tomorrow, and we can talk, okay?"

"Yes," Vera said. "Thanks."

As she had promised Lenore, Vera walked to the messenger service office after leaving the bookstore. A squirrel behind the desk was happy to write down her message onto the special paper used for express wingmail. Vera's message was brief: "Can you recommend the name of a reliable attorney for criminal law who is based in the city? Asking for a friend. Please respond express. Vera."

She gave the squirrel the name and address of Chloe McKibben and paid the fee. She was confident that Chloe would have the message by the end of the day, and she expected a response shortly thereafter. With luck, she would have a good name to give to Bradley by the next morning, and soon he would no longer be bothering her.

She was already feeling more cheerful at the thought of getting Bradley out of town. Talk about ruffling fur (and feathers)! Bradley Marvel was a walking disaster.

Once again, she considered Orville's previous notion of Bradley being the victim. From the perspective of motive, it wasn't difficult to believe. After all, most folks who knew him seemed to dislike him at best, while some felt considerably worse.

And then there was the fact that Bradley lived in a city teeming with creatures, meaning that the sheer number of folks who might have a grudge against him made it even more of a possibility. Mockingbird Court seemed easy enough to get in and out of for a determined individual, and murderers were nothing if not very determined individuals.

But was it possible that someone could have mistaken a fox for a wolf? The idea wasn't as outlandish as it might seem. The general outline of both creatures was similar. They both had long pointed ears, a snout of the same general shape, and a fluffy tail. True, wolves were larger than foxes, but in a darkened room, or if the killer was nervous, a smaller creature might have appeared larger, particularly if they were expecting to see a wolf, for it is a well-known fact that most folks see what they expect to see.

So there was a possibility that Rick's death was in fact a *mistake.* Vera pictured the scene. The killer sneaks into the apartment, knowing that Bradley is out, and they hide in a dark corner of the main room, ready for him to return. After some time, the door opens, and a figure walks in: pointed ears, the distinctive snout, perhaps even wearing the same type of hat. The killer springs into action, knife at the ready. The deed must be done quickly or else the victim will make a noise or fight back. So, one swift stab, and it is over.

The victim falls to the floor in the middle of the room. The hat rolls off the head, and there is nothing more to be frightened of. But the killer must ensure that the victim really is dead. So the killer lights a lamp, brightening the room, just enough to see the body and verify that it is not breathing, and there is no heartbeat. They turn around, facing the now illuminated scene before them. And this is the moment, Vera imagined, that the truth is revealed.

It is in fact . . . the wrong creature! Yes, they have the same general shape, but now in the light, one can see that the coat is red instead of gray, the body much smaller than it would've seemed in the tense and shadowy moment in which the killer made their move. The killer has no idea why Rick is here at all, considering Bradley isn't with him. It makes no sense, and it certainly isn't fair. But the fact remains that there is a body, and the killer is holding a knife, and this is a situation that must be resolved.

The killer drops the knife near the body and extinguishes the lamp. They peek out of the open door into the hallway and see no creature. This is their moment. They slip outside and start walking away. Perhaps they intended to latch the door behind them, but in that moment, they make a tiny mistake (following that much larger mistake they made in the room). The door opens inward once more after the killer has walked off. Nobody in Mockingbird Court remarked on having seen the killer in the public areas of the apartment building—or else surely there would have been some mention of it in the reports from the newspapers. The only thing residents noticed was that open door, and the dead body within.

And that would bring the whole situation to the exact moment when Bradley entered the scene. Having returned home from dinner, with Darcy in tow, Bradley finds the body in his own apartment, and he can't account for why his editor might have been there, nor why his editor was killed—but all the blame and all the suspicion fall squarely on him.

It was an interesting theory. Unfortunately, Vera had no ability to prove it true one way or the other, not without gathering more evidence, or being able to prove that another creature was in that apartment. But it did cast a little more doubt on the notion of Bradley as a coldhearted killer. And it brought into question a lot of assumptions about the killer's motives if in fact they had killed the wrong creature. Vera shook her head. Well, it wasn't her problem, anyway.

Too bad it *felt* like her problem.

Chapter 6

Vera woke before the sun the next morning. She'd slept poorly again, disturbed by old memories and new theories, all of them unwelcome. Her kitchen was still full of blue shadows when she got up and set the kettle on to boil. She lit the fire, noticing how cold the house had gotten overnight. Summer was truly just a memory now. In the woodlands, autumn came swiftly, bringing these chilly mornings and the scent of frost in the air, even this early on.

She sipped some tea while gazing into the flames. Half her mind was in the past, turning over all her memories of Rick, and trying to reason just how everyone's paths might have crossed so much that Rick could have ended up dead in Bradley's home, killed by an unknown creature. Then Bradley had to rope her into the business, without even knowing her past link to the victim. She shuddered when she realized another coincidence she had yet to consider, which was that she herself had been in the city at the time the crime occurred. How ironic, considering that she'd left the place years ago and kept her visits few and far between since then. Vera had only spent two nights in the city! And yet, in that short span, Rick had been killed.

But by whom? If Rick's attitude had remained the same as it had been when she knew him, he'd probably made lots of enemies, not just Bradley. And Vera didn't really believe Bradley was a killer at heart—the wolf was all talk, playing at being dangerous. Look how he'd reacted the moment he truly was in danger . . . he'd run away, straight to Shady Hollow. That wasn't what a coldhearted murderer did.

If it wasn't Bradley Marvel who killed Rick, someone else must have. She immediately thought of Darcy, the lynx who so competently managed Bradley's work and life. That assistant was a cool customer—not many creatures would witness a crime in their boss's home, then arrange a private charter and pack some bags to tag along afterward (*not* on a privately chartered boat, Vera noticed). Clearly, Darcy had her own reasons for doing all of that. It was above and beyond her job description, that was for sure.

Vera set down her mug and stood up. Yes, she had a direction for her own inquiries now. She'd find Bradley's clever assistant and learn a little more about her . . . including whether or not she could be a killer.

After putting on a warm, emerald-green felt coat and draping a soft scarf around her neck, Vera packed her reporter's gear in her bag (paper pad, pencil, camera, enameled tin mug for emergency coffee breaks) and headed out. As she pulled her front door closed, her paw lingered on the knob. Should she lock it? She remembered all too well the unpleasant shock on finding Bradley inside when she first got home. She didn't want a repeat of that experience.

But this was Shady Hollow! Vera would not cave in to fear just because she'd been startled once. She deliberately turned away from the door, still unlocked, and walked down the street toward the center of town.

The walk to the bed-and-breakfast wasn't long, though the air was crisp enough that Vera was glad to reach her destination, the cul-de-sac off Main Street. She knocked on the front door of the inn and heard a cheerful "Come in!" from the inside. Opening the door, she stepped into the foyer. She saw Geoffrey Eastwood in the main dining room further back, getting things ready to serve breakfast to the guests when they came down.

"Sorry I barged in so early," Vera said in apology to the chipmunk. "But I was hoping I could speak to Miss Montrose—the lynx—before things get busy today."

"Wait here a moment," Geoffrey said. "I'll go up and knock. What's the exact message?"

"Vera Vixen would like an interview, here or wherever Darcy would feel comfortable talking."

Geoffrey nodded and hurried up the stairs. While she waited, Vera examined the sitting room to her left and the study to the right. Both rooms had been designed for maximum cozy relaxation, with comfortable wingback chairs placed near the fireplaces and the windows. Shelves of books—old and new—meant that everyone could find something good to read. There were also several charming, framed paintings and sketches, most of them highlighting some woodland scene that Vera recognized. However, there were also a couple of portraits, including a large one above the study fireplace that showed Geoffrey and Benjamin together in the very same suits they wore at their wedding. Both chipmunks beamed with joy, and Vera felt that there could be no better advertisement for Bramblebriar's welcoming tone.

It seemed to be taking an inordinately long time for Geoffrey to deliver a message, so Vera decided to go upstairs and see what was the matter. She heard the chipmunk speaking softly to someone at the end of the hall. She peeked in an open door and saw Geoffrey, his back to her. She was not quite in view herself, but she could see the two speakers. Darcy was dressed in pajamas, but clearly awake. She was at the desk in the room, papers arrayed before her. The portable typewriter was open on the desk as well.

Odd, thought Vera. She had assumed Bradley had taken possession of the item as soon as he'd got it, in which case it ought to be in his room, instead. *Well, perhaps he prefers to use a pen for drafting, and she types it all out for him later.* Many assistants acted as typists. Though why either of them thought Bradley would have much time for writing when he was evading the police was another matter.

Then she caught the drift of the conversation. Geoffrey was saying, "Miss Vixen is a real journalist. She's not interested in gossip . . . though if you're approached by a hummingbird named Gladys, I should advise you to be *very* circumspect. But you can trust Vera to be objective."

Darcy muttered something Vera couldn't quite catch to which Geoffrey said, "No, I don't think so. You could certainly ask her yourself."

Vera decided that whatever Darcy's concerns might be, it wouldn't help to barge in now. She crept back downstairs and waited in the front room again.

Moments later, Geoffrey returned. "Miss Montrose will be down shortly. She was fast asleep, you see."

"Of course," Vera said, making a mental note that the chipmunk excelled at what might be termed *the hospitality lie*. "I'm happy to wait."

When Darcy came down, she immediately suggested a short walk to another location. Judging by the way the lynx kept glancing up the stairs, Vera guessed she didn't want Bradley to stroll in and interrupt the meeting. Vera felt much the same way, so she suggested Joe's Mug. Darcy was quite willing to follow along, especially at the mention of coffee.

The two creatures settled into a quiet booth overlooking the main street, where more creatures were moving to and fro on their way to work or school or wherever their busy lives were taking them.

"You know," said Darcy, "I spoke to Chief Braun yesterday afternoon."

Vera did know that, but she hadn't been able to sit in because she was working at the *Herald*. "Yes, but I hope you'll be able to tell me a little more."

"I guess. Don't know what you want to know that I didn't already tell him."

"Maybe nothing, but let's try." Vera opened her notebook. "First of all, I think it's important to get *all* the things that you can remember recorded, so that you'll be able to give a full report to the metropolitan police later. You didn't speak to them before you left the city?"

Darcy shook her head. "I left as soon as I could, only several hours after Mr. Marvel. He told me that it was most important for him to avoid the publicity that would come with an interrogation by the police. He instructed me to pack some of his things and gather a few essential items and follow him on the next ferry up to Shady Hollow."

"But Mr. Marvel was here last year on his book tour," Vera said. "Were you not his assistant then?"

"Oh, yes," Darcy said. "That's right. I planned his whole tour, and I did remember the name, after a little while, because he overstayed his welcome and was almost late to his next event."

Vera suppressed a smile at Darcy's unexpectedly accurate phrasing. "So you packed things up and caught the next ferry upriver. Wait a moment. Surely the apartment was occupied by police from the moment the body was discovered, or shortly thereafter. And yet they let you take things?"

Darcy clarified, "Not from the apartment. Bradley also keeps some things at the publishing office. He doesn't work there much, but he keeps it ready in case he's stuck on a tour and needs items sent. I just grabbed those things."

"Ah." That did make sense. Vera said, "If it's all right, I'd like to ask you some specific questions about what you saw at the crime scene. You understand how important it is to be able to have all the details to be accurate."

"Sure, ask me whatever you want." Darcy sipped the coffee in front of her.

"In your own words, will you tell me what you saw when you came up to the apartment? Why don't you start from the moment you entered from the street."

"We were returning from a dinner meeting," Darcy began.

"Um, just to be clear," Vera said. "Was this a meeting or a date?"

Darcy looked appalled. "Ew! It was a meeting. Have you seen the types he dates? Flashy models who couldn't tell the difference between a novel and a brick. And even if he did ask to date me, he's way too old for me!"

"Did he ever ask?"

"No, thank goodness. Bradley's an insufferable boss, but he's not creepy, you know?"

Vera did know, in fact. "I'm glad to hear it," she said. "So you never dated Bradley?"

Darcy snorted. "Of course not. I'm an idiot, but I'm not that much of an idiot."

"Okay, thank you for being so honest. Go on."

"The apartment is on a small street called Mockingbird Court, which is also the name of the building. And because it's a rather posh building, there's always an attendant at the front door. It was a weasel working that evening, and he opened the door for us, said good evening, adding a 'Welcome home' to Mr. Marvel. The weasel told him that a package had been delivered while Mr. Marvel was out. Bradley assumed it was another box of fan mail and said it could wait until morning to be brought up. At that point, we walked through the foyer and up the stairs."

"And what time was that?"

"It must've been just after seven o'clock. I don't remember the exact time."

"Okay, so you walked up the stairs to Bradley's floor. And which floor was that?"

"Fifth. He lives in 5A."

"The penthouse, he called it."

Darcy rolled her eyes. "He would. It's a nice apartment, but Mockingbird Court doesn't have penthouses."

Vera made a note to remind herself to double-check all of Bradley's claims. Then she said, "So at the fifth floor, you left the staircase and walked down the hallway to his door. Did you see anyone in the hallway?"

"Yes," said Darcy. "There were two creatures: a mouse and a groundhog. The mouse was dressed in an evening outfit, as if she had been preparing to head out. The groundhog was wearing a nightgown and a dressing robe."

"And what were they doing?"

"They were both standing right by Bradley's door, looking in."

"What did you do next?"

"Well, of course we hurried to where they were, and Bradley pushed them aside, rather rudely. He was yelling at them for trespassing, said he hated it when fans hounded him. But it was obvious that they weren't fans; they were just other tenants in the apartment building. He has no idea who his neighbors are."

"Were you just behind Mr. Marvel at this point?"

"Yes, we reached the door at almost the same moment. Bradley stepped in first, and then I came in right after him. I stopped short because I could see what was in the middle of the floor, and why those other two creatures had been looking in."

"Please describe what you saw, as precisely as possible."

"I saw the body of Rick Renard, the editor at our publishing house, dead in the middle of the living room. He was lying on the rug in front of the sofa with a knife next to him, and there was blood everywhere. A big pool of blood, like a red lake," she added, her eyes losing focus for a moment.

"How did the rest of the apartment look? Did it seem to be disturbed in any way? Was anything missing?"

"It looked more or less the same as what I had seen on previous visits. I'm afraid I wasn't paying attention after I noticed the body. It was horrible. Bradley was yelling about a robbery, some crime gone wrong. I don't know why he said that, because there was no way he didn't recognize Rick the same moment I did. Maybe he was in shock."

"Would you say that his reaction appeared to be genuine? Do you believe he really was surprised to find the body there?"

"Oh, yes." Darcy nodded vigorously. "There is no way he would have behaved that way if he'd known what was coming. I told him to stop yelling about a robbery, because there was no reason for Rick to come to the apartment and steal anything. There wasn't anything worth stealing, not for him." Darcy's tone had acquired a certain bitterness just for a moment, which Vera noted silently. But she moved along, not yet ready to discuss an idea that was forming in her mind about the clever assistant.

"What did you do then?" Vera asked.

"I tried to calm Bradley down. I said that we needed to contact the police immediately, and the mouse who had been at the door said that she would run down to the building manager and let them know. I thought that was a very good idea. But Bradley spun around and yelled not to do it. The mouse was already gone, though."

"Why didn't he want the police to come?"

Darcy gave her a look. "Why do you think? He'd already started to work out the angles, and he decided that one of the angles was very bad publicity, and he didn't want to risk it. He shut the door to the hallway and turned to me and said he had to get out of town."

"He wanted to flee immediately?"

"Oh, yes. He told me to pack a few things, get the typewriter, and then buy a ticket on the next upstream ferry to Shady Hollow. He said it was the perfect place to go because the cops in the city wouldn't even know it existed. He said he would go right away, even if he had to pay for a private boat. He said I should take the next ferry, and that all I had to do was lay low for a few hours because the cops wouldn't think to go to my place for at least a day or so." Darcy shook her head. "I can't believe that he was already thinking like that. I don't mean to say that it was premeditated. Just . . . it was as if Bradley Marvel for a moment became Percy Bannon and knew what a secretive international agent would do in that situation, which is of course the exact opposite of what a normal citizen should do." She laughed softly. "I guess he really does like to play the role when he can. Even when it ruins everybody else's life."

It was obvious that by everybody else's life, Darcy meant her own. Vera drank her coffee and tried not to allow pity to show on her face.

After Vera finished up her interview with Darcy, the lynx returned to Bramblebriar, and Vera remained to study her notes. There was something that Darcy wasn't telling her. Maybe it didn't mean she was the killer . . . but she was holding back. And innocent creatures generally didn't do that. But then again, there were many reasons why someone might keep a secret—to protect a friend, or a career, for example—and Darcy did seem like the sort of creature who could keep a secret.

As Vera was sipping her coffee, she looked up to see Orville standing in the doorway of Joe's, scanning the crowded restaurant. Vera assumed he was looking for her, so she raised a paw and gave a wave. The bear nodded and approached her table.

"Snack time already?" she teased.

"I wish this could be a date, but there's no time. Vera, sorry to ask again today, but could you please come to the police station with me? The cop from the city has arrived, and he has some questions for you."

"Me?" she asked, puzzled. "He wants to talk to me?"

"Yeah. Before he interviews Marvel and his assistant. Not sure why, but I did tell him you're a reporter, so maybe he wants to talk about what all you've heard so far from Bradley and Darcy. Want to follow me?"

She didn't, but she had very little choice.

Chapter 7

The fox was more than slightly alarmed, but she gathered her notes and left a tip on the table for Esme. Orville was wearing his most professional expression, probably because he felt nervous at the idea of a city cop observing his own more relaxed methodology. (*Methodology* being a word he only recently incorporated into his work vocabulary. This wasn't surprising, considering that his predecessor Chief Meade's *methodology* had involved taking most days off.) Vera wanted to ask questions as she followed him to the station, but she kept quiet. She would find out what was going on soon enough.

When the pair arrived, Vera saw a bison wearing the smart uniform of the metropolitan police force—all sharp pleats and shiny buttons—pacing slowly back and forth in front of Orville's desk. His eyes appeared small in his massive head, but they had a sharp look to them.

The bison didn't wait for Orville to make introductions. He said, "Hello there. I'm Detective Wendell Knox, Metropolitan Police." He tapped his badge with one hoof, as if there could be any doubt. "And you must be Vera Vixen."

The fox acknowledged that with a nod. She was still feeling somewhat nervous. Although she was innocent of any crime, Vera was nevertheless wary around any law enforcement creature she didn't know well.

The bison loomed over the fox, as he probably loomed over most creatures. It likely helped to establish his authority. She was determined not to be afraid. She had done nothing wrong. However, she *really* did not want her past relationship with Rick Renard to come to light.

Detective Knox gestured to a chair on the guest side of the desk. "Won't you take a seat, Miss Vixen? As I'm sure you're aware, I'm investigating the murder of one Mr. Richard Renard, which occurred in the city a few days ago. Naturally, the department is working hard to interview his wife, his family circle, and his colleagues. But Chief Braun here tells me that you're a journalist, and that you've spoken to both Mr. Marvel and Miss Montrose about what they, er, witnessed."

She relaxed slightly. If he only wanted to get Vera's impressions of a few suspects, or perhaps just glean some extra facts that he didn't already know, this would be painless. She said, "Yes, that's true. I was naturally curious about whatever had caused Mr. Marvel to be so alarmed as to come here, and I also know that it's better to get a witness account as soon as possible after an event. Memories tend to play tricks on us after a while, and details can get lost or confused."

Detective Knox gave her an approving nod. "The very thing I always tell recruits, Miss Vixen. I'm glad you recognize the importance of such matters. And because you were fortunate enough to be able to speak to Marvel and Montrose, I do hope that you can share what you learned. Obviously, neither of them was around to give official statements after the murder." His voice was mild, but the implication was clear: the two made a very big mistake in leaving town.

Vera pulled out her notebook. "I have everything here. I could copy it out for you?"

"Why don't you just summarize it for the moment, if you please." He leaned back in the chair with an interested expression.

Vera dutifully recited the particulars, going over first what Bradley had told her and then proceeding on to Darcy, noting carefully the few spots where their accounts differed. Knox sometimes asked a question about times, but for the most part he sat and nodded along. On the other side of the desk, Orville remained in his chair and watched Knox, perhaps eager to observe a big city cop in action.

"I'm happy to copy this all out for you to add to your case file," Vera said in conclusion. "I really have no intention of writing an article about this—I just did the interviews because I believed it could be important."

"Very helpful of you, Miss Vixen," the bison said. "Now there's one more thing I'd like to clarify. I understand that you knew the victim, Richard Renard."

She gaped at him. How could Detective Knox possibly know that? She stammered, "Ex-excuse me?"

Orville put his paw on the desk as he rose. "Hold on a minute! That's absurd!"

"Er, Orville, stop," she said, waving anxiously at him.

He turned to stare at her in bewilderment. "Stop? Why? This cop strolls into town acting all friendly and then starts lying about you? Maybe he's upset that you got the witness statements, and he didn't, but this is unacceptable! I'm going to report—"

"No, you're not, Orville," Vera said, her voice a little louder now. "Detective Knox is correct. I did know Rick Renard. He and I worked at the same newspaper. It was my first job out of college. He was my editor."

Now Orville gaped at her. "You knew him, and you didn't say?"

"It's . . . complicated." Vera cringed at the expression on Orville's face. This was worse than she dreamed.

"Why should it be? It's a weird coincidence, but you haven't lived in the city for years and who cares if he was a co-worker from way back when?"

Detective Knox said, "Perhaps Miss Vixen and I ought to discuss this without a third party present."

"I'm not letting you harass Vera just because you happen to be investigating this case. You're not talking to every creature in the city who used to work with Renard, are you?"

"Not yet," Knox said, unperturbed by Orville's outburst. "For now, I'm confining my conversations to those individuals who had a more than casual relationship with the victim."

"More than . . ." Orville trailed off. He crossed his forepaws and gave Vera a look that he reserved for the worst offenders.

So much for Vera's hope that the past would remain buried.

"Yes," Vera spoke carefully, aware that Orville was paying very close attention to each word. "We worked together, and we also dated." Vera was determined not to be ashamed or embarrassed. She was a modern female and thus entitled to have lovers. They had discussed their pasts briefly when they started dating, but not any specific details.

Orville coughed. He stepped back from the desk and muttered, "I need to go to Bramblebriar to let Marvel know that he'll be expected here for a formal statement later today. Miss Montrose too." He glared at the bison. "Anyone *else* you'll want to chat with while you're visiting?"

"Not at the moment, thank you."

"I'm going. If there's some emergency, you know where to find me."

The bison nodded his big head in acknowledgment, and Vera said nothing. She did not want to relate the details of her disastrous affair with Renard, and certainly not in front of her current beau.

Orville stalked out of the police station, and Vera was left alone with Detective Knox.

"He seems protective of the town's citizenry," Knox observed in that deceptively mild tone. "Or is it just of you?"

Vera rolled her eyes, refusing to answer that. "You have questions for me, Detective. Why don't you ask them while we've got the place to ourselves?"

"I appreciate your eagerness to cooperate, Miss Vixen."

"I bet," she grumbled.

The bison continued with his line of questioning. "When did you last see Mr. Renard?"

"It's been years. I haven't seen Rick since I left the city and moved to Shady Hollow, four years, five years at least. And you still haven't mentioned how you knew!"

"I'm not at liberty to share that information, Miss Vixen. So, you admit to being a former co-worker. But he was in fact your boss, correct?"

"Yes. He was my editor. He assigned me stories and reviewed everything I wrote. He had final say on what got printed in each edition—for our section, that is. That's how it works."

"What section was that?"

"Local politics and community affairs, mostly."

"Hmmm. Speaking of affairs, it would be correct to describe your personal relationship with him as an affair, yes? You knew he was married."

She sighed. "Yes, I knew. Not at first. I was young and naive and didn't ask any questions. But later, I did meet his wife a couple of times when she came to the newsroom." Suddenly, Vera had a vivid memory of the glamorous and elegant figure Mrs. Renard cut.

"Are you sure that you didn't see him recently? Such as when you were visiting the city?"

Vera was startled that the bison was aware of her recent movements. "Who told you that I was in the city?"

"That's not important. I happen to know you were there for three days and two nights, leaving the very day Renard was killed. In fact, only about an hour or so after the hour we've set as the time of death."

She inhaled sharply. "You've got to be joking. Are you suggesting that I'm a *suspect*?"

"Your words, not mine, Miss Vixen."

"No," she replied firmly. "I never saw him. I don't even know where he lived. I didn't know where he worked until Bradley mentioned it. As it happens, I was in the city to interview someone and to see an old friend. My former roommate, Chloe

McKibben. I did *not* see Rick Renard. I have had no contact with him since I moved away from the city."

"Well," the bison replied, "I'd like to take your word for it, Miss Vixen. However, because this is a murder investigation, I will require a more detailed account of your movements when you were in the city."

"Of course. I can write it up, along with the interview notes that I took. Unless I'm your sole suspect and those questions about Bradley and Darcy were just chitchat?"

"I'd love to see everything you can provide," he said, as if she were granting him a favor. Knox had a way of not actually answering one's question, and Vera didn't like it. "Oh, yes. One more thing."

The police officer pulled a little cloth bag from somewhere inside his coat and untied the string at the top. He pulled out a thin notebook, opened the front flap, and read out: "'Property of Vera Vixen, Shady Hollow. Reward if found.'"

She stared at him. "I don't understand. How did you get one of my notebooks?"

"Are you telling me you can't guess?" the officer asked her.

Vera shook her head. "No, I can't. I have a dozen of those, I go through them like some folks go through snacks. I use them for all my work."

"But you recognized it immediately."

"Well, of course! Wait, let me see it."

He showed two pages splayed open but refused to let her hold it. Vera leaned forward and saw notes from her interview with the architect of the bridge.

"Yes, that's mine. I used it in the city for a long-form article I'm working on, but I got so distracted when Bradley popped up here that I haven't had time to review anything or work on the article. I hadn't even noticed it was missing," she said. "But I don't understand why *you* have it." She frowned at the identical notebook she was still holding in her paws.

Detective Knox said, "This piece of evidence was found in Bradley Marvel's living room, not far from the body."

"What? *What?*" Vera could hardly breathe. "That's impossible!"

"And yet it happened. Isn't that curious, Miss Vixen." Knox stood up, tucking the notebook back into his pocket. "Well, I do have a few other folks to chat with, and I hear there's an adorable little festival going on. Perhaps I'll see you there. Because I'm quite sure you won't be leaving town any time soon. Good day, Miss Vixen."

Chapter 8

With that pronouncement, the bison strolled out of the police station, whistling a tune, presumably off to hector and interrogate some other innocent creatures.

Vera remained in the chair, too stunned to move. Had that really happened? How had the detective gained not only the knowledge of her recent trip, but also a years-old mistake she'd worked hard to forget? And the notebook! She must have misplaced it at some point during the trip to the city, but how could it possibly have made its way from any of the places where Vera had spent time, down to the neighborhood by the bay, to the very apartment in Mockingbird Court—a place Vera didn't even know existed until that wolf decided to show his face in Shady Hollow and tangle her up in his tale of woe.

She almost wondered if there was a conspiracy against her. Could Bradley have been aware that she was in the city and had her followed? Could he or his assistant somehow have nipped the notebook while Vera wasn't looking, and planted it at the scene? But then why would he come to Shady Hollow, risking his own reputation by acting like a fleeing suspect? Perhaps to see her own humiliation up close? (Vera *had* made Bradley leave Shady Hollow by means of a rather forceful threat last year.)

She'd have to figure the truth out on her own because she was officially a suspect now. Knox had told her specifically not to leave town, and the fox had never felt more guilty for something that she *knew* she didn't do.

When a shadow darkened the doorway, Vera knew two things almost immediately. Orville was back, and he was angry.

"Vera! What were you thinking?" the bear began right away. "How could you not tell me that you were acquainted with the murder victim?"

Vera turned to Orville, saying, "I can't talk about this now."

He slammed his paw down on his desk in frustration. "No? You too busy or something?"

"Yeah, because I have to clear my name of a murder charge! It's really going to upend my schedule!"

"What?" He stared at her, dumbfounded.

"Knox didn't tell you? They found evidence linking me to the crime scene. I'm probably the prime suspect!"

"Vera!" he roared.

Vera gulped, holding back tears. Without another word, the fox gathered up her things and left the police station.

She hurried to the bookstore, her mind completely overthrown by the detective's accusation. Her initial reaction, which was that the idea was too ridiculous to even contemplate, fought with the secondary impulse to flee from the threats. Vera had spent so much time over the past few years of her life trying to forget Rick ever existed. To be confronted now with the absurd notion that not only was she still thinking of him, but that she plotted an elaborate operation to return to the city for the purpose of luring him to an unexpected location, only to kill him! That was too much.

Unsurprisingly, the beautiful early autumn day hardly penetrated Vera's thoughts. She didn't notice the brilliantly clear sky, complete with a crescent moon hanging high in the west before it set down below the distant mountain ridge. She ignored the many touches of color along the street and sidewalk, including the cheerful sunflower swags that had been carefully constructed by the residents of the retirement home, each one hung on a lamppost to brighten the view.

She replied automatically and without thinking to the greetings offered to her by others who were out and about, such as the badger Mr. Unterwald, who doffed his hat as he passed, and even the rather concerned sounding Dorothy Springfield, a rat who was prone to dreamy and abstracted moods herself, but who *always* noticed when another creature wasn't all there.

Vera entered the bookstore, hoping that it would be a slow hour. In this, she had guessed correctly, and she saw Violet Chitters leaning on the front counter, leafing through the latest issue of a literary magazine.

"Oh, hullo there, Miss Vixen," Violet said, with a smile. She closed the magazine with one paw and stood at attention. "Is there anything I can help you find today?"

"Marvel's not here, is he?" Vera asked, looking around.

"No, he signed pretty much everything here that could

take ink, so he won't be in for a bit. Though he did suggest an impromptu reading in a day or two, which Lenore snapped up, as you can imagine."

Orville would hate that, Vera couldn't help but think. Aloud, she said, "It will be well attended. Lenore is who I'm looking for, actually."

"In her office, filling out some orders. I'll ring for her." Violet reached over toward a silver bell that was on the counter. She tapped it three times, the preestablished code to let Lenore know that she was needed.

A moment later, the raven flew down from her office at the very top of the silo portion of the store, fluttering past history, politics, fiction, poetry, and the other subjects that occupied the shelves wrapping around the inside of the silo on each floor.

When she landed, Lenore took one look at Vera and immediately recognized that her friend was in distress. She said to Violet, "You're in charge for the next hour. We'll be back."

Violet nodded, but couldn't keep a trace of apprehension from her voice when she said, "Where shall I find you if there's a problem? Not that there will be!"

"We'll be at the Bamboo Patch," said Lenore.

Vera nodded at this decision, already craving the peaceful setting of the restaurant.

As the two friends left the bookstore, Lenore said in a quiet tone, "Don't talk about anything yet. We'll get our table and some tea before you have to spill. But I can tell something's gone wrong, hasn't it?"

"You could say that again," Vera muttered as she negotiated the busy sidewalks next to her friend.

Fortunately, Shady Hollow was not large, and so, even though the Bamboo Patch was more or less on the other end of the little downtown area, it didn't take long to reach the cross street and turn toward the restaurant, which was almost entirely concealed behind a thicket of tall bamboo that had been planted a few years ago when Sun Li first opened his restaurant.

To walk through the light green shade of the bamboo grasses and hear a few of the stalks knock against each other with a hollow sound was to step away from the ordinary world of the bustling little river town and enter a different place, one that encouraged a creature to breathe a little slower and enjoy a few moments of serenity . . . ideally, along with an exquisitely prepared meal.

There were certainly other customers enjoying the restaurant, for all during the Harvest Festival, visitors were looking for places to eat as well as novel experiences. But the eatery was designed in such a way that many of the booths and tables felt rather private, even though they were no further apart than in most other restaurants. Nonetheless, Vera requested that their hostess take them to the most secluded table available. It was in the corner overlooking a beautiful little patio, which was surrounded by a bed of multicolored chrysanthemums, and rising behind it, the green wall of bamboo.

They ordered tea, and once the hostess had left, Lenore leaned forward and said, "Okay let's hear it."

The cozy restaurant exuded warmth and calm. Vera and Lenore sat across from each other, cups of steaming tea in front of each of them. Other customers enjoyed their meals around the pair, and the delicate clink of teacups and the soft hum of conversation combined to create a tranquil atmosphere. Vera took a deep breath, willing herself to absorb the calm.

It didn't really work.

Vera sighed. "I'm so glad you could take a little time away. It feels like ages since we've had a proper chat."

Lenore nodded. "I know, right? This hasn't exactly been an easy week for you."

"You have no idea."

They took a sip of their tea. Vera had ordered the cinnamon plum, and she savored the comforting warmth.

Then Vera said, "Ugh, I can't get into it yet. It's . . . it's infuriating! Tell me something normal first, anything normal. Have you read anything interesting lately?" She grasped at this, knowing her friend always had an answer ready.

Lenore's eyes glowed. "Actually, yes! I just finished *The Elephant's Memory*. It's enchanting—so beautifully written."

Vera frowned. "Wait, is that the one where the elephant's friend turns out to be the memory of a long-dead ancestor and they've really just been talking to themself the whole time?"

"Yes!" Lenore fluttered her wings, which she did when getting enthusiastic about a book. "It sounds morbid, but it's incredibly moving."

"What drew you to it, aside from it being morbid?" asked Vera.

"Do I need another reason?" The raven cawed, but then looked thoughtful. "Well, it's a unique perspective—the one of a dead character, I mean. Death adds this poignant touch to the whole narrative. You should give it a try."

Vera nodded over her teacup. "I will if I ever get the chance. Thanks for the recommendation."

"Live to serve," Lenore said. "Now how about you tell me whatever is about to make you burst with rage."

Vera inhaled, then practically hissed, "I'm a suspect, Lenore. That stupid detective from the stupid city sat in his stupid chair and played me for a stupid fool and then casually informed me that I'm a suspect in Renard's murder."

The raven was suitably stunned. "Uh . . . how? Why?"

The moment had come to tell Lenore about her connection with the murder victim in Bradley Marvel's case. Vera took another sip of tea and then put down her cup with precision on the table.

"Lenore," the fox began, and the raven fixed her gaze on her friend.

"You know that I don't like to talk about my past before I came to Shady Hollow, but recent events have shown me that nothing is ever truly behind us. I'm going to have to tell you everything.

"When I finished college," Vera began, turning her teacup around in her paws, "I was anxious to begin my life as a journalist."

Lenore nodded but did not speak, not wishing to interrupt the flow of Vera's memories.

"I desperately wanted to move out of my parents' house and do what I had dreamed of doing. They didn't approve of my studying journalism. That's when I met my best friend, Chloe. We shared a small apartment—nothing much, but it was so exciting to have our own place! She was a law student, while I'd gotten a job at a city newspaper. And my editor was Rick Renard."

"Oh, no," Lenore said in a low voice.

"Yeah, you can probably guess what's coming. He paid attention to me from the very beginning. He was charming and flirtatious. I was so green that I didn't even realize he was married until it was too late. By then, I was completely in love with him. We dated for a few months, and it was a whirlwind. He kept saying he adored me and that he intended to leave his wife.

Of course, it turned out that he had a reputation for carrying on with young reporters and office assistants and such. But no one warned me, and even though I thought I was a journalist, I didn't ask questions."

Lenore's expression had grown wide-eyed. "Oh, Vera, I'm sorry."

Vera stopped talking for a bit and poured herself some more tea from the large pot on the table. She refilled Lenore's cup as well.

"It gets worse. Somehow my mother got wind of what was going on—don't ask me how. She invited me over to the house for dinner, and she and my father told me flat out that they didn't approve of my relationship with my boss and that I had to end things, for my own good. I was shocked, as you can imagine. Rick told me to keep it a secret, and I thought that it *was* a secret. I responded much like you would expect from a young creature in love for the first time. I yelled at my parents that they didn't know what they were talking about, and Rick and I would always be together, and his wife didn't understand him, and all other kinds of nonsense."

At this point in the story, the fox teared up a bit at the memory, the feelings still unexpectedly sharp. Her friend slid one of the cloth napkins across the table. Vera wiped her eyes and thanked her.

"I can't believe that I'm still upset about this. I mean, it was ages ago. I'm much more emotional about the rift with my folks than I was about the way things ended with Rick. My mother was of course right, and things did end poorly with Rick. But he didn't just break my heart; he also managed to destroy my career."

"Wait, what?" Lenore gasped.

"One night," the fox continued, "Rick and I were in his office after-hours, which happened a lot. Virtually everyone else at the paper had gone home. Well, I happened to see some correspondence on his desk about the upcoming mayoral election. This was a hotly contested vote between the incumbent, a stoat named Connor Warburton, and a newcomer, a beaver called Henry Mallory. Mallory was considered the favorite to win, but it was by no means a sure thing. When Rick left the office for a moment, I took a closer look at the papers on his desk."

"What'd you see?"

"Something I never expected: Rick was taking bribes from Mallory to print articles that were favorable to him and portrayed Warburton negatively. Of course, I was appalled, but managed to recover myself by the time Rick returned to his office with a bottle of wine. Rick wanted me to stay and drink a glass or two with him, but I said that I had to get home. I was astonished by what I had discovered, and I even tried to tell myself I'd made a mistake. I needed to be alone to think about what it all meant."

Lenore nodded sympathetically.

Just then, Sun Li, the panda who was the proprietor of the Bamboo Patch, stopped by their table with a fresh teapot of hot water and removed the empty one. With his usual tact, he made no comment since it was apparent that the two friends were in a serious conversation. He merely gave a friendly nod and moved on.

Vera continued with her story.

"I went home and went right to my room. I didn't even want to talk to Chloe about the situation until I had figured out my course of action. She was a lawyer, and I was worried she'd jump right into the legal aspects. I couldn't think about that yet! I thought I was in love with him, and I just couldn't believe that Rick would do something so unethical. After a lot of tossing and turning, I resolved to have a private conversation with him when I went in to work the next day."

"How'd that go?" Lenore asked.

"Well, when I got to the newspaper in the morning, the whole office was in an uproar. Elspeth Wickers, an elderly rabbit who was the office manager, was waiting for me by my desk. She told me that I was fired! I was to collect my things and leave the office immediately. I was completely shocked, and it must have shown on my face because she patted my paw with as much sympathy as I had ever seen her exhibit, and then she left."

The fox could see that her friend had lots of questions at this point, and she hurried to explain what had happened.

"Somehow, a rival newspaper had discovered that *someone* on our paper was taking bribes to print articles about Mallory in a positive light and to malign Warburton. They threatened to expose the creature responsible. Rick was tipped off early and managed to divert the paper trail that led to him . . . directly onto me instead. The creature that I had thought loved me instead framed me for the crime that *he* committed. Then Rick appeared at my desk!"

"He did *not*." Lenore looked furious.

"Oh, yes. He looked all concerned as he spoke, but what he said was that I had a lot to learn about the world. No hard feelings, but if I made a fuss, he'd tell everyone about our relationship and that I used him to get an edge in the newsroom, and then no paper would hire me.

"I was all fire at that point, and I said that I'd expose the truth.

He just chuckled and told me that I was a naive little thing. No one cares about the truth unless they can profit by it, and what profit could I offer?" Vera sighed. "The worst of it was that he was right. I hadn't taken any of the items on Rick's desk, so I couldn't prove what I'd seen the night before. He completely outmaneuvered me. I felt so betrayed that I couldn't even face him. I just wanted to crawl into a hole with my shame."

"I'd have gone for his eyeballs," Lenore said, "but I get it. What did you do?"

Vera snorted in laughter despite the seriousness of the conversation. "What could I do? I gathered my belongings in a box, my notebooks and pens, and my mug that read NUMBER ONE REPORTER, which in retrospect I might have purchased a little too early. I left the newspaper offices without a word to any of my colleagues. I made it to the sanctuary of my apartment before I started to cry. Fortunately, Chloe was at work. I didn't feel up to explaining things to her. I made several decisions as I packed a suitcase. I'd leave the city and take the ferry to someplace that looked promising. I left a note for Chloe with money for the next few months' rent. I just said I had to leave—I didn't explain anything about Rick's scheme or how he got me fired. And I didn't tell my parents because I just couldn't face the *I told you so*'s."

Vera drank some more tea and then finished up her story.

"I'm sure you're wondering why the scandal was never made public. I sent a message to Rick before I left the city. I told him that I would go quietly, taking the blame for his appalling actions, and that I would never contact his wife about our relationship . . . as long as he squelched this story. I said that I didn't care how he did it, but the story about the bribery of the mayoral candidate would never see the light of day. I never received an answer from him, but I anxiously scanned the newspapers for weeks afterward, and I never saw anything in print. I don't know how he did it, but he must have convinced that rival paper to kill the story. He always had a lot of influential friends."

Lenore asked, "Then how did you end up in Shady Hollow, and what did you do before you came here?"

Vera took another sip of tea. "I hopped on the southbound ferry with all my worldly goods—well, all that I could fit in my bag—and got off at one of the very last stops, a little place called Stumphole Landing. I took the first job I could find, in a coffee shop, and I worked hard and saved money. I was able to rent a small apartment with what little I had saved. For several weeks, all I did was go to work and come home and read whatever newspapers I could get my paws on. I didn't go out or really talk to my neighbors. I sent Chloe a message, asking her to contact my parents. I wanted them to know that I was safe, but I was too ashamed to speak to them directly."

"You were only guilty of being young," Lenore said in a gentle tone that was unusual for her.

Vera just shook her head. "I knew I didn't want to sling coffee for the rest of my life. I still felt the call to be a reporter. There was a small paper in town, just a weekly that amounted to a little bit more than a broadside. It was called the Stumphole Landing *Intelligencer*, and it was run by a stork who was—to say the least—rather eccentric. He was on the older side, and always dressed in the most formal style, whether he was stopping to buy bread from the bakery, or meeting a client, or sitting in the park."

"Sounds interesting."

"He was. He was born and raised in that little town, but

somehow or other, he got a hold of pretty much every book I had ever heard of. He'd read all the classics and could quote from them by memory. I don't remember a single time that I asked him for the meaning of a word, and he didn't come back with it immediately along with the correct spelling and usually a quote from some beloved literature that used it."

"And he hired you?" Lenore asked.

"Yes. I don't think he needed anyone else working on the paper, but when I expressed interest in doing some reporting, he very kindly took me under his wing and gave me a beat. He didn't really care to report on news originating outside the region. He considered himself an expert on local matters and was far more interested in that, rather than news coming from the city or elsewhere in the world.

"But as it happens," Vera said, "I was *keenly* interested in every scrap of news I could get from the city, so it was my job to visit the tiny library and the tiny police station and the tiny office at the docks, which were all the places news from 'abroad' was likely to show up. I would talk to the police chief to find out if any news had come by boat or wingmail that might be of interest to readers. And I talked to the librarian, who always seemed to have word from her correspondents in other parts of the world. Every week I'd compile all the tidbits that I felt were interesting enough, and then write a column for the weekly."

Lenore nodded. "So you did get to be a real reporter!"

"Sort of. My compensation for the work was hardly enough to buy breakfast, let alone provide me a living, but it kept me in touch with news from the city. Plus, I was learning more about the business of keeping a newspaper running than I had ever learned in my journalism classes. After about a year, I felt like I was ready to find a full-time job as a reporter, and to his credit, my boss agreed. Said it was time for me to spread my wings . . . metaphorically speaking."

"Not everyone has our particular advantages," her raven friend admitted, fanning out her feathers.

"He reached out to several colleagues he knew to find out if a position was available. As it turned out, there was one in a town further north. It was in the foothills, a really beautiful place called Acanthusville. The job was a full-time position, and I jumped at the chance. I did that for a couple of years and learned even more and started to get a sense of what type of reporter I really wanted to be. While I was grateful for the work I'd done in Stumphole Landing, and again in my new town, I knew that I really enjoyed working on longer pieces. So I looked for a position that would allow me to do so. It took a while, another few years, and another few jobs, but eventually one of the stories I researched required me to travel to Shady Hollow to talk to a few folks I couldn't reach otherwise."

"I remember when you arrived," said Lenore.

Vera smiled, recalling her first impressions of the town. "Something about this place just made me feel like I wanted to stick around. Luckily, there was an opening for a reporter at the *Herald*, and Stone was impressed enough with my résumé and my references that he hired me on. And, of course, I've been happy here ever since."

"You never wanted to go back to the city?"

Vera shook her head. "It's funny. While I was working at that job, I read every single newspaper that came out of the city. I scanned every column and every inch for news of Rick and that politician to find out what happened. It was odd, because *nothing* was ever mentioned in print, but I always felt like the next day I'd read my own name in an article, and everything would come out. Of course, sometimes I thought about hopping back on a boat, going downriver, and visiting the city again. Plus, I really wanted to talk to my mother and father, to give them some closure about my abrupt departure, and to explain what had really happened. But the fact was that the more time went by, the harder it got to picture myself going back. I wrote a few letters and sent some postcards to keep in touch. I never wanted my parents to worry . . . but it was just too difficult to go back. My father, I think, understood better than my mother. In his letters to me, he always said that he'd be glad to stop by. But that was his way of saying that he'd never dare visit unless I asked explicitly. And I never did. And, no, I never visited them in the city either."

"Not at all?" Lenore asked.

"The city started to feel like a dream to me. Even though I had grown up and spent so much of my life there, it felt like all of that had happened to somebody else, like my past was a story I was only reading about, a story that didn't involve me at all anymore."

"Your friends and family would always welcome you," Lenore said.

Vera sighed. "I know that, but I didn't want to hear my parents say, 'I told you so.' I just wanted to pretend that it had never happened. Eventually though, I began to heal, and I think Shady Hollow was a big part of that."

Vera sat back in her chair and heaved a sigh. It had been a hard story to tell, but she felt so much better that she had shared it all with Lenore.

"So now you can see why the police from the city are interested in me," Vera continued. "Naturally, I've had no contact with Rick Renard since I sent him that final message before leaving the city. But the cops don't believe that. They want to know what I was doing in the city a few days ago when a creature who definitely wasn't me murdered my former lover. If Bradley Marvel is innocent, and I believe he is, the police need another suspect."

Lenore sipped her tea, processing the personal and painful tale that Vera had shared with her.

"I'm so glad that you confided in me," the raven said. "And I'm sorry that you had to go through that ordeal, but I'm also glad that it brought you to Shady Hollow. You've done so much for this community, and I'm so happy that we're friends. Believe me, I know that when a creature isn't close with their birth family, they can create a second family out of their close friends. You and I have both done that, and our lives are all the richer for it."

The raven rarely expressed any feelings that were not sarcastic, and the fox was grateful that she did so now.

I will not cry again, Vera said to herself sternly. And then aloud, she said, "I'm so happy that we're friends too, Lenore. It means the world to me."

Sensing that the two companions had their fill of both tea and emotion, Sun Li drifted over to their table.

"Will there be anything else, ladies?"

"No, thank you, Li," Vera responded. "We'll take the check. We both have to get back to work."

The tea was just the respite Vera needed. She'd been buffeted lately by far too many unpleasant reminders of her past. She walked back to the bookstore with Lenore. At the door, the raven advised her, "Whatever happens, just remember that you've got friends on your side."

"So you're saying I should just hold tight and let justice prevail?" Vera asked with an edge of disbelief.

Lenore shook her head, stepping back into her shop. "Nah, justice doesn't happen when folks sit around. We're going to work together to make our own justice. And if anyone decides to get in the way, well, they're going to be sorry. Sooner or later."

Chapter 9

Vera decided to take a walk through town to absorb all that she could before being summarily tossed in a cell or sent downriver in the custody of the city's finest. Her route required passing by the Shady Hollow Harvest Festival, which was just starting to hit its stride. The annual event existed to showcase the bounty of the surrounding farms and forest during this most delicious of seasons. Vendors set up tables and booths all along Main Street and in the small park in front of the village hall, ready to welcome not just the town residents, but all those who traveled from the outlying neighborhoods and other hamlets too small to sponsor their own festival.

Today, boats were heading upstream and downstream, filling up the docks along River Drive, and even inventing makeshift landings along the river as farmers and entrepreneurs and visitors all hurried to get the best position for the celebrations. Little rowboats gently knocked together in the current, though each one was secured to a post or tree branch with a long rope. And throughout the town, the side streets were much busier than usual as creatures trundled carts to their destinations, each one filled to the top with crates and boxes, plus vast piles of squashes, apples, potatoes, bundled-up cornstalks, and countless other items.

Vera loved the festival since it provided such a wonderful opportunity to sample every offering from local bakers and cooks, not to mention the ale and wine and cider and other delicious drinks dreamed up especially for the event. She passed the large table that was hosted by the rabbits of Cold Clay Orchards and accepted an offering of a beautiful, burgundy-skinned apple from one of the workers behind the table.

"Excellent year for the crop! Perfectly crisp and wonderfully sweet," he told her cheerfully. "We'll be eating apples into February; these will keep so well."

Vera thanked the rabbit and tucked the apple into the satchel slung over her shoulder.

Another vendor held up a small tin pie plate. "Hello there! Did you want to try some apple pandowdy?"

Under normal circumstances, the answer would almost certainly have been an unqualified yes. But Vera was in no mood for the happy chatter that always accompanied the samples. At the moment, she was far too preoccupied with the murder of Rick Renard, and what it might mean for her personally. Would she be vilified for her past mistakes, even if she could prove her innocence of the murder? Would she have to leave Shady Hollow forever?

As the fox walked among the booths, her thoughts chasing one another in circles in her head, she spotted a welcome sight just past the cider table. A little red popcorn cart. Vera made her way over to where Muriel Lodge, a hedgehog and relative newcomer to town, was dishing up bags of her delicious popcorn. Muriel made a fine living by trundling her mobile popcorn cart to various events around Shady Hollow. Sometimes, she parked it in the middle of town and made the local business creatures come to her. Vera had immediately become a regular, given her penchant for sweet treats. Muriel offered plain buttered popcorn as well as delicious, gooey caramel popcorn. Often, she added a seasonal flavor, which was currently a luscious-smelling pumpkin spice.

"Hi, Muriel," she called, catching sight of the small creature hard at work bagging her treats and popping fresh corn.

"Good to see you, Miss Vixen. Can I get you your usual?" the hedgehog inquired. Vera regularly enjoyed a mixed bag of buttered and caramel popcorn. Muriel had a head for business, and she never forgot an order.

The fox sighed and shook her head. "Actually, no, thank you, Muriel. Perhaps another time."

Muriel's mouth dropped open. "Uh." She had been in town just long enough to understand that this was a highly unusual situation. It was not in the hedgehog's nature to pry into her customers' personal lives, so she didn't ask questions. She merely wished Vera a good day and carried on with her work of filling individual bags to the brim with popcorn. Vera could feel Muriel's inquiring gaze hit her back as she walked away.

As Vera left the popcorn cart without a little bag of crunchy goodness clutched in her paw, she pictured the next day's headline: *Local reporter skips her snack! This is a first in Shady Hollow history. What could be bothering Vera Vixen?* The fox laughed at herself and felt just the slightest bit better. Then she saw Detective Knox ambling toward her, and her mood plunged back down.

"Miss Vixen," he said in a perfectly pleasant voice, as if he were an old friend happy to be reacquainted with her rather than someone intending to destroy her life. "I told you we'd meet again. And I was right before."

"About what?" she asked warily.

"It's a wonderful festival. Did you know they've got these things . . . what'd the badger call them . . . pumpkin puffs? Delicious."

"Pardon me, Detective Knox, but I'm not exactly in the mood to make small talk."

"Large talk then?" he suggested with a wry grin.

"How about true talk." Vera nodded to a picnic table under a tree not far from where they were standing. "If you're going to be forthright, I *am* interested in learning more specifics about the crime scene," she said. "I know that the body was found in Bradley Marvel's apartment, but I don't know much beyond that. Why don't you ask him? He's probably here at the festival." Vera looked around, half-expecting the wolf to emerge from the crowd.

Knox shook his head. "He'd better not be. I stopped by the inn where he and his assistant are staying and advised him that a low profile would be best, at least until more facts are uncovered."

"You mean until he's eliminated as a suspect."

"That would make things easier," Knox agreed. "But in any case, I think I made myself clear that he should not be indulging his basest celebrity tendencies. He can walk around town, but no dramatic events or speeches should be happening. A lot to ask for Mr. Marvel, I know."

"Well, perhaps he'll be relieved. Then he can write uninterrupted."

"His assistant suggested that very thing. She seems very sharp. I expect that if Marvel does behave, she'll be the reason."

"Yes," Vera said thoughtfully. "Darcy is very sharp."

"But enough of that. Let's chat." Knox smiled. "Though you do understand, Miss Vixen, that as a suspect yourself, it would be inadvisable for me to share certain details with you."

"But if I were the killer," said Vera, "then I would already know all of this information and thus you wouldn't be giving me any new clues that I didn't already have."

That earned her a small laugh from the bison. "I suppose that's true. I'm rather intrigued anyway, so I'll play along, at least for a little while." He moved to the picnic table and took a seat. Vera perched opposite him.

"Let's begin with the basic facts," he said. "The victim, a fox, male, known to our prime suspect, was found in the living room of the apartment, owned or rented by another suspect, Bradley Marvel (wolf, author, famous, annoying). The body was found in the middle of the room on a small, woven rug, green in color, which made the red fur and darker red blood of the victim stand out by contrast."

"That's how Darcy described it. But how was the body positioned? Was he lying faceup or facedown? Was the knife still in the body, or had the killer removed it and dropped it nearby?"

"Guess," said Knox, looking at her steadily.

"I have no idea," Vera said, a little annoyed. "It all depends on whether Rick knew that he was about to be attacked, or if the killer snuck up on him, or waited until his back was turned. And even the way the body fell would depend on the strength of the blow, and even the height of the attacker. Bradley did mention that he recognized Rick right away, so I assume that means his head and face were visible, which makes me think he must've been lying on his back. Were there signs of a struggle?"

"As a matter of fact, not that we can tell. Of course, it's difficult to re-create such a scene based on purely material evidence, but in the city, for better or worse, we have a large archive of similar crimes to measure it against, so it's easy enough to form a hypothesis."

"And what is your hypothesis?" asked Vera. "If you've got one that doesn't involve me."

"Oh, I do. My guess is that Rick came to Bradley's apartment with some sort of threat or ultimatum. If it was a legitimate business offer, Rick would've called Bradley into the publishing house office rather than meet privately. But Rick didn't count on Bradley's reaction to whatever threat or offer he made, and thus was unprepared when Bradley reacted in a violent manner."

"That is a lot of speculation," said Vera. "According to Bradley, he had been returning from dinner along with his assistant, Darcy, and Rick's presence in his apartment was completely unexpected. He didn't previously arrange a meeting there."

"Well, that's just what a suspect would say," Knox noted. "And of course I have to be highly skeptical of any alibi Bradley offers, especially when his supporting witness is compromised."

"Compromised? In what way?" Vera asked, puzzled. "Darcy has appeared to me to be a very sensible and competent creature, whom I would guess plays a vital role in Bradley's work. I think that she would know what she saw."

"I'm not questioning her competency. I am questioning her objectivity."

"That's where I have to disagree with you," Vera said. "You're asking me to believe that an otherwise intelligent and sensible creature would be willing to not just lie, but also to accept the fact that she's covering up a murder. In my experience, most folks balk at the idea of being made accomplices to a crime, or when they're asked to condone something as heinous as a murder. Even if Darcy was in love with Mr. Marvel—which she's assured me she isn't—seeing him kill another creature, particularly someone she knew, would make her think twice about staying on Bradley's side."

"In my experience, Miss Vixen," he said, "love is an incredibly powerful emotion, and it can make folks do irrational and dangerous things. Now, it is possible that Bradley Marvel's alibi holds up, and in that case, it means that Darcy's does too. My colleagues are conducting interviews and chasing down a few leads related to the alibi. But until I hear definitive proof that Bradley and Darcy were far away from his apartment at the time of the killing, they remain very high on my suspect list."

"But I'm still at the top, am I? That stupid notebook!" Vera sighed. "Let's get back to the actual crime scene, then. I'm curious about why the murder weapon was still in the apartment. Wouldn't it make sense for the killer to take it with them?"

The bison shook his head. "No. Think of how suspicious it would look to be carrying a bloody knife through a hallway, or down onto a street. The killer had no need of it after the fact, and indeed, any connection with the knife would be dangerous. And since it had been taken from Bradley's kitchen, why not leave it there?"

"I guess that makes sense," said Vera. "Do you think the fact that the knife was from Bradley's apartment indicates that the killer didn't intend to hurt Rick? It was a weapon of opportunity, rather than something brought to the scene specifically, which we would expect in a premeditated crime."

"Yes, that's true. It doesn't rule premeditation out, but it would bolster a theory that the murder was the result of an argument gone wrong. Unfortunately, it is still a murder, and it is my job to find who did it and arrest them."

Vera nodded. "Bradley mentioned that his apartment door was open when he returned to the building. He also said that other residents were looking in, so what is the significance of that fact? Again, if I *were* leaving the scene of a crime," Vera mused, "I would want to delay the discovery of that crime for as long as possible. I would be quite sure to close the door behind me. Why do you think the killer didn't bother?"

"Naturally, you would say that you would do the opposite of whatever we found at the scene."

Vera frowned at him. "Don't be absurd."

"I am being perfectly serious. But to answer your question, it could have been a mistake. Most killers are not in command of their emotions or reactions afterward. They get nervous, jittery. They're not paying attention. Perhaps the killer thought they closed the door, but it didn't latch properly and bounced back. Or perhaps we are dealing with a different type of killer who was perfectly content with the idea that the body would be dis- covered very quickly. Mockingbird Court is a busy apartment building, with many residents. The idea that the hallway would've been empty for very long at that time of the evening was unlikely. To my mind, it's almost as if the killer wanted the crime to be discovered quickly."

During this chat, Vera had been drawing a rough map of the room as she understood it from Bradley's description. Now, she pushed that drawing across the table to Knox. "Take a look at this and tell me if the dimensions and the placement of the important objects in the room are right. I based it off what

Bradley explained to me, but I don't find him to be the most reliable of witnesses."

The detective spun the paper around and looked at it for a long moment. He took the pen that was on the table and made a few notations on the paper. "The body wasn't as central in the room. It was more to the side with the windows. It is true that the knife was located on the rug, but it was closer to the victim's forepaws."

"Was the victim dressed for the outside? What I mean is, was he wearing a hat or a scarf, something that would indicate he was about to leave, or did he look like he was in the middle of a visit?"

"Good question," said Knox. "The victim's hat, a brown felt fedora, was on the floor near his head, which suggests he was wearing it and it got knocked off when he fell. He wasn't wearing a coat, but the weather had been very warm that day, so he may not have been wearing one in the first place."

"I know you're operating on the assumption that Rick was killed shortly before the discovery of the body. Did your medical examiner confirm the time of death?"

"Yes, she was sure that the death could not have occurred more than two hours before the discovery of the body."

"Two hours is a fairly big window."

"Well, as I said, it had been unseasonably warm that day, and that made it more difficult to determine the exact time of death. Mr. Marvel himself said that he left his apartment for dinner at 5:30 p.m., and we have confirmation from the weasel who was on duty at the door that Mr. Marvel left Mockingbird Court at that time."

"So you do have witnesses who attest to all the times that various residents or visitors came and went? It seems to me that would make it easy enough for you to determine whether Bradley Marvel, or Darcy, or anybody, came and left."

"It's not so simple. There are multiple doors in the building. Granted, most residents use the front door through the foyer. That's where the mailboxes are, and where the main stairs are located. But there is also a back door for deliveries, or whenever a resident moves in or moves out, and for taking out trash. There are three other side doors at the bottom end of each wing of the building in case of fire. None of those doors are watched with regularity, so it is entirely possible for someone to leave out the front and then immediately circle around and re-enter through one of the other doors."

She frowned. "But surely those doors lock automatically."

"They do, but how easily could one be blocked open, or the killer have an accomplice waiting on the other side?"

"I don't suppose your colleagues have found any witnesses that saw either a fox, a wolf, or a lynx use one of those doors that night?" Vera asked.

"If I did, I certainly wouldn't tell you. That's information that we would need to withhold. However, I will say that this is a stickier case than I'm used to seeing. It is true that Bradley Marvel had the motive and means and opportunity, not to mention that the crime scene is conveniently located in his own apartment. But there is something else about this case that I don't like."

"What is that?"

"Bradley Marvel is a well-known writer who requires a certain . . . ahem, acceptability . . . for his public image. Would he be so foolish as to jeopardize his entire career? Would he really *kill* his own editor? And if he did, wouldn't he be able to hide the fact of the crime long enough to clean up the crime scene, or to stage a more plausible scenario? I find it difficult to believe that he has the sangfroid to kill another creature, and then go out to dinner."

"I don't believe that Bradley is a killer," said Vera. "I think he doesn't have the gumption."

Knox nodded at her. "Keen observation, Miss Vixen. You have noticed something in his emotional makeup that very few creatures have. I happen to agree with you. Marvel doesn't have the gumption to carry out such a . . . definitive act, especially one with such tremendous consequences. However, I wonder if *you* do. Do you believe yourself capable of murder?"

Chapter 10

D o *not* answer that question!" said a voice from behind her. Vera wheeled around at the sound, but it took a moment for her mind to catch up. Yes, it was true. Standing in front of her was her old roommate, Chloe. She gasped, "Chloe, what are you doing here?"

"Your wingmail said *asking for a friend*. I assumed that meant you. And here I arrive to find you getting grilled by a metropolitan cop."

Chloe reached for Vera's paw and hauled her up. She turned to Knox. "Vera Vixen is my client as of this moment. You will not speak to her without my knowledge, and it must be in my presence. My card." The cat whipped out a silver case and offered a creamy ivory card to the detective.

He read out, " 'Chloe McKibben, attorney at law. *Let sleeping cats lie.*' Sends quite a message, counselor."

"That's the idea. Good day, sir."

Chloe hustled Vera away from the picnic table. She said, "I came directly here from the docks, because someone told me you'd be at the festival. I'm just glad I didn't stop to tour the town first!"

"But I still don't understand why you're here! I only asked you for a recommendation."

Chloe smiled, two little fangs glinting briefly in the light. Her feline expression was sharp, alert, and inquisitive. "I couldn't imagine that you were *casually* inquiring about a criminal attorney, not if you were sending express wingmail to ask the question. And anyway, if it had been a casual inquiry, you certainly would've brought it up when we were just together in the city."

Vera nodded. "I guess that's true. As a matter of fact, I was asking on behalf of someone else when I sent the note. But I'm very glad you're here, because I probably am the one who needs an attorney after all."

"Listen, if I am to represent you in any capacity, I'll need to know everything. Why don't we go someplace where we won't be disturbed, and you can explain how you managed to get into this whole heap of trouble since I saw you last week."

Vera led Chloe back to her home, the cozy little den in which she always found refuge from the outside world. Chloe looked around the front room and nodded, as if this was exactly what she expected to find—a quaint and homey little space with a few pieces of rustic furniture, a shelf of books, and even more books piled up on the floor nearby. "You really are living the life up here in a little town in the woods. The complete opposite of what we called 'home' back in the city."

"It certainly is different," Vera admitted.

She thought about the tiny little flat that she and Chloe had shared. Vera saw the cracked plaster walls, the shabby regifted rugs and chairs. She remembered the table with the wobbly leg, and the constant sound of other tenants' paws pattering on the ceiling above them and in the hallway outside. She could even smell the overcooked food that always wafted in from other kitchens.

"When I first moved into that place," Vera reminisced, "I thought I'd really arrived. Living in the city, and away from my parents? It was an achievement . . . even if the place wasn't so glamorous."

"Not so glamorous? It was a dump!" Chloe laughed and took a seat in the oak ladderback chair at Vera's kitchen table (none of Vera's chairs matched—she liked it that way). "Do you have anything to drink? Because we have a lot to talk about, and that means we'll both need to stay awake."

By this point in the day, Vera usually preferred milder beverages. Today, however, she brewed a pot of strong coffee and sat a small bottle of Cold Clay's apple brandy on the table, just in case. Her former roommate nodded approvingly. Vera poured them each a large mug of coffee. Cream and sugar were already on the table, but Chloe opted for a healthy dollop of brandy. Vera added only cream to her mug.

Her friend picked up a pen. "Okay. Let's start with what Knox suspects happened, and then we can get into what really happened." Chloe was not wasting any time.

"As far as I can tell," Vera replied, "Detective Knox thinks that I went to the city a few days ago not to do my interview for my article about the bridge project, but instead to meet Rick Renard. He thinks I got upset with him as a former lover and that I murdered him in the heat of the moment. Although what he thinks either of us was doing in Bradley Marvel's penthouse, I couldn't tell you." She proceeded to give Chloe a summary of everything she knew about the crime so far, including Bradley's and Darcy's own statements.

Chloe took careful notes as the fox talked.

"So, the connection between Rick Renard and Bradley Marvel was that Renard was Marvel's editor at Fieldstone Books?"

Vera nodded as she sipped her coffee.

"And that's how Knox thinks I'm connected too. But he's wrong. I swear I've not had any contact with Rick since I moved out of the city. I didn't know that he had left the newspaper, let alone that he'd shifted fields and was working as a fiction editor. And since I barely know Bradley Marvel either, I had no idea that the two of them were even colleagues."

The cat studied her notes and added more brandy to her coffee mug.

"It seems that Knox is making an awful lot of assumptions. Purely circumstantial evidence."

"Well, it's worse than that. One of my notebooks was found at the crime scene."

"What?" Chloe squeaked, astonished.

"I have no idea how it got there. But Knox showed it to me, and it *is* mine. I had been using it earlier on my trip. All I can think is that I lost it somehow, or that someone stole it and placed it there."

"Do you remember the last time you definitely, *definitely* saw it?" Chloe asked intently.

"Sure. The last entry is dated because I took notes for my interview. I'm sure I put it back in my satchel when I left my subject's place. That was the day before Rick's murder, almost a day and a half, if he was killed in the evening."

"Okay. That's not great, but I'm sure we'll figure out how this could have happened. If this Detective Knox tries to charge you with anything, I'll stay in Shady Hollow for as long as it takes, or if you need to come to the city, we can deal with it there."

"If I have to go back to the city," Vera pointed out, "it will mean things have gone very badly."

"I hate to bring up the possibility that things could go awry," Chloe said then, putting her pen down and giving Vera a steady look. "But if the very worst comes to pass . . . you could always just leave."

"Leave?" Vera echoed. "Leave where? My house?"

Chloe peered around the living room as if looking for some hidden door, but then she replied, "This place is just what you're calling home for now. It's not exactly the den of your foremothers, is it? You've lived other places before, and you'll live other places after. I'm not talking about a residence, Vera. I'm saying that you could leave Shady Hollow. Leave the woodlands, in fact. There's a whole world out there, and you're an enterprising creature. You could disappear from here and reinvent yourself somewhere else. You've done it before."

Vera was flummoxed by the matter-of-fact way Chloe laid this all out. "Where?"

"Anywhere! Cross the mountains, cross the sea. Maybe the desert appeals to you. All I'm saying, Vera, is that it's an option. If you need it."

"If I left, everyone would assume I'm guilty!"

"But you'd be free," Chloe said softly. "Which is infinitely preferable to being righteous in prison, yes?"

"I'm not sure about that."

"Look, I do believe you're innocent. Of course I do. You're one of my oldest friends. But you also have to believe me. Justice does not always prevail in matters of the law. Prisons are filled with perfectly innocent creatures who just assumed that everything would work out because they explained to the cops and the prosecutor and the judge and the jury that they hadn't done anything wrong. And they're shocked when the verdict comes back, and then it's too late. Do you want to trust a system that you know to be imperfect, Vera?"

"It may be imperfect, but that's no reason to run away. I'm innocent, not naive. I'll fight this accusation to the very end!"

Chloe stared at her for an achingly long moment, then gave a sharp nod. "Good! I'm glad to hear it."

Vera gaped at her. "Wait, was that a *test?*"

"It's important to know what a client will do when they're heading for the waterfall downstream . . . metaphorically speaking," Chloe said, with a little shrug. "Some of them are happy to grab at any branch offered. They don't care about clearing their name; they just want to be out of danger."

"I care!"

"Well, you did run away before," Chloe observed. "After the whole . . . thing." She waved a paw to encompass all of Vera's youthful ideals and indiscretions.

"That was different! I didn't know what was happening, and I panicked. And besides, there were no cops asking me to stick around then. Leaving wasn't a criminal act."

"Technically, no. And let us hope that the police never decide to explore that old situation. You don't want the label of 'criminal' attached to your name if this current mess ever does show up in front of a jury."

Vera winced. "Chloe, you're not being very reassuring."

"It's wise to consider the worst possible scenario. Trust me, Vera. I know what I'm doing. Police, judges, juries . . . they always end up doing exactly what I tell them to."

"Really?"

"Well, most of the time. It helps to pick cases I think I can win." Chloe smiled. "Leave everything to me, Vera. Do what I say, keep a low profile, and this will all be over soon."

This plan of action was comforting for Vera. It helped to know that she had a creature on her side, especially one as legally experienced as Chloe. *She* knew that she was innocent, but she didn't know how to prove it.

"I'm delighted that you're here, and I would love for us to be roommates again, even if it's just for a little while. But the fact is that I don't really have guest accommodations, and I'd hate to ask you to sleep on the living room floor."

"Oh, don't worry about me. I'm sure there's somewhere else I can stay."

"Well, yes, there's the Bramblebriar Bed and Breakfast. The only problem is that Bradley Marvel and Darcy Montrose are both staying there. I don't know how you feel about living in the same place as two murder suspects."

Chloe laughed. "I'm not afraid of them. They might be suspects, but I'm a lawyer. And no one messes with me. Why don't we wander on over to Shady Hollow's most charming inn and see if a room might be available?"

By this point, it was evening as they walked back through town to the inn on its little cul-de-sac. Of course, there was indeed a room available for Chloe. Ben was pleased to offer her accommodations on the floor just above the one on which Darcy and Bradley were staying.

As the trio went up the staircase, a raven was making her way down.

"Oh, hullo, Vera, Ben. I was just going to stop by the festival for the evening talent contest. It's all music, and I've been assured that all those who entered are actually competent."

Vera hid a snort of laughter.

Chloe smiled as well. "Lenore Lee, right? You run Nevermore Books."

The raven shook her head. "You've mistaken me for my sister. Lenore does run the bookshop, but I'm Ligeia. I've got a room on the top floor. I'm staying here while on sabbatical from my university."

"I'm so sorry. I should have introduced you," Vera said belatedly. "Ligeia, this is Chloe McKibben, my old friend from the city. Chloe, this is Professor Ligeia Lee, a much newer friend I met very far from the city!"

The two nodded at each other, then Ligeia excused herself.

"Shady Hollow is a popular place!" Chloe said. "And here I thought it would be a sleepy little burg."

They proceeded to the room. Chloe gushed about how picturesque it was—and also managed to finagle a promise out of Ben to bring up a pot of herbal tea and a couple of extra cookies for Vera, even though she was only visiting.

Ben winked. "A few of Geoffrey's cookies seem like a small thing to ask, considering that your recommendation nabbed us another guest."

Vera sat while Chloe unpacked her bags. Her friend had certainly made a success of herself, to judge by her wardrobe. The cat's outfits were all excellently tailored and made from the finest of fabrics. A silk top in a shell-pink hue with a big bow that tied around the neck looked particularly fetching. Chloe also hung up a suit in the closet. "I always bring one just in case I need to look lawyerly on short notice. This is the suit I wore when I got sworn in, after I passed the bar. I spent a little too much, probably, considering I hadn't even gotten a position in any firm yet, but what do they say? Dress for the job you want."

"You must have wanted to look like the best attorney in the city," said Vera, loyally.

Chloe gave her a smile. "You bet!"

Chapter 11

Vera felt much better after Chloe's arrival in Shady Hollow. It wasn't that she didn't have faith in her friends who lived there, but Chloe had known Vera for years; plus she had the right background to help when Vera needed it most. If Orville decided he was angry at her, then she couldn't exactly count on him to help.

News traveled very fast, and the next morning, most of the town seemed to know all about one Chloe McKibben. When Vera took her to Joe's Mug, Joe greeted her like a local and motioned them to take a seat anywhere in the diner. Despite the early hour, Chloe was dressed in a puffy blouse in a soft mint shade over black-and-white checked trousers. She sashayed across the floor like she owned it.

Several customers watched them—mostly watching Chloe—but a few whispered to one another and nodded toward Vera. Oh, no. It seemed the fact that Vera was a suspect in the "big city" murder case must have gotten out, too.

They chose a booth toward the back. Lucy, a mink, was on duty that morning, and she poured two mugs of coffee the moment they sat down.

"Coffee cake to go with that?" she suggested with a smile. "We've got cinnamon or plum."

"Ooh, plum," Chloe said. "Vera? How about you?"

"I'm not sure I'm hungry."

"Nonsense," Chloe told her. "You have to keep your strength up. She'll have the cinnamon," Chloe announced. "And we'll both take the cheesy hash browned potatoes, and I'll have a waffle with that, too . . . and Vera will take the pancakes, short stack but the regular amount of whip."

Lucy nodded smartly as she jotted the order down. As she left, Vera looked at Chloe. "You remembered my old breakfast order!"

"How could I forget? You must have eaten that exact meal a hundred times at the Sunnyside Diner."

"You're right! The midnight special really kept us going, didn't it? You think they still do that?"

"The place closed last year," Chloe said, taking a sip of coffee.

"Oh." For some reason, that felt like a personal blow to Vera. "Really? It was so beloved."

"It was on a choice corner. Going to be a shiny new building with a high-end brunch place on the ground floor. Fruit parfaits and seven kinds of orange juice, you know the type."

"Ugh. Students won't be able to afford that."

"I think that's the point. That's city living, though. Just when you get used to things, they change." Chloe gave a philosophical shrug.

Lucy arrived with their coffee cakes and a promise that the main meal was coming up. They both took a few bites. (Vera's appetite did indeed return on tasting the crumb-topped delight.)

Then Chloe took out some papers, shuffled them in her paws, and said, "I've done a little research in the short amount of time I've had. The murder was big news even in the city. My firm makes a practice of collecting all such news on current and recent cases in the event that we'd be contacted in connection with them. We like to be ready ahead of time. I made sure to grab copies of the Renard Case file, as they're calling it. I read through them on the ferry up."

"Wow." Vera took some of the clippings and started to skim them.

"Yeah, not much beyond the basic facts, and a lot of what-ifs, as is typical for the crime beat," Chloe was saying. "I also asked a few of my sources for more information about everyone involved. Obviously, you already know about Bradley Marvel."

"More than I'd like to, really," Vera said.

Chloe chuckled, then went on, "There's not a lot on the assistant, Darcy Montrose. She's been working for that publishing company for three years; she is unmarried and doesn't have a criminal record. Though there's a first time for everything."

"Are you referring to marriage or crime?"

The cat grinned at her. "Good one. Anyway, that's the extent of my info on her. Apparently, she lives alone in a small apartment in the River District."

Vera was familiar with that neighborhood, which teemed with students and workers living close together in extremely modest accommodations, which is not to say that it was an unpleasant place. However, no one would be caught calling the River District fancy.

Chloe held up another file. "As for the victim himself, he apparently had a long track record of romantic affairs, and he was known for . . . let us say, failing upward. He would leave a job rather abruptly, always ending up in a better-paying or more prestigious position within the next few weeks or months. He seems to have known an incredible number of influential creatures in the city and made use of those connections. One of those types who knows everyone."

Vera nodded. "Yes, that matches what I remember of him. He was always so proud when he could name-drop anybody. Every time he went anywhere, he was running into somebody he knew. Lot of paw-shaking and backslapping, you know?"

"I definitely know the type," Chloe said with a sneer. "A lot of my colleagues are like that. In a way, Rick's disposition makes it a little easier to cast doubt on any one particular creature's motive. The fact is that Rick knew so many different folks, it isn't hard to believe he made a lot of enemies. First as a journalist with the power to print an embarrassing or incriminating story, and then later at the publishing house, where as an editor he had a lot of power to publish a book that could influence a lot of opinions. He was very fond of publishing memoirs and tell-all books."

"How did he end up as Bradley's editor then?" Vera wondered. "Bradley writes fiction."

"Not sure, but it's worth digging into."

"I'll do just that," Vera said, making a note. "It could be important. Regardless of Rick's unsavory behavior, things still look pretty bad for me and Bradley and Darcy. I mean, *all* of us had a connection to Rick."

"Don't you worry, Vera. I am going to fight this to the very end if it comes to that. I know you're innocent, and anyone who thinks otherwise is going to have to go through me to get to you." She held up a paw, her claws extended. "I'm not afraid of a fight."

Vera smiled at her friend, remembering the many times that Chloe had gotten into passionate discussions with other creatures while they were roommates. Chloe never backed down, and she relished every opportunity to outmaneuver an opponent, or make someone come around to her side of an argument. She was meant to be an attorney.

"Maybe we can get witness statements from some of the other creatures Rick harmed in some way. His wife, for example, or some of his previous paramours?" Vera suggested.

"We can certainly try," said Chloe. "Though we ought to be careful, because I think she's an excellent suspect."

"And she may have an alibi."

"Creatures of her class always do, no matter what day it is. She's off to her knitting circle on Tuesdays or her playwriting class on Thursdays, and everyone else there will swear up and down that they saw her."

"And all the while her husband is running around behind her back," Vera added.

"A common tale but upsetting every time. If she is behind it, I can't say I don't understand her motive." Chloe's face had drawn into a scowl as she described the likely situation. She seemed truly offended on behalf of every creature who had been taken advantage of in that way. Vera sympathized too, of course, and she was glad that her friend was not only realistic about what happened in the world, but also had compassion for those who were victims of it.

———————

After her breakfast meeting with Chloe, Vera hurried to the bookstore to give the good news to Lenore.

"My friend Chloe didn't just send a reply! She *was* the reply! She's here, and she's going to represent me."

Lenore wasn't quite as overjoyed as Vera had expected. She said, "Your lawyer pal is already here? She must have had a bag by the door when your wingmail arrived." Lenore ducked her head a few times, a habit when she was thinking hard.

Vera chuckled. "Lucky for me. But yeah, she didn't waste any time."

"Are those all billable hours?" Lenore asked.

"It's not like that." Vera realized her friend was worried about the newcomer. And why not? After all, Chloe was well-known to her, but a complete stranger to Lenore, and vice versa. It was interesting to contemplate how these two spheres of her life— one from the past, and one from the present—were now colliding. "She was worried and came to find me. You'd do the same, right?"

"Of course. Is she staying with you?"

"No, she's got a room at Bramblebriar, same as your sister. It's funny, we ran into Ligeia in the hallway last night, and Chloe thought she was you."

Lenore snorted. "Ugh, ravens don't all look alike!"

"But you and Ligeia totally do."

"Chloe can't know what I look like either. But obviously you told her about me. It's fine, whatever."

During their dinners together on Vera's visit to the city, Chloe had been very interested in what Vera had been up to the last few years, asking a ton of questions about Shady Hollow and who lived there. And who wouldn't be? It was such an interesting little town. Vera had surely mentioned that Lenore was the owner of Nevermore Books, and she probably also shared the whole tale of how Lenore's sister Ligeia had come to visit the town as well. A good story is a good story, after all.

Vera said, "Lenore, I think you'll really get along with Chloe. You both have the same sort of attitude about the world . . . in the sense that neither of you are exactly sunshine and rainbows."

"Well, I'll take your word for it. You said you two were roommates back in the day?"

Vera nodded. "Yes. We were finishing up with school and finding our first real jobs. We had so much fun."

"Oh, so you weren't working *all* the time?"

"Not exactly." Vera smiled. "We had lots of late-night dinner parties with other students around the school, plus some of our workplace colleagues. I remember one time waking up at three in the morning to find Chloe baking cookies with a friend. They had decided that gingersnaps were a *necessity*, and all the stores were closed. So that was how we ended up at a ginger tea party before dawn." She laughed at the recollection. "Sometimes we got on each other's nerves. But that's always the way with roommates. Chloe would get upset with me when I didn't wash all my dishes. That kind of thing. But I was always running off to work because I didn't want to be late. That's just how things go sometimes!"

"And what did Chloe do that annoyed you?" Lenore asked.

"She had a habit of flinging her sweaters and coats over the backs of all the chairs, and I always had to move them if I wanted to sit down. I got so annoyed, but no matter how many times I asked her to toss her clothes on her own bed, she kept doing it. Nobody's perfect."

"I second that," said Lenore. "And now your old roommate is your new lawyer. Who would've thought?"

"Well, she's giving me some professional advice, at least. I can't believe that detective is even entertaining the notion that I could be the killer! And Chloe seems even more upset about it than I am. She said she's going to make sure that cop gets totally embarrassed if he tries to press charges against me. I'm lucky to have her around—it's not every day you have to ask someone to defend you against an accusation of murder."

"Well, I believe that you didn't do it. I'm just sorry I don't have a law degree to help you out."

"I don't come to you for legal advice. I come to you for book recommendations and sarcasm." Vera smiled at her friend. "You're one of the reasons that I decided to stay here in Shady Hollow. I don't know what I would do if we weren't friends."

Lenore looked away and ruffled her feathers a bit. But Vera knew that she was pleased with the comment. The raven always affected an attitude of not caring what others thought of her, but everyone liked to feel appreciated.

Lenore glanced toward the window, saying, "No matter what, your cat friend is right about the need to prove you innocent. I honestly don't care if that cop takes Bradley Marvel back downstream with his paws tied behind his back, and that Darcy creature could do a lot worse than to kick that wolf into the river and get a new job entirely. But it's absurd to suggest that you went down to the city, killed the boss you haven't worked for in years, and then came back home like nothing happened. At the very least, I know you would've had a cover story that wouldn't have put you in the city at the time of the killing. You're way too smart to get caught for a murder this stupid."

Now it was Vera's turn to feel bashful. "Thank you, that's very sweet. I do fancy myself to be a little smarter than the average killer. It's true that I left on very bad terms with Rick. But it's also true that it was so long ago. I hadn't thought about him in years until Bradley showed up here saying his name. It's so strange how the past seems to be washing up again into my present. Bradley shows up—who I first met last year—and then I hear my old boss is dead. And now Chloe is here too! An old friend from my old life."

"Well, they are all connected, aren't they?" Lenore noted. "You don't get one without the other. It was Rick's death that brought Bradley here, and it was Bradley's ridiculous decision to flee the scene that got Darcy and then the police detective following him. And then the police detective started asking questions about you and uncovered this strange coincidence about Rick, as well."

"Do you believe that it is just a coincidence?"

"What do you mean?" asked Lenore. The raven looked at her with a curious light in her dark eyes. "How could it not be a coincidence?"

"I mean, it is a coincidence, of course. But it does feel so strange: everything is echoing around me. And all these old names keep sounding in my ears: Rick, his wife Priscilla, and Chloe, and Bradley, too."

"And what are you going to do about it?"

"Well, as it happens, I'm going to travel back into the past."

Chapter 12

Vera needed to learn a lot more about Rick's life after she had left the city. She went to the newspaper office and descended to the basement level, where the archives were kept. The bulk of the collection was made up of back issues of the *Herald*, but the archives also contained a number of other papers from surrounding towns as well as from the city, kept in the event that reporters needed to reference major events. Vera approached the desk of Mrs. Binsley, the rabbit who oversaw the archives (and who had done so for apparently the last hundred years or so). There was virtually nothing that the creature couldn't put a paw on within a few moments.

"Mrs. Binsley, I'm looking for some information regarding publishing companies in the city. Within the last five years."

"Certainly," the rabbit replied. "Let's first take a look in the index, and find out if there were any standout moments; otherwise you'll be down here a long time going through the papers issue by issue."

Vera nodded and followed the rabbit to the file cabinets against a nearby wall. Mrs. Binsley was muttering under her breath as she approached, saying things like *publishing, mergers, bought and sold,* along with the names of several large companies in the city.

Vera said, "The publisher I'm most interested in is Fieldstone Books."

"Oh, that makes this much easier." The rabbit went straight to the drawer for the letter *F* and began examining the contents. She pulled out a few files. "Looks like there was a sale a few years ago. BW always wants to know what's happening across the publishing industry, whether it's books or newspapers or magazines."

Vera took the files to a table lit with one lamp, a pool of light in the otherwise rather dark environment. She sat down in one of the wooden chairs and opened the file in front of her. The index did not contain the actual articles, of course. It was just a list of titles, along with the dates on which they appeared and the section of the paper they were in. It made it much easier to do research, because one only needed the papers for a particular range of days (and perhaps a day or two on the other side), rather than needing to leaf through every single one.

Vera noticed immediately that Bradley's publisher had been in a rough spot a few years prior, to judge by the titles listed in the index: "Publisher set to close," "Historic publishing house Fieldstone on the rocks," and "Marvel's publisher needs a miracle."

Mrs. Binsley had followed Vera to the table, knowing that she would soon be needed to fetch the papers in question. Vera pointed out the dates, and Mrs. Binsley gave a crisp nod. "I'll have them out for you shortly."

Not long afterward, Vera was reading the articles themselves and learning all about the sale of the respected publishing company, which had been acquired, oddly enough, by the Burnside family . . . which Vera recognized as the name Priscilla Renard bore before she married Rick. *That's an interesting development,* Vera thought. If it was indeed Rick's in-laws who purchased the publishing company, he must have finagled the position of editor that he had still been enjoying at the abrupt end of his life.

Still, there had to be more to the story. Vera continued reading and went on to learn that despite the strong sales of the Percy Bannon books, the profits simply hadn't been enough to keep the company afloat all on its own. It was the acquisition of those titles, and by extension, Bradley Marvel himself, that had driven the price of purchase as high as it had been. One article mentioned that while the Burnside family was the main investor, the reclusive business genius Maverick Brown also had a large stake. Vera whistled at that news. One more reason, she thought, that someone could have felt very strongly about making sure they kept control of things . . . perhaps even to the point of eliminating Rick.

The acquisition of Bradley's old publisher created a new company, because the family already owned a small publisher, one focused on what might politely be termed "newsworthy" topics. That publisher was known for putting out nonfiction books on current events and notable figures, which was something that Rick might *actually* have been suited to deal with as an editor.

The business deal explained the apparent disconnect between the fiction and nonfiction sides of the new publisher, in addition to shedding light on how Rick most likely secured the lucrative and prestigious role of editor in chief.

Vera paused upon reading a quote from one article: "We are extremely excited about the direction of Fieldstone Books as we enter a new era of publishing. As editor in chief, Rick Renard will bring his journalistic background and knowledge of the city and its culture to a whole new slate of titles that every bookstore will want to carry because we will offer something for *every* reader."

It feels a little random, Vera thought, but she tapped her paw on the name of the creature who had been quoted, Priscilla Renard. She was Rick's wife, and he must have sweet-talked her into offering him the position during the negotiations. Vera shook her head, imagining how he must have played his wife for a fool, garnering all the advantages from the strategic marriage while hiding his own reprehensible activities from her. Just then, Vera had another idea. She hurried back over to the files and pulled one marked *Renard, Priscilla.*

The file on Rick's wife contained several snippets of society news, mostly charitable committees or fancy weddings and the like. But Vera noticed a brief article from some column called "Talk of the Town," dated a couple of years back, with a byline from a creature named Bianca Wellspring. Vera studied the tidbit with interest:

> Did you attend the metropolitan media awards gala last night? Well, I did. All the newspapers' and magazines' best and brightest could be seen in their fin-

est evening wear in case they should be called to the stage to accept a coveted Voice of the City statuette. But some made news last night: a certain foxy couple had a very public argument after Mr. Foxy was seen canoodling with a young journalist who was most definitely not Mrs. Foxy. After smacking her husband over the head with her elegant crystal-beaded clutch designed by up-and-coming couturier Sylvester Vestris, Mrs. Foxy loped out of the gala. I guess the rich aren't all that different from us, except that they don't stay for dessert.

Vera decided that the gossip writer could give Gladys Honeysuckle a run for her money. There was probably much more material for such a column in the city simply because there were more creatures, and thus more drama occurring daily. She added this to the long list she kept in her head of reasons to be grateful that she now lived in Shady Hollow. And now she had even more evidence of Rick's consistently bad behavior—if a gossip columnist had mentioned it, he wasn't even trying to hide it. She wondered why his wife tolerated him for so long. Perhaps she finally lost her patience!

So, where did that leave Vera? Priscilla Renard certainly had motive, and now Vera understood a little more about how Rick came to oversee the publishing house in the first place. After carefully putting all her notes away, Vera stood.

"Mrs. Binsley, I'm done here. Thank you so much for your help."

"Didn't do much," the rabbit noted, surveying Vera with a quizzical expression. "Find anything of interest?"

"I hope so. A few questions answered, anyway."

"Did you look up that city detective? I have some questions about him. Strolling into our town and accusing one of our own of murder! Can't be very good at his job if he's that clueless."

"You mean Detective Knox? Unfortunately, I think he *is* good at his job. But he does seem to think I'm a prime suspect."

"Then he's made a mistake, and that's all there is to it." The rabbit sniffed and put her nose in the air. "Maybe I'll do a little research myself."

Vera bit back a smile, imagining the bison cowering as the elderly rabbit peppered him with her archival evidence. "I may be back, but this will do for now. Are you coming to the Harvest Festival later?"

"After I close up here, yes. The theatrical evening will be worth it."

Vera bid Mrs. Binsley farewell and left the basement level to return to the ground floor and out into the open air of the street.

It was rather crowded already, since there were multiple activities scheduled that afternoon before the main event. Vera saw the unmistakable fedora worn by Bradley Marvel and overheard him talking to a small crowd of admirers, offering a dramatic reenactment of some scene or another from one of his Percy Bannon books (judging by the audience's reaction, they were eating it up).

Rolling her eyes, Vera moved past them, intent on reaching her next destination. She stopped once to make a small purchase and then carried on. The fox had been putting off this most unpleasant task, but now she had to face it.

She had to apologize to Orville.

Chapter 13

The police station was on the main street, under a stand of oaks that were just starting to turn the same russet color as the brick of the building below. Vera took a deep breath and went in.

Orville was sitting at his desk . . . well, he was leaning back in his chair so far that he was almost reclining. A small pile of acorns sat on the desk blotter (no doubt gathered from the trees above—the acorns tended to clatter down onto the roof every autumn, or when there was a high wind). He'd placed an empty coffee mug on the floor in the corner of the room and had been flinging acorns into the mug, presumably as an exercise to defeat boredom.

"Slow day?" she ventured.

The bear looked over at her, surprise on his face. Then he looked away again, resuming his brooding. "The Harvest Festival visitors are a law-abiding bunch. I'll walk over later to make sure no one's enjoying too much of the autumn ale samples."

"Where's Detective Knox?"

"Who knows."

"Um, you? You're both cops."

"He's just fine on his own, wandering around, probably waiting for more anonymous tips."

"More? He got one?"

Orville launched an acorn, which clattered off the rim of the mug and bounced into the corner. "That's how he knew about you."

"Wait, what?" Vera said. "I thought he found out about me because of the notebook that somehow made its way to the crime scene."

"There's nothing in the notebook about Renard," Orville reminded her. "You were interviewing creatures involved in the bridge project. He got your name from the notebook, but he told me later that he learned that you'd been involved with Rick because some creature called the metropolitan police and told them."

Vera sat down abruptly, stunned by the news. "I don't know what to think about that."

He shrugged. An acorn pinged into the mug.

She hated when they fought. And judging by Orville's solitary game and the number of acorns scattered around the room, he wasn't having much fun either.

"Look, can we talk?" she asked Orville.

"That would be very mature of us as a couple, wouldn't it?"

he replied, flinging another acorn into the coffee mug. His aim was surprisingly good.

"I can't tell if you're being sarcastic," she confessed.

"I'm not."

She inhaled. "I'm sorry I didn't tell you about knowing Renard immediately. I was so thrown by the news. And until that city cop sprung the question on me, I honestly hoped it would never come up. Because I haven't seen that fox for years, and I had no idea where he even was. It was just an unlucky coincidence that I happened to be visiting the city the same day he was killed."

"I never thought you killed him," said Orville. "Frankly, I'm a little offended that you'd think I would."

"I didn't think that," she said. "I wasn't thinking at all, if you want to know." She had been *worrying*, which was a rather less useful practice.

"Vera, you either trust me or you don't. If you'd told me you knew the victim, I could have helped you prepare for exactly the sort of situation that detective surprised you with. Surprised both of us with. And now we're both in a bad spot."

"*You're* not a suspect."

"I told Knox he was an idiot. Which I don't think endeared me to him. Especially because he was correct. Law enforcement works better when we're not attacking each other."

"I'm sorry. I made a mistake."

"You did." Another acorn rattled into the mug. "What did you want to talk about?"

"Besides saying I'm sorry?" she asked, puzzled.

"Yeah. The apology is a good start, but you've got that look in your eyes like you've got a good story. Or a clue that you're *maybe* going to let me in on."

She nodded, holding up her notes. "I went to the archives."

"The newspaper archives? Here? What could you learn here about what happened in the city?"

"Lots. I'm going to tell Chloe what I found later, but I know she's busy looking over some legal questions like statutes of limitations and jurisdictional lines, and that can take a while. So, do you want to go over this with me?"

He leaned forward, pushing the last of the acorns to the side. "What'd you get?"

Vera spread her notes over the desk, pointing out specific items as she spoke. "The good news is that I think I understand now how everyone is connected," said Vera. She displayed her diagram of all the suspects and their links to the victim. "The bad news is that I wasn't able to eliminate a single suspect, not even myself."

Orville took a few moments to peruse the paper in his paws. Then he looked up at Vera. "I think that we may be able to eliminate you. Remind me what you did that day starting in the morning through to when you went to bed. You went to do an interview about the bridge that was never built. With the squirrel who designed it, right?"

"Yes, but that was the day before. For the interview, I went to the Furlong Building on Juniper Street, which was where the squirrel I was interviewing for my article asked me to meet. That interview started at nine thirty, and I was done around ten o'clock. The rest of the day I spent chasing down leads in the big public library, mostly with no results."

"And then?"

"Well, I had a rather late night that evening because I'd gone to dinner with Chloe, and I didn't return to the hotel until nearly midnight. So on the day of Rick's murder, I slept in and didn't even leave my room in search of coffee until well after eight o'clock."

Orville picked up another piece of paper on his desk, the one that must have been provided by Knox. "Yes. The hotel staff have confirmed that you walked through the lobby and headed outside shortly after eight."

"I got coffee at a little place on the corner. It was called Full Circle Coffee. Their sign is a picture of a coffee cup seen from the top. I sat there for about a half hour. After that I went to the museum for a few hours. There was an exhibit on Early Woodland Culture I was interested in seeing."

"Did you save the ticket stub?"

"I think so. It's probably in my travel bag. I could find it. Why? It's no good for an alibi; it was hours before the killing."

"Helps to 'build the veracity' of your general statements." He patted the *Big Book of Policing* with one paw.

"Well, look at you!" Vera said.

"I'm trying. So, was the exhibit any good?"

"I thought so, though I'm not an expert. I must have stayed in the museum until almost one. I had lunch at a little café near the museum that looked across the avenue toward the park. I can't remember the name of the café, but I had a squash and coconut soup that was really tasty. My appointment with Keats Loring wasn't until three, so I stayed at the café and read a book until I left and walked through the park to the building where Keats lives. He and I chatted for almost an hour, and he gave me a copy of some of his newest poems. They're on my shelf at home now."

"I believe you. And Keats can surely confirm all that."

"He'd better. At about four, I returned to the hotel to collect my bag, which I had left there."

"In your room?" he asked sharply.

"No, I'd checked out first thing and asked the bellhop to keep my bag until I called for it. They have a room near the desk for situations like that."

"So pretty much the whole day, someone could have snuck into that room and riffled through your bag."

Vera blinked. "Maybe! But they'd have to have known it was there."

"If someone wanted to frame you specifically, Vera, they'd be watching you. They'd know."

She shuddered at the thought. "Ugh. Anyway, I got my bag back at the desk shortly before five. I walked all the way to the ferry station, knowing that there was a little food stand near the docks. I intended to get something to eat before I got on the boat. I took my time because the ferry wasn't going to leave until eight o'clock sharp. I just ambled around the harbor until I was sure that they would be allowing passengers on."

"What did you get at the food stand?"

"I got a baked potato with a harvest salsa topping. I didn't get coffee because it was too late in the day. I made sure to keep the receipt for that meal because I wanted to submit it as an expense."

"The records of the ferry company have you marked off as a passenger who boarded," said Orville. "Unfortunately, the records don't state the time of boarding, only whether a passenger actually got on or not."

Vera sighed. "Naturally. I think I probably boarded around a quarter to eight."

"Knox made a point to me that a creature *could* get from Bradley Marvel's building to the harbor and get on that boat before it leaves. Though I think that it would probably require hiring one of those buggy drivers."

Orville was referring to the vehicles run by enterprising creatures who were strong enough to haul the two-wheeled carts with a passenger seat up and down the broad avenues of the city. The entrepreneurs who operated them tended to be badgers, mustangs, bears, or hogs. Riding in one would certainly speed up the process of getting from the heart of the city to the harbor, which was nestled on the southern side of the city along the bay.

Vera shrugged. "I suppose it's possible. It would be extremely difficult to prove either way, considering how many creatures own one of those carts, and how busy the city streets can be. You'd have to spend days asking every single operator if they remembered their fare from that evening. And I wonder how much an operator would remember after each ride. As long as the fare was paid, there probably isn't much to differentiate one customer from another." Vera looked up at the cuckoo clock, mentally retracing her steps from the evening in question. "So, is Knox convinced that the murder took place between 5 and 7 p.m.? That same gap in time when both Darcy and Bradley left each other alone for a bit?"

Orville gave a nod. "It seems the only time that's possible. It can't have happened too much earlier than the moment when the open door was discovered. There are a lot of residents in Mockingbird Court, and tenants are always nosy about their neighbors. I can't imagine too many residents would have walked past an open door without peeking in and noticing a bloody body. But for what it's worth, unless Knox could prove you were actually in the building . . ."

"Which he can't, because I wasn't," Vera said quickly.

Orville allowed the point. He continued, "There's absolutely no definitive evidence to prove you were there, and there are no witness accounts saying a fox was seen in the building during the crucial time."

"Yet," she amended miserably. "With my luck, some resident will call in an anonymous tip saying they saw me."

"Speaking of that, you ought to make a list of everyone who knew anything about you and Renard."

She shook her head. "No point. I kept it a secret from nearly everyone. My parents knew somehow, but I don't think they would have called the cops. They were disappointed in me, but I doubt they think I'm a murderer."

"School friends? Other colleagues at work?" he asked.

"No. I never even told Chloe that I'd been dating him. She knew I was with someone, but I kept the details from her. And even when I got fired from the newspaper, it was because I had been blamed for the blackmail scheme. I didn't get fired for dating my boss."

"Well, someone knew about it, Vera. And you're going to have to find out who."

Chapter 14

Following her talk with Orville, Vera ambled around the millpond to think over what he'd said. She paused at the marshier north end of the pond, amid reeds and cattails that grew so tall she couldn't even see the town from here—and likewise was hidden from view herself. The reeds, which had been green and lush all summer, had begun to turn the color of straw—a pale, warm gold that somehow made the waters of the millpond look even more blue. An errant breeze knocked the reeds together in a hollow symphony, sounding higher-pitched but similar to the sound of the big shoots surrounding the Bamboo Patch.

Out of curiosity, Vera made her way down a particular

narrow path, which was even narrower than she remembered, being nearly overgrown now. The path led to a modest dwelling scarcely distinguishable from the mud with which it was built. The door had been boarded up and a faded, tattered sign nailed to the wood. It said:

KEEP OUT

BY ORDER OF THE POLICE

ALSO, OTTO WOULD SAY THE SAME IF HE COULD

She smiled upon reading the note, remembering the cranky toad who once lived here. She liked to think that Otto would have appreciated the efforts to preserve his old home. Or perhaps he'd be contrary about it and grumble about why everyone was being so sentimental and letting a perfectly good house go to waste. She could almost hear him now—how sharp the memory of his tone still was! Otto had been a part of the town's very fabric. She was glad she'd had the chance to meet him.

Was that what folks meant when they talked about being a local? The idea that if someone said, "Oh, you're as cranky as old Otto," no one had to ask, "Otto who?" If so, then Vera was happy to be a Shady Hollow local, and she'd put her paws down hard if anyone tried to take her away from this place.

Which meant that she really needed to solve the mystery of Rick's murder if she hoped to remain a local! Orville had suggested that she make a list of everyone who knew of her clandestine relationship, and so she'd been racking her brain, trying to remember if there was anyone else who possibly could have known the truth. But she'd been forthright when she told Orville that the list would be a short one. Vera could think of only a few names: herself and Rick, obviously. Her parents, who'd found out by some means, but refused to tell her who had passed on the information. She shied away from even thinking of the task, but she'd likely have to ask if they remembered. Ugh. Who else? Not Chloe or anyone from her circle of college friends, though Chloe certainly heard Vera's initial swooning accounts of Rick's handsomeness. Vera had been particularly cagey, so excited about having a secret affair that she was somehow able to avoid spilling the beans. So, who did that leave? It had to be a work colleague! The problem with working at a newspaper, Vera reflected, was that it was filled with reporters, all of whom were constantly on the trail of a story, and who loved getting the scoop before anyone else.

But as she mentally toured the office where she'd once worked, stopping by each desk in her mind, recalling the names and faces of those who sat at each one . . . none of them seemed likely candidates for the creature who had sussed out a secret, kept it for years, and only informed the police the moment Rick went cold. She was missing something, but what?

The only other creature who might well have known about the relationship was Priscilla Renard, but Vera could hardly ask *her* for confirmation. (Not least because even the metropolitan police couldn't locate her.) Vera didn't like to contemplate the notion that a wealthy and well-connected fox could have it out for her, possibly to the extent of framing her for a murder, or even simply assuming that Vera was truly the killer.

She continued around the millpond and passed the sawmill, observing the final preparations for the crowning of the Harvest Queen at the soiree that constituted the ultimate event of the Harvest Festival. Gladys Honeysuckle was there as well, probably trying to learn about some surprise planned for the party. She saw Vera and flitted over.

"Vera!" she buzzed. "Everyone is talking about the latest developments in the big city murder case. Tell me it's not true that Detective Knox wants to arrest you!"

"I wish I could, but it's a possibility," Vera told her. It wasn't worth it to conceal anything from Gladys. The hummingbird would likely just make up a more salacious version of events to write in her column, anyway.

"The *nerve* of him!" said Gladys. "Coming up here on the trail of Marvel and his assistant, and then turning on you just because he couldn't drag Marvel back immediately! Doesn't he know he's not in the city anymore?"

"Maybe he's just a big fan of harvest festivals," Vera suggested. "Who knows? He might come back for the ice-carving contest in the winter."

"He'd better not!" Gladys zipped around Vera, her wings a blur but her expression clearly outraged. Vera was surprised at the bird's intensity . . . but then again, Gladys was intense about everything, so perhaps it made sense.

"Will you excuse me, Gladys? I've got to get going, and I don't want to interrupt your work," she added diplomatically. She didn't consider gossip to be quite on the same level as journalism, but she couldn't deny that Gladys's column was popular and served a role in the community.

Vera continued along and stopped in at the bookstore. The main doors were flanked by a shock of dried cornstalks on each side, surrounded by massive pumpkins in shades from pale yellow to rich red—uncarved as yet but undoubtedly destined to be changed into spooky, candlelit creations for Mischief Night, now only a few weeks away. Inside, Lenore and Violet were busy helping customers since the festival brought a lot of new shoppers into town. Vera and Lenore agreed to meet for breakfast the next day to discuss the latest developments.

"Will Chloe be joining us?" Lenore asked.

"Not sure. She's not exactly an early riser. And she told me she's been reading several case files that might be of help. I bet she'll be up half the night."

As it happened, Chloe did not join them for breakfast, having informed Vera that she was always sharper after a good night's sleep. "But find me later and fill me in," she ordered.

And so, the next morning, which proved to be rather cloudy and dreary, the coppers and golds in the trees muted until the sun returned, Vera and Lenore met at Joe's Mug, a place that defied the gray day outside, thanks to the chatter of happy patrons and the smell of fresh coffee wafting up, mingling with spices from the bakery.

Esme brought two mugs and a coffeepot to their table in the corner.

"Good morning!" the beaver said brightly as she poured fresh coffee into the mugs. "I'm making a wild guess that you both want coffee?" She winked.

The fox and the raven each greeted her and said that yes, it was the correct assumption. Vera grasped her mug with grateful paws while Lenore looked over the menu.

"We added a few cardamom pods to this brew—hope you like it! Ooh, hold tight. I'll be right back to take your order," Esme said as she caught sight of a vole and a muskrat coming in the door.

The beaver seated the newcomers and poured them some coffee as well. Then she returned to the table with her order pad.

Vera looked out at the iron-gray sky and decided she needed something cheerful. "I'll have the autumn fruit salad and a pumpkin-cranberry muffin, please."

"Same," Lenore said.

"You got it." Esme scribbled it down and made her way into the kitchen to place their order. Vera gave thanks for the day that Esme decided to give up the life of an heiress and work at Joe's instead.

"What's going on with the investigation?" Lenore asked in a lower tone. "Has that detective been harassing you again?"

"Not since Chloe arrived," Vera replied. "I'm nervous about being a real suspect. I know I didn't kill Rick, but there are an awful lot of clues pointing in my direction. Not to mention Orville has found out about my past with Rick, and he wasn't too pleased. I mean, I'm not very proud of my behavior either. Carrying on with another creature's husband."

"Piffle," said Lenore. "It was a mistake, but you were young. Orville knows that you had an entire life before you met him. I'm sure that he will respect that. Or at least he'd better if he wants to lead a peaceful life."

"But how will it look if the *special friend* of the police chief of Shady Hollow is arrested for murder?" Vera wailed. "And what if BW fires me from the *Herald*?"

"Now, Vera." Lenore tried to soothe her friend. "You know that neither of those things are going to happen. You didn't kill anyone, and Chloe will make sure you're not arrested. You'll make sure that the real murderer is found. And as for BW, he's probably delighted to have a notorious figure in the newsroom. He'll say it'll sell more papers."

"He is nothing if not reliable," Vera agreed.

The fox was grateful for Lenore's confidence in her, but she was still terrified that Knox might arrest her for murdering Rick, and Orville would leave her, and BW would fire her from her job at the paper. She also feared that Lenore would turn her back on her. She could not fully articulate these fears to her friend, but they loomed large in her imagination.

"The newest edition of the *Herald* included a choice line in the gossip column."

"Oh, no." Vera groaned. "Now what?"

"You might like it." Lenore read out, "'Rumor has it a certain vixen is being sought after by a big city constable. Does the tourist intend to take back a souvenir? You know what they say about visiting rural spots: take only pictures, leave only hoofprints.'"

Vera blinked in surprise, both at the fact that Gladys had decided to include a crime-based item in her gossip column, and that it sounded . . . rather fierce. "Um, did Gladys just threaten Knox via gossip tidbit?"

Lenore chuckled. "Maybe. Anyway, it looks like the fact that you're on Knox's suspect list is common knowledge now. So you might as well make the best of it."

"Great."

Just then, Chloe came in the door, dressed in an elegant, long, belted coat in a heather-purple shade, with a little round black-and-white hat that covered one ear.

Across the restaurant, Esme stopped brewing coffee and simply watched as Chloe made her way to the table where the two friends sat.

"You came after all!" Vera said, extraordinarily pleased.

"I decided that I'd make the sacrifice of an early wake up so that I could be part of the discussion," she said, sliding into the booth next to Vera. "Otherwise, I'll just have to ask you to repeat everything later. Oh, do I smell coffee? Excellent."

Esme had rushed up with a fresh mug in one paw and another coffeepot in the other. She didn't put the mug on the table, but in an unusual move, poured the beverage while holding it away from them. She explained, "Wouldn't want to get a coffee stain on your coat. That's from Luna Markham's fall collection, isn't it?"

"Good eye," Chloe said, clearly surprised. "You must follow fashion if you know Markham."

"I used to *wear* Markham, before things changed for my family." Esme sighed. "Still got an old dress of hers in my closet. Anything to eat, ma'am?"

"Maybe later," Chloe said. "For now, the coffee is all I desire."

Esme nodded and told them to holler if they needed anything.

Vera turned to her friend. "I was just telling Lenore that I found out from Orville that Knox received an anonymous tip about me. Hence his misunderstanding about my feelings about Rick—namely that I still thought about him at all, let alone enough to make a special trip just to kill him."

Lenore was grim. "I think it's worse than a misunderstanding. An anonymous tip that sends the police straight to you? Someone's got it in for you, Vera."

"That's ridiculous! The only creature I could possibly call an enemy is Rick himself, and he's dead! I doubt he left an anonymous tip from the dark forest beyond."

"You must have another enemy. Someone you haven't thought about. Did you cross anyone while you were at school?"

"Not that I can remember." She looked at Chloe. "Anything spring to mind?"

The cat wiggled her nose as she thought for a long moment, then said, "Nothing. We had a good friend group, and everyone we knew was mostly focused on their own studies and jobs. We didn't have time for drama."

"How about your job? Did you work anywhere before the newspaper with Rick?"

"Just a couple of internships, which were short and unremarkable. Rick is the only creature who ever had an interest in ruining my life."

"Well," Chloe said slowly, "I can think of one more."

"Who?" Vera asked her blankly.

"His wife. Priscilla Renard."

Vera nodded. "I've been considering that too. But I barely even met her! I only ever saw her a few times in the newsroom."

Chloe lifted a paw to forestall Vera's objection. "It would be a mistake to think that Priscilla was unaware of Rick's behavior. Let's suppose she did know. It's quite possible she blamed you rather than him."

"Chloe, are you suggesting that she's the one who offered the anonymous tip?" Vera asked.

"It's a real possibility. You tried to keep the relationship secret, but who knows if Rick cared as much? He certainly proved to be completely untrustworthy in other parts of his life, as you found out."

Vera felt so foolish. "He might even have admitted the affair to his wife, if she confronted him."

Lenore nodded. "The fact that she's still married to him *and* that she gave him the job as editor in chief suggests that she tends to forgive him. Or look the other way. It is possible he lied to her, and she chose to believe it."

"It's not pretty, but it's also not unusual," Chloe pointed out. "Perhaps we can re-create Priscilla's movements the day Rick was killed. She certainly had motive if she finally snapped. And why not blame the crime on a former lover? Kill two birds with one stone."

"Or two foxes," Vera muttered.

Chapter 15

Naturally, Vera was well aware that *she* did not kill Rick Renard, but that didn't mean Detective Knox believed her. After all, things looked pretty bleak from the outside. She and Rick had a relationship long ago that had ended badly. If a creature wanted to believe the worst, it was entirely possible to suppose that she held a grudge all this time. Or worse, that she had continued to see Rick on and off since she left the city. It was terrifying to think that she might not be able to prove her innocence. She could lose her job and her relationship. Not to mention be convicted of murder and sent to jail! Her mother would never get over *that*.

Although she was an adult with her own life, she still cared about her parents' opinion of her. Foxes and their families were very close. Vera knew that her folks were hoping that she would marry and have kits of her own. She had no idea how she would explain her relationship with Orville.

The fox shook herself to keep her thoughts from spiraling down such a dark path. She would simply have to redouble her efforts to find the real killer so as not to stand accused herself. She didn't think that Bradley Marvel was guilty, but what about Darcy, or even Rick's wife?

It was so frustrating to Vera that the murder occurred so far away! True, she was intimately familiar with the city itself, having been born and raised there and having walked the streets for much of her life. She could practically draw a map from memory, with all the streets labeled and all her favorite spots marked down.

But now it felt so far away, as if the murder had occurred in the lost past rather than merely separated by distance. As a reporter, she relied on being able to visit a scene and absorb it with her own senses, looking around and noticing things with her own eyes. She could sniff and know the last meal that had been eaten, or the favorite perfume of the last resident, or even whether the building was new or old or neglected or well cared for. She could pace the perimeter of a room, reach out and touch a painting on a wall, or a knitted sweater flung casually over a chair, or the stones of a fireplace and know how long it had been since a fire warmed the spot. She could tell so much about the space and its inhabitants simply by being there.

But in this case, she was wholly dependent on the reports of others—others who had every reason to misremember, or even lie about what they heard and saw and felt during that crucial interval.

For a moment, she contemplated the wisdom of catching a

ferry downstream and returning to the city for the sole purpose of visiting Bradley's apartment, to see for herself what others had described. But even if she had been free to do so (assuming that Bradley—and Knox—would give permission), the scene she so needed to experience had already evaporated. It had been nearly a week since the murder, and the apartment had no doubt been visited by a dozen or more creatures intent on their own particular tasks: removing the body, searching for evidence, lifting books, moving furniture, cleaning the rug, opening the windows, closing the windows, running water from the tap . . . Every single move and gesture inexorably altered the reality of the space. Even if Vera could stand in the middle of the room and use all her senses, there was little guarantee that she would sense anything of value.

Never again would she take for granted the privilege of front-line experience with the mystery at hand. Attempting to solve a murder without being anywhere close to the crime scene was like trying to paint a picture in the dark. Not only could she not see the canvas, but she didn't even know what color of paints she was dipping her brush into! The result would be predictably horrific. How could anyone expect a revelation from that randomness?

Vera took a deep breath and pulled herself together. She was a journalist by profession, but a truth-seeker by vocation. Surely others had faced more difficult situations. She could find a way to get through this one and come out the other side with the truth. All she needed to do was be open-minded when it came to the possibilities and ruthlessly logical in sorting through them.

First, she had to consider which resources she had been ignoring. It was too late to return to the murder scene and observe it in anything like its initial state, but she *could* request police reports through Detective Knox, and perhaps even gain access to photographs that an investigator had taken on that first night or the morning after. She knew she could also ask those who worked at the publishing company to help determine what Rick was up to in the last few weeks of his life.

She could always look at a map of the city to visualize the neighborhood in which Bradley lived and plot out possible scenarios for how the murderer might have gotten into and out of Mockingbird Court unseen (or at least unnoticed). Above all, she had her own relentless determination. And, she remembered, she had friends and colleagues who would assist her in her endeavor. Even if she couldn't do it alone, she could do it with the support of those who cared about her. Orville would be glad to discuss aspects of the case with her from the perspective of a police officer, and he could forward a request to the city police in a manner that would make them more likely to respond. Lenore was always a reliable sounding board for her ideas and always offered a new perspective that Vera hadn't considered. The raven also had many books at her disposal, and who knew which one might hold a crucial fact that would help them put together all the pieces of the puzzle. Chloe had known Vera for many years, and she was also intimately familiar with the workings of the justice system. She would help Vera navigate the complexities of any legal issues coming her way, and she would serve that crucial role of childhood friend (well, young adulthood friend) who would always be there. Someone who would vouch for Vera's innocence and also fight for it. And of course, there were others in Shady Hollow as well, like Joe and Sun Li and Professor Heidegger. If she called on them, they would lend whatever assistance they could.

Really, Vera thought with a smile, considering all the advantages she had, it would be nearly impossible for her to *not* solve this case.

"Well," she said out loud, "that does make me feel a little bit better. Though I better not mention it to Lenore. Optimism always makes her queasy."

Chapter 16

Vera spent the rest of the morning assessing each suspect in the case, searching for gaps in what she knew. As she looked over her notes, she decided it was past time to talk to Darcy about some key details. Darcy was holding something back, and she was fairly certain she knew exactly what it was. So that afternoon she tracked down the lynx at the bed-and-breakfast to inform her they were going to have another chat. She found Darcy in her room, sitting at the desk with the type-writer, though her attention was firmly on the small plate of cookies nearby. Her paw hovered over one, then another, as she agonized over the decision.

"I'd go for the leaf-shaped one with the red icing," Vera

advised. "Geoffrey mixes in sumac, which gives it a nice citrusy flavor. Great for a pick-me-up."

"I need that," said Darcy, grabbing the red leaf.

Vera stepped into the room and closed the door. "I'd like to ask you a few more questions."

"I don't have to talk to you," Darcy replied in what would have been a haughty tone if she weren't speaking while chomping a cookie.

Vera smiled, showing teeth. "No, but if you don't chat with me, I'm going to dig through your job, your life, and your past until I find out what I want to know."

Darcy got up as if to flee, except that Vera blocked her way out.

"Or you could just talk to me," Vera coaxed her.

"Not here," Darcy said, glancing around as though someone might be lurking in the closet. "We've got to go somewhere where we won't be overheard."

"Let's walk then." Vera took the lead, heading down the main street with the goal of walking around Maple Heights, a part of town where they'd be unlikely to run into anyone who'd be interested in their conversation.

"So what do you want to know?" asked Darcy, once they'd ascended the slope and could look down on the part of Shady Hollow that hugged the river. Looking over the changing leaves of the trees and the strips of the streets dividing them was like viewing a giant patchwork quilt from above.

Vera pulled out her notebook and pen. "First, why don't you tell me a little more about your side of things than you admitted before." She looked expectantly at Darcy. "How long have you worked for Bradley Marvel?"

Darcy sneered. "Way too long to suit me. When I first got the job, I thought it was a dream come true. I was just an intern at the publishing house, and an editor called me into their office and told me that there was an opportunity to get an inside track on becoming a real writer. They said that a major author had just lost his assistant and needed a new one, and I had all the qualifi-cations to fill the role."

Vera scribbled down the words. "So you took the job."

"Of course I did. I would've been an idiot to say no. But as it happens, I was so excited that it didn't even occur to me that there could be a downside to this new gig. When I found out that I would be working for the great Bradley Marvel, I screamed. I mean, you see his books everywhere. Everyone knows who he is. And everyone knows who Percy Bannon is. I've read all his books. I was dazzled by him. At least, I was at first."

"How long did that last?" Vera asked.

Darcy shrugged, then said, "Maybe three months? It was a whirlwind. I was doing everything he asked me to do, all typical assistant type of stuff. I fetched coffee. I ran manuscripts from his apartment to the publishing house and back again. I did errands around the city for him so that he wouldn't have to waste time doing ordinary things instead of writing. I didn't mind doing all of it because I thought I was part of something special. But whenever I asked how the new book was going, he brushed me off."

After noting it all down, Vera looked steadily at Darcy, not saying anything. In her experience, creatures often opened up when they got antsy. Silence was a tool.

Darcy squirmed a little and rather deliberately gazed at the larger and more ostentatious homes in the neighborhood. Most of them had elaborate harvest decorations on the doors and porches. "I don't know what made me do it," she said at last. "Actually, that's not true. I do know. It was curiosity, pure and simple. I was carrying these papers back and forth in a big enve- lope. Every couple of days I would go to the publishing house and drop some off and then pick up other ones and bring them back to Mr. Marvel."

"Okay," said Vera, encouraging her to continue.

"Of course I never looked at them," Darcy said. "Until one day . . . I did. He'd been especially rude to me after I brought him his coffee in the morning. Maybe if he hadn't been so rude that day, I would've been able to ignore my curiosity. But as it was, I decided if he was going to be mean to me, he deserved it. So, when I was a couple of blocks away from the publisher, I stopped at a little diner and got a cup of coffee. I pulled the envelope from my bag, and I opened the flap. It was only tied with string. It wasn't sealed. If folks want to keep a secret, they should try a little bit, don't you think, Miss Vixen?"

Vera said, "You may have a point."

Darcy smiled at her. "Well, in any case, I opened the envelope and pulled out the papers inside. Do you want to guess what I saw?"

"I would assume you saw some pages of Marvel's new manuscript."

Darcy shook her head. "I saw *nothing*. I saw blank pages. I was shepherding blank pages back and forth around town, spending hours of my time doing a useless errand, all for show!"

Vera said, "Maybe it was just a simple mistake? Perhaps he gave you the wrong envelope that day."

"No." The lynx looked angry. "I know that isn't true. Because along with that blank stack of paper was a small note writ- ten by the editor, Rick. It said that if Bradley didn't produce something within the next week, he'd be forced to make it public. And he would have to make a big announcement that the new Bradley Marvel book wouldn't be coming out when everyone expected it to be, and that Marvel wouldn't get paid, and the editor wouldn't get paid, and his assistant wouldn't get paid, and no one would pay for any books because there weren't any books to buy . . . and that might mean the end of Bradley Marvel's career."

Vera was digesting Darcy's words. "So what did you do?"

"Well, it took me a while to understand what I was really looking at," said Darcy. "I must have sat there for twenty minutes before I fully realized that the great Bradley Marvel wasn't writing *anything* when he was sitting in his apartment all day. And then, I just got angry. Because I had taken this job, thinking that it was good for me, only to find out that my employer was going to get me laid off, all because *he* wasn't working. It wasn't fair."

"Some folks might think that would be a good motive for murder," said Vera.

"Yes, if it was Bradley Marvel who died," said Darcy. "And believe me, there was a moment when I wanted to kill him. More than one moment, actually. But what I did was go back to Marvel's apartment and show him the blank papers. I demanded an explanation for what was happening, and why I was toting blank pages around the city."

"What did he say to that?" asked Vera.

Darcy laughed, then said, "He tried to deny everything at first. But it was clear that this had been going on for a while, and eventually he told me that he wasn't able to come up with anything for his new Percy Bannon novel. At first, the pages that I had been carrying back and forth did have some words on them, but the words weren't very good, and Rick kept sending them back with nasty notes. Eventually, Bradley just started putting blank pages in the envelope. And those are what I found." Darcy sighed. "Even then, it was hard for me to stay angry at him. You have to understand that I admired him. He was a great success, a famous author, and I wanted to be like him . . . or at least be as successful as he was. I always thought that I was going to learn from a master. Instead, all I was learning was that I was going to be out of a job."

Vera felt sympathy for the young creature. She knew very well how anxious one felt in a new job, in the city, when starting a career. You wanted to do everything right, and you were terrified of making the wrong move. Vera put away her pencil. "What happened then?"

"Bradley made a suggestion. He said that he trusted me, and since I was his assistant, I could *assist* him in getting started on the new book. He said that we would work together in the mornings at his apartment and maybe generate some exciting new ideas and plots. He said it was difficult being a solitary genius. No one understood you! You were all alone, thinking great thoughts, and eventually it was difficult to think anymore at all. But if he had someone to talk to, perhaps the ideas would come out of the corners again."

Vera knew where this was going, but she wanted to hear Darcy tell it in her own words. "So you accepted. And how did the process work?"

Darcy said, "I got excited all over again because this seemed like such a unique opportunity. And it turned out that it was, just not in the way that I thought it would be." She looked down to where the main street of Shady Hollow was filling with visitors, a wistful expression on her face. Then she looked back at

Vera. "He really is very charming. You understand that, don't you?"

Vera nodded. "Yes, I could see how you would think that of him. Especially because he devotes so much time to that image."

Darcy gave a little laugh. "That's true. I wish I'd known that right away, but I was very naive. Anyway, once I accepted his offer, it seemed impossible to stop, even after I realized it wasn't what I wanted to be doing."

Vera retrieved her pencil. "Go on."

"What I mean is that I wasn't just assisting Marvel by listening to him give ideas or working out scenes. Instead, I became a sort of stenographer, recording his words, then more and more often suggesting words of my own. And writing them down. It was exciting at first. I felt like I was being listened to. And I'd read all the Percy Bannon novels over and over, so I really knew the story. It felt very natural to suggest new places for Percy to go and new cases for him to solve. Even new creatures for him to meet." At this last line, she blushed a little bit. "But it turned out differently."

Vera sighed. "It was you doing all the work lately, right? You started writing the books."

Darcy exhaled, as if relieved the words were finally out. "You got it."

"I started to suspect not long after you arrived. Bradley was very vague about his process and his progress on the new book. Most writers won't shut up about that sort of thing. Then, I noticed that you were the one who kept the typewriter in your room at the inn. And all those little cutting remarks you made about him sitting down to write while he was here. He couldn't respond because he wasn't writing at all."

"Yes, it's true. And Rick Renard knew. Or at least he guessed right away. It must've seemed funny to receive all those blank pages one day, and then the beginning of a whole entire novel a couple of days later. Bradley came clean after Rick asked him what was going on. And he explained that I was helping, and that I was the best assistant he'd ever had." Darcy rolled her eyes at her past self. "You can't imagine how proud I felt when I heard him say that. I was such an idiot."

Vera shook her head. "No, you weren't."

But Darcy laughed again, more harshly. "I was. I let a little flattery blind me to the fact that both Bradley and Rick were taking advantage of me. Sure, Rick said that I would get a promotion eventually. Sure, Bradley said that I was so smart, and he introduced me to some of his writer friends, and I felt so special and so important. But the fact was I was covering for Bradley's writer's block, and he was very happy to let me do it."

"Maybe he regrets it," Vera suggested. "He could have felt trapped by the situation too."

"If he does, he hides it well. But I'm glad you know the truth, Vera. It's not a fun secret to keep."

"I can understand that." Vera finished writing down what Darcy had said, and then asked, "And how long ago did this all occur?"

Darcy took a breath, then said, "Do you know the name of Bradley's newest book?"

Vera asked, "You mean the one that came out earlier this year?" She knew all too well the title of that book. *"The Quick Dead Fox."*

Darcy nodded. "And the book just before that?"

Vera nodded. *"Hard Pass,* I think. Or was it *Hard Fall?"*

Darcy snarled, *"Hard Fall.* I know because I came up with the title. I wrote that book, too. I wrote that book pretending that I was Bradley Marvel. And then I wrote the next book, pretending that I was Bradley Marvel. And they wanted me to write another book after that, pretending to be Bradley Marvel."

Vera wrote down the titles, figured the dates in her head, and then looked up, a feeling of horror coming over her. "Wait, *how* long has this been going on?"

Darcy said, "It must be two and a half years now."

Despite having suspected the truth, Vera was still shocked. This had been happening the whole time she had known Bradley Marvel! Even longer than that. She saw with her own eyes how the wolf had blown into town for his author event, acting like he owned the place, behaving like a celebrity, and in general being intolerable. But everyone tolerated it because he was a successful artist. Now it seemed he wasn't that at all.

Then Darcy said, "And you know, I still do all the other work. I still bring him coffee. I still get his laundry. I still pick up groceries from the corner store. Because I'm an assistant, and that's my job. That was the agreement that we all seemed to come to so long ago. I was promised that this would be the start of something bigger for me. But Bradley didn't want it to change. And Rick didn't want it to change. Why would they? The way things were was perfect for them. Bradley got his fame. And Rick got his money-making books and the prestige of being the editor of such a successful franchise." She nearly spat Rick's name out.

Vera didn't write that last part down. She didn't have to because she didn't think she would ever forget the words. Earlier, Darcy had said that anger would've been a great motive if Bradley had been the victim. But Rick was the victim. And Darcy's bitter confession revealed that the lynx did indeed have a motive for wanting Rick gone.

He had been complicit in the secret arrangement that forced

a young, female writer to do the work that her wildly successful, older, male boss got all the credit for. Vera remembered all too well how hard she had worked at her earliest jobs, only to see others like Rick—and even Rick himself—take the credit. She could feel the anger returning when she recalled how she had been tricked. Darcy doubtless felt the same.

She might even have felt murderous.

Chapter 17

Vera had a lot to think over following Darcy's revelation. It was one thing to suspect something, but quite another to hear it confirmed. She decided to let all the new information settle in her mind before she acted on any of it. And the best way to do that was to get a good meal in her belly. Luckily for Vera, today was a special day. The Harvest Festival soup contest was being held just outside town in Cold Clay Orchards, and it was slated to start around four o'clock. She'd made plans to meet Chloe there, and Vera was excited to show her friend all that Shady Hollow had to offer, especially at this time of year. While she knew Chloe was a city cat at heart, part of her wondered if she, too, might someday choose the slower pace of the woodlands.

Darcy opted not to attend the event, parting ways from Vera at the street corner near the bed-and-breakfast. "I just want to mope for a while," she confessed. "Honestly, I'd be back in the city by now, except Bradley will go to pieces if I leave, and then I'll have to deal with *that* on top of everything else." She sighed. "Did you know Maverick Brown has a stake in the publishing house? Maybe I can get transferred over to be *his* assistant, somehow."

"I've heard Brown is incredibly eccentric," Vera warned.

"So what? It has to be a better gig than this." The lynx padded off, her head low. Though Vera could barely call her a friend, she nevertheless wished she could help improve Darcy's situation. But alas, the only creature who could really do that was Bradley Marvel.

All too quickly, it was time to meet Chloe. Vera could hear the din from a block away, and she smelled the wonderful aromas long before she saw the crowd bustling amid the rows of fruit trees. Chloe was waiting near the entrance, and she waved a paw at Vera to get her attention.

"Hurry up!" the cat called. "I'm starving and I'd hate to miss out!"

The Harvest Festival's "Soup's-On Soup-Off" was always well attended, partly because folks got to try a lot of soup samples, and partly because it was great fun to watch the contestants hurl good-natured challenges and insults at each other. Anyone was allowed to enter the contest, whether they were a professional cook like Joe or Sun Li, or just an amateur with a ladle and a plan.

Sun Li had won the competition last year with his Soup's *In* Pumpkin and Wild Rice Soup Dumplings. A few of the judges had wept actual tears of joy, the recipe was so good. The panda graciously decided not to enter this year, to give others a chance at winning. Instead, he'd been invited as the Judge of Honor.

This year, several booths were set up under the trees in a section of Cold Clay Orchards. The soup challenge was extremely popular. Every creature loved soup, and the weather was still sunny, but getting crisp.

Vera and Chloe approached the booths, but Vera stopped to wait upon seeing Orville nearing from the other direction. When he reached her, he said, "A couple of boats got tangled up and drifted downriver. I was called in to coordinate the retrieval. I was worried that we'd take too long, and I wouldn't get to try the soups."

"Now that would be a real crime," Chloe said with a smile.

Orville nodded. "You understand completely, Miss McKibben."

"I hope all the boats are back?" Vera asked.

"Exactly where they should be." He gave her a slight bow and then escorted her toward the front entrance of the orchard. Vera thought how nice it was to be on good terms with her beau once again.

They purchased their soup tickets at the gate (all the proceeds went to charity). "Thank you!" a rabbit said as he gave them their tickets. "Five each, but you can buy more inside. This year we're all soup-porting Goody Crow's Restful Home for Aged Creatures!"

They all groaned at the pun and went to join the bustle. Orville was looking around at each pot and cook, trying to decide where to start.

"Let's begin with Joe's booth," Vera suggested. "I think he said that he's been trying several new recipes, so I'm sure he's got a fantastic entry this year."

"Good idea," Orville agreed.

They saw Joe's antlers from some distance away and walked over. But Vera stopped short when she heard a strident voice ring out. Esme von Beaverpelt was shaking a paw at Detective Knox, who was in line for his own soup sample.

Esme frowned. "You're that city cop! The one blaming Vera for a crime?"

"It's not as simple as that, ma'am."

"Well, here's something simple for you, sir. We're out of soup!"

"I guess I'll get chili, then," he said, shifting to the next place, where a squirrel was ladling out the spicy mix into a little bread bowl.

The beaver shot dark looks at both Joe and his son, and then further down to catch the attention of the various other chefs. "Anyone who serves *him* can say goodbye to fresh coffee next time they stop into the café! Understood?"

"Esme, that's not really necessary . . ." Vera began to say.

"Stay out of this, Vixen," the beaver snapped. "I said, *understood?*"

"Yes, Miss von Beaverpelt!" several voices shouted in chorus.

The squirrel with the chili slowly retracted her paw, still holding the cup she'd been about to give to Knox. "Sorry, sir. I seem to be out of chili."

Esme nodded curtly on hearing this. Though Esme worked as a server at the diner, it was well to remember that she was a born-and-raised scion of the town's most influential family, and she still knew how to command attention. She regarded Knox with a steady gaze, her paws curled up and set just where she'd tied her apron around her waist.

"Er. I'll just wait over there," Knox said, edging out of line. His hulking form came to linger under a large oak, just beginning to glow with yellow highlights.

Since an essential quality of bison was that they were unmovable, Vera was frankly impressed and not a little intimidated that Esme had forced Knox back with words alone.

Orville followed him, perhaps out of professional solidarity, while Chloe stayed close to Vera. "Wow," she murmured. "Wouldn't want to get on her bad side."

"Indeed," Vera whispered back.

Upon seeing the retreat of the detective, Esme nodded once more, then turned to Vera. "Red lentil or the potato leek? The lentil is Joe's, the leek is Joe Junior's."

"Um, lentil please. And another cup for Orville . . . if he's allowed."

Chloe said, "I'll take the leek."

The line of soup tasters recommenced its winding progress, and the two friends shuffled off to allow more hungry folks to step up. Vera walked over to Orville and wordlessly offered one of the cups.

"Smells good," Knox commented mildly.

Orville said, "Sorry about that. Esme's not usually so . . ." he trailed off.

"Partisan?" Knox suggested.

"Folks do have their opinions," Orville agreed.

"And the consensus seems to be that Miss Vixen is without flaw."

"Let's not go *that* far," said Orville, glancing at Vera.

"Be careful what you say, Chief," Chloe warned playfully. "I've known Vera much longer than you have, and I have agreed to defend her."

"Noted," Orville said with a little mock salute.

"Still, I'm impressed at the vehemence with which your neighbors defend you," Knox told Vera.

"It's a good town," was all Vera could say in response. She wasn't foolish enough to think that the detective would simply determine she was innocent because a few creatures said so.

"How's the soup?" he asked then.

"Terrible," Orville replied as he slurped the whole cup down and chomped on the bread bowl. "I'd better go get seconds to be sure."

Vera walked to dispose of her used spoon in a nearby wash bin, and then turned around to see a familiar face.

"Why hello, Mr. Fallow!" Vera paused to chat with the dapperly dressed rat, stepping to the side of the main path to allow other creatures to pass by. Mr. Fallow was an old-school gentlerat, and he always doffed his hat when he met a lady in the street.

"Good afternoon, Vera. You're looking well. I hear that you've selected Miss McKibben to represent you, and I assume she is the well-dressed feline over there. Is it true?"

"Yes," said Vera. "No disrespect to you, of course. But I know that you don't deal with much criminal law . . ."

He held up a paw. "No need to explain, Vera. The choice of attorney is a deeply personal one, and you should always choose someone you feel will be the best option for you. And you're correct. I am much more familiar with civil matters. Besides, Miss McKibben has a stellar record, so I'm sure you'll be fine."

"Wait, you've heard of her?" Vera asked.

He smiled. "Not till she arrived here in town. But I requested a reference check once I learned of the situation."

"Wow." Vera was nonplussed. "Just out of curiosity?"

He smiled diffidently. "Partly that. Partly professional . . . let's call it pride. Any attorney operating in my bailiwick ought to be good, whether it's me or someone else. And the association reported back that McKibben is well regarded in the city."

"Well, that's great to hear!" Vera wanted to kick herself for not thinking of doing the same thing, because as a reporter on a story she would have checked a creature's credentials immediately. But, she reminded herself, Chloe was her friend, not some stranger. "Thank you for letting me know."

"Of course. And should you need any further advice, you know where my office is."

"Thank you, Mr. Fallow. I'll remember that."

He strolled off, perhaps in search of more soup.

Vera was touched by the rat's concern. Mr. Fallow had always been a very gracious creature to her, whether she came looking for information for a story, or she just happened to pass him on the street. It wasn't surprising that he'd quietly verify the status of a new arrival, just to protect the residents and the reputation of Shady Hollow. It was a measure of how close-knit and caring this community was.

Vera returned to Knox and Chloe, and they continued through the fairground.

"Who's next?" a voice called in a challenge. "Who's ready to take up the ladle and face me? I dare you! What? What's that? I can't hear you; I've got chowder in my ear!"

A crowd was gathered around a tall wooden structure, laughing and exchanging jokes with the creature inside.

"Oh, it's Lefty's turn in the pot," Vera said, as Orville reappeared by her side, now with a fresh cup of onion soup.

"What's that?" Knox asked. "I thought cruel and unusual punishment was no longer practiced in the woodlands."

Orville shook his head. "That's not a jail; it's a game. For charity. Whenever a cook decides their soup is too old, or over-cooked, or just not suitable to be tasted, they can take it over here to the Soup Pot. Folks can pay to throw old soup at whoever's volunteered to stand inside. If you hit them, you win a prize. But it's mostly just a silly way to raise money for a cause. In summer we do a similar one, but with tomatoes that have gone too soft."

Lefty stood upon a narrow ledge, dancing around as if he had a whole ballroom floor. "Come get me! What'll it be? Chowder? Bisque? Bouillabaisse? Hurl any flavor you like for a mere pittance! Buy three cups, get up to three chances to soak me! All proceeds go toward the new addition to Goody Crow's Restful Home. Great cause! Feed me and help your neighbors. It's a win-win."

Orville strolled up and offered a bill to the squirrel running the game. "Three chances, right?"

"You got it, Chief. Any particular flavors?"

"I'll take what comes." Orville raised his voice to bellow at Lefty, "This is for the honey incident!"

Lefty started waving his paws, jumping in alarm. "Oh, no, no, no! Help! Abuse! Brutality! And me, an innocent raccoon with hardly any priors!"

The whole crowd burst into raucous laughter.

Orville grinned and hefted his first missile (the soups were spooned into hollowed-out bread rolls that had gone stale—the game doubled as a way to reuse all the old food before it got composted). "Ready, Lefty?"

"Give me a sec, Chief! Maybe you want to spin around first? Or close your eyes? Something?"

Orville went into a pitching stance. "Nope."

Lefty threw his front paw over his forehead. "Woe is me! Remember me to Rhonda, everyone!"

"I'm right here, you dolt," Rhonda called from the sidelines.

"Oh, hey, sweetie. Listen, I love you! If this is the end for me, the loot is buried in—"

A bread bowl of corn chowder flew through the air and smacked sideways into Lefty, covering his face and snout with thick, chunky liquid and bits of stale bread.

The crowd cheered, several creatures starting a chant of "Or-VILLE! Or-VILLE!"

Lefty went silent, licking off the goo as best he could. Then he said, "This must be Parson Dusty's entry. He always adds a little too much dill."

The squirrel nodded to Orville and gave him a red ticket. "Congratulations, Chief. You can redeem this over at the prize booth."

"Wait, I don't get to throw more soup?"

"You've already won!"

"But I wanted to hit him again."

"Sorry, Chief. Rules are rules. *Up* to three chances. Letter of the law, you know."

Orville grumbled but accepted the ticket. Then he whirled around again and yelled, "Wait, what loot?"

"Oh, nothing to worry about, Chief!" Lefty called back, grinning now. "You wouldn't be interested. Real boring! Good night! Okay, who's next? Come on, it's for charity! Step right up!"

"Come on, Orville," Vera said. "You need to pick out your prize."

Chapter 18

At the prize booth, Orville was dithering over an extra-large jar of pickled watermelon rind (which he loved) and an extra-large sack of chestnuts (which he also loved). While he and Knox discussed the pros and cons of each, Vera scanned the crowd.

She waved to Howard Chitters and his family, then spotted a figure slightly further on. She narrowed her eyes and told Orville she'd be back.

"Wait, where are you going?"

"I need to collect some facts," she said, already moving out.

Detective Knox started to say something, but she heard Orville warn him off. "She's using her reporter voice—it's best to stay out of her way when that happens. Pickles would keep longer, wouldn't they?"

Vera advanced on her target. With his well-tuned sense for being noticed, Bradley had already stopped and turned toward her, a grin on his face as if he were expecting a fan photo to be taken. But when he realized it was Vera, his dashing grin evaporated, and he looked to the side, possibly trying to sidle away.

"Marvel, I've got some questions for you."

"Oh? Maybe just some follow-up on that fantastic interview your pal conducted? Happy to talk more about my books!"

"Oh, good, because that's exactly what I want to ask about. Come on."

"Where are we going? Where is everyone else?"

"This is an *exclusive* interview," she muttered.

She half-dragged him to a spot well away from the crowd, which had only grown since her arrival. Twilight was turning the sky to amethyst, and shadows were gathering under the trees. Paper lanterns hung from branches all around, and a few creatures were steadily working to light them all, so it seemed like comically large fireflies had begun to appear in the orchard. The muted sounds of attendees laughing and chatting and the strain of a stringed instrument made everything feel so peaceful and normal.

Except, of course, for those creatures under suspicion of murder.

Vera turned to Bradley and told him that she knew all about what Darcy was really doing in her role as assistant.

He grimaced at first, then started to look sick. "You can't tell anyone, Vera! Please! It would ruin me!"

"It was your choice to involve Darcy in your mess," she told him, unwilling to let him off so easy.

"I know, and I never intended it to go so far. It was just meant to give me a little space, a little time to figure out what was wrong. But the thing is, she's good, and the longer she did it, the more I kept asking myself why I wasn't doing it."

"Seems to me that you know you're in the wrong."

"You think I don't worry about it every day? Of course I do! If the public found out that Darcy wrote the last three Percy Bannon novels, they might ask if she wrote the earlier ones, too."

"And did she?" Vera demanded.

"No! I came up with the whole idea, and I wrote the first several, no problem! And readers loved Percy, and they just wanted more, more, more. What will they do when they discover they've been lied to? They'll hate me. They might ask whether I'd written any of my books. They might think I didn't even write *Weaver's Luck!*"

She rolled her eyes. "Oh, please, I listened to you yap to poor Barry about it for an hour. I'm very sure you wrote that."

"But all it takes is a seed, Vera. A hint of plagiarism, or trickery, and it's all over. If one reviewer or publisher or agent in the city even dreams that book isn't mine, no one will work with me again. *Weaver's Luck* is the reason I got a break in the first place! It's the only truly excellent thing I've ever written! And if I can't ever get past this writer's block, I'll never do another thing like it. I can't lose *Weaver*, you understand?"

"What would you do if I did write the truth in the paper?" she asked.

Bradley moaned. "No, don't! I'd have to leave the city. All cities. I'd have to go somewhere so far away that no one has ever heard of Bradley Marvel or Percy Bannon or maybe they don't have books at all . . . somewhere! I'd never show my face again to anyone I know. Don't do it, Vera. You've got the power of life and death in your pen. I'm begging you."

She inhaled. Desperation was practically rolling off Bradley, but he never once threatened her. His impulse was to run. Which was exactly what he'd done before.

"No promises, Bradley," she said quietly. "But I know you need a chance to fix this whole mess. So you think about how you'll do that, in a way that won't hurt Darcy or anyone else. Got it?"

"Got it," he said eagerly. "I'll make it work, Vera. I can do it. As soon as this murder is solved, that is. I can't think straight while I'm a suspect!"

She knew the feeling. "I'm doing my best to get the answers to the murder, too," she said. "Unless the real killer can be identified, it will destroy a lot of folks' lives, not just yours or mine."

He nodded, then said, in a hopeful voice, "Can I help?"

Vera remembered all too well how intrusive Bradley's "help" had been the last time she was solving a mystery. She said, "You can help by staying out of my way and trying to remember anything you might have missed about what happened with Rick. The smallest detail could be key."

"Okay," he said. "But if there's any chance of a more . . . heroic way to help, let me know?"

Vera had to take pity on the dejected wolf. "I'll do that, Bradley."

"Great!" He beamed. "You know, I think this is giving me an idea for a story!"

Vera returned to where Orville was waiting with Knox. The soup contest had come down to two contestants. Cassia Brocket entered her family's famous beer cheese soup. Mr. Gobble, a turkey from the distant village of Northfield, offered a barley and parsnip soup that had proven a surprisingly formidable competitor.

At the final round of tasting, Sun Li sat at a table with a bowl of each in front of him. The crowd surrounded the table, waiting for his verdict. Both chefs stood nearby, looking quite nervous.

The panda dipped his spoon delicately into the beer cheese soup and tasted. He nodded once. "A blend of cheeses, to allow for proper melting consistency. And not too much beer—the vegetable broth base is still present, with the herbs providing depth. Very well done."

Miss Brocket heaved a sigh of relief.

Sun Li turned to the barley soup. Tasted. Pondered. He said, "The parsnips were roasted before being added, yes? And I think . . . the barley toasted in a nut oil of some type?"

"Walnut oil, pressed fresh last month," the turkey bawked.

The panda nodded in approval. "Wonderful choice."

He tasted each soup again, and the crowd held its collective breath.

Then Sun Li stood up. "What an honor to try each of the entries, and to taste the best the earth offers us, lovingly prepared by our friends and neighbors. All the contestants should be proud of their work, and this last round has been a challenge for me to judge. A delicious challenge," he added. Then he lifted the bowl of barley and parsnip soup. "I declare this the winning entry. For flavor, yes, but also innovation and attention to detail. Congratulations, my fellow chef!"

Everyone broke out in a cheer, and Mr. Gobble stepped up to accept his award: a ladle carved from cherrywood. Cassia gave the winner a gracious hug and placed a chef's hat on the turkey's head.

After that, there was music and dancing, but Vera excused

herself, wishing to be solitary for a while. The crowd was a little too jubilant for her mood. She waved goodbye to Orville
and promised to stop by the police station tomorrow to let him
know any developments. She threw a look at Detective Knox.
"And you should watch out for the locals."

He gave her a solemn nod. "I understand they can be rather
partisan, Miss Vixen."

Vera had spent the entire morning at the newspaper office,
attempting to perform her usual duties while simultaneously
fending off questions from other reporters and explaining to
BW that *no*, she would not be writing a memoir from the city
jail, so he didn't need to plan a special edition for it.

"Just consider it, Vera. I'm not saying I *want* you to be thrown
in jail. I'm just saying there's a silver lining to every cloud. Think
of the opportunities for the first serial."

"I'm going to find lunch," was her reply to that. She stood up
and pushed past her ever-so-profit-minded boss.

Barry Greenfield gave her a wink as she walked by his desk.
"Don't worry. We'll visit you in jail, Vixen."

"Thanks, Barry. Means a lot." She couldn't stop a chuckle
though. Reporters all thought they were comedians.

Vera opted to stroll down River Drive, watching the boats
knocking along the docks and the many creatures hurrying
about, all intent on their various tasks. A barge was being pulled,
heavy with a shipment of crates from the city. The stevedores
called to each other with jargon that made sense to them but
sounded mystifying to outsiders. Vera appreciated the cheerful
efficiency with which they worked.

She continued, and finally halted at the door of the Riverside

Pub, where the proprietor had placed a wooden easel that was painted on both sides and chalked with the day's specials. Today, the pub was advertising a spicy potato and pumpkin soup, and a red lentil, carrot, and apple slaw that claimed to be the "best of this season."

That was promising. Vera walked in. She was about to slide onto a stool at the bar when a voice behind her said, "Won't you join me?"

She turned and saw Detective Knox in a booth. She narrowed her eyes at him. "You trust me not to poison your slaw?"

"It's a risk I'm willing to take." He gestured for Vera to take a seat in the booth opposite.

Despite everything, Vera found that she rather liked the detective's unflappable demeanor. She just wished he didn't consider her a suspect!

As if he read her mind, he said, "Don't worry. I won't arrest you over lunch. That would be very rude. And if I had to gamble on it—which would be illegal and unethical—I'd bet that you'll never be formally accused of Renard's murder."

"Yay, I guess?"

They were interrupted by a stoat carrying a large tray. He stopped at the table and set down a bowl of soup and a plate with several little tidbits, along with a glass of amber ale. Vera looked at Knox's meal and ordered an exact duplicate. "But no ale for me," she added. "I'll have the apple fizz."

The stoat nodded and hurried off.

"Humph," Knox said, huffing out the sound so it was almost a snort. He was frowning at a piece of paper in his hoof, which appeared to be some kind of communication from his department. He then glanced toward her, a thoughtful expression on his face.

"What is it?" Vera asked. Probably something dire if recent events were any guide. "Got a new clue that links me to the murder weapon? A witness who saw a fox stroll into the lobby of Bradley's building?"

He looked surprised, then held the paper up to the light. "Can you see through this?"

"What? No! I was just making things up! You're telling me that someone is trying to link me to the murder weapon?"

"No, it's not that. But someone *did* see a fox enter the lobby of Marvel's building."

Vera gaped at him. "But I didn't . . ."

"Not you, Miss Vixen. This witness reads the society pages, and they seemed to recognize Mrs. Priscilla Renard."

"Wait, Rick's wife was there, too?"

"According to the witness, another resident of Mockingbird Court, Mrs. Renard walked in about an hour before the witnesses first discovered the body. Isn't *that* interesting? The witness saw her begin to climb the stairs, but since they lived on the second floor, they couldn't say whether she continued all the way up to the fifth."

"But that's a huge development!" The reporter in Vera wanted to whip out her notebook. "Is one of your colleagues going to question her?"

"Already went to her house, hence this message." Knox waved the paper in question. "But here's an even more interesting development. Apparently, Mrs. Renard has left the city, and her household staff has no idea when she'll be back."

Vera had to take this news in for a long moment before she could even formulate a reply. At last, she said, "Mrs. Renard just left, without leaving word at all?"

"So it seems. Perhaps the grieving widow simply needed time away from all the attention."

"As if! No creature is grieving Rick, and in any case, what's her excuse for going to Bradley Marvel's place at all, let alone the one evening that Rick just happened to be going there too? Mrs. Renard's a society fixture, not a working creature. She wouldn't have any business with Bradley, and if she wanted to see Rick, she could wait for him to come home."

"Unless the business she wished to discuss with Rick would be better conducted in someone else's home. No one wants their own clean floors covered in blood, and I'm sure her floors are especially clean, what with the maids and all." Knox's tone was mild, but the implication incendiary.

"Could Rick's wife really be the killer?"

"She certainly had motive. It can't be pleasant to endure years of infidelity, especially when Renard seemed so blatant about it."

"And her alibi?"

"Not sure about that yet. And I must be careful. The fact is, Miss Vixen, it's obviously important to have an alibi confirmed and to carefully assess all the evidence one can put their paws on. But it doesn't amount to much if the psychology doesn't match up."

"What do you mean?" asked Vera. The stoat returned with her food, and the two of them began to eat as they discussed the case.

"What I mean is facts are all well and good," Knox went on after sampling the slaw. "But facts can be manipulated. Or they can be misunderstood. Let's say for example, you walk into a room, and you see a knife on the floor, with little red drops all around it. And even more smearing the blade. Now a reasonable creature might immediately think, 'Aha! That's blood, and this knife has been used in a crime.' If they were to study it and notice any telltale signs, such as a paw print, or perhaps a bit of fur that had been stuck to it, they would automatically assume that evidence belonged to either an attacker or the victim."

The police detective continued, "However, another creature walking in and seeing the same scene, but who wasn't looking for a crime, would only see a knife dropped on the floor with ketchup around it, and conclude that some poor creature was quite clumsy in making their lunch, and was called away on some errand before they could clean it up. Which scenario is true? I can never know the entirety of what is happening in the world. I can only see the particular moment, or perhaps listen to a few key witness accounts, which may or may not agree with one another.

"My method is to not only look at facts, but also to look at the psychology, and to make sure that those two things are in harmony. In your case, everyone that I've spoken to is adamant that you could not possibly have committed such a crime. Some of them suggested that while you are capable of great emotion, and occasionally perform some overly dramatic action not fully thought out"—Vera assumed *that* was Orville talking—"none of them would countenance the idea that you would murder anyone. So you see, while a few of the facts lying before me would indicate that you are indeed a suspect, the psychology does not match. And I'm not suggesting that psychology out-weighs facts. All I am saying is that when I only have *one* of those things pointing toward a particular conclusion, I need to be extremely careful before proceeding to that conclusion."

"That makes sense," said Vera. "I've never heard it explained exactly like that before."

"Well, I've been on the force a long time. I don't imagine I would've explained it like that my first year on the beat." Knox took a sip of ale, then leaned back in the booth.

"So you don't suspect me of the murder. But I noticed that you're not exactly proclaiming my innocence yet."

"Well, I do like to keep my options open. And I hesitate to declare anyone innocent until I know exactly who is guilty."

She asked, "Do you have any particular theories about who is guilty? Does this news about Priscilla change your ideas?"

"Oh, I have several, some of them quite outlandish. As I said, the psychology and the facts often don't agree, even within my own theories. I prefer to keep those theories private. But what about you, Miss Vixen? Do you have any theories?"

She nodded slowly. "Also several. Some of them probably even more outlandish than yours. One thing that I can't forget is how angry I was at Rick the last time I saw him, when I left the city all those years ago. And it occurred to me that if such a nasty situation had happened to me, it must've happened to other folks as well. Creatures tend to be predictable. They behave the same way over and over until they're given some reason to change their behavior. If I was angry at Rick, then I have to believe there were other creatures just as angry, or maybe even more so. His wife, certainly, but others as well."

"It's true that he made enemies as well as friends. It's not difficult to find a city official or politician, or some society paragon, who was on the wrong end of Rick's reporting, or later, one of those tell-all books. He loved a shocking headline, and he wasn't above the kind of journalism that valued sensation over solid reporting. He would never outright lie, but he would frame things in such a way that strongly implied something about a creature . . . then he was always able to walk it back if the objections became too loud. Like he was always playing a game."

Vera gave a nod. "Yes, that sounds like Rick. And like anyone who plays a game like that, it's really a kind of gambling. Maybe this time he pushed someone a little too far. And that creature decided to take action."

The cop gave her a look of approval. "The same thought crossed my mind. I've got several creatures in the department combing through Rick's old columns to see if anything interesting pops up. We're also looking at the books that he'd recently edited at Fieldstone, though in that case, you would think that the offended party would go after the author instead."

"What if it's a book that isn't available yet?" she suggested. "Maybe the killer was trying to stop something from coming out."

"That's very possible. I'll make sure to get a list of the books that are expected over the next several months, and perhaps we can have a look through his papers to find out if there was anything else in the works."

Vera shook her head slowly. "But the psychology for that doesn't really make sense either, does it? I mean, as you say, if someone was writing a book that would expose a nasty secret, the killer would go after whoever wrote it, not the one responsible for editing and publishing it. Unless Rick and the writer were in it together somehow." Vera sighed. "I don't know. It's hard to keep track of all the possibilities. For all we know, the simplest and most obvious conclusion could be the right one. Maybe some burglar really did break into Bradley's apartment, and found Rick there for whatever reason, and just panicked." But she didn't like that idea, and she could tell Detective Knox didn't like it either. Because it didn't explain why Rick was there in the first place.

"What we need . . ." both of them said at exactly the same time.

Vera broke off and chuckled. "Sorry, you go first."

Knox said, "What we need is to concentrate on Rick's movements that day so that we can understand *why* he went to Bradley's apartment. To me, that's the key to this whole case."

"I'm happy to give you the notes I took from my additional interviews with Bradley and Darcy," Vera offered. "But they were clear that they had no idea what Rick was up to. Maybe his colleagues at the publishing house would know."

"We're working on that. And of course I've sent messages to his wife. Haven't heard back yet."

"Well, I've got to get to the *Herald* offices," she said. "I'm easy to find if you have any more questions."

"Thank you. Oh, one more thing, Miss Vixen. I suggest that you not make a big announcement about the fact that you're not really a suspect anymore."

"Why is that?" asked Vera.

"Because it can sometimes be useful to withhold information. The police do it all the time. It gives you a little more to work with in case you need to change the game."

"Are you using me as bait?" asked Vera.

"Not exactly. But you can observe folks' reactions in a different way if they think that you're still a suspect, and that could be quite enlightening."

He didn't say more, and Vera was feeling a tad overwhelmed.

"Oh, 'course, I'm not the only one on this case. And there is still the matter of the notebook." Knox said. "Regardless of my theory about psychology, a jury would have questions about how it got there."

"This is ridiculous," said Vera. "I am no more guilty than I was before, which is to say not guilty at all. The introduction of some flimsy piece of evidence—literally, figuratively—isn't proof of guilt. That notebook could have been stolen. It could have been lost. It could have been lost and then stolen. It's purely circumstantial."

"The circumstances of it being found in the very same room as the dead body of a creature you had every reason to hate is going to make a jury think quite hard." The cop continued to look at her steadily. "I strongly suggest, Miss Vixen, that you focus less on your little harvest festival and more on the very real possibility that you could yet wind up behind bars."

"Very kind of you to offer me advice," said Vera dryly.

Knox took a sip of his ale. "Well, what can I say, Miss Vixen? For what it's worth, I do think you have a chance to solve the whole thing. You've got pluck."

"And will my pluck keep me from going to prison?"

"That's entirely up to you. But it would look rather bad if I spent a week in the woodlands and came back with not a single suspect to charge, and the crime still unsolved."

Chapter 19

The next day, Vera woke up before the sun (which was itself waking up later and later every day). Feeling restless, she donned her favorite coat, wrapped a beige scarf knitted in the traditional woodland crossover stitch around her neck, stuck a snack of smoked almonds in her pocket, and headed outside.

It was chilly, and a low mist crawled over the ground, making the town look half submerged. The sky was that crystalline pink that happens only when the air is totally clear and the sun is just below the horizon. Within moments, it would begin to turn first light blue, then deepen to the usual shade everyone who woke later would assume the sky always had.

And soon enough, the streets would be bustling, as visitors and residents did their best to enjoy the last days of the festival. The

Sawmill Soiree would cap everything off, but until then, there were preserves to purchase, hats to try on, and pies to sample. A big day indeed.

But for now, she seemed to be the only creature out and about. Vera deliberately turned away from the town, choosing a route that took her down the exceptionally quiet residential streets, then near the millpond, and back onto the North Track that would eventually take her to Mirror Lake. She inhaled deeply, breathing the misty air into her lungs.

She loved these northern woodlands, and she very selfishly didn't want to leave them behind. She surely did not want to leave them in cuffs, en route to prison for a crime she didn't commit. And she didn't want Bradley or Darcy to be blamed either. She was certain that both were innocent (Bradley was annoying as all get out, but that wasn't exactly a crime).

A shadow seemed to block out the sun. Was this a harbinger of her dismal future in a dank prison cell?

"What do you want from me?" Vera shouted at the shadow . . . then she realized the shadow was Lenore.

Lenore landed with a soft thump. "Wow. Good morning to you too."

"Sorry about the less than friendly greeting. I thought you were a dark omen of my future."

"Aw, you're so sweet!" Touched by the notion, Lenore preened for a second, then got serious. "I went to your place with an offering of those red bean buns Sun Li makes. When you didn't answer your door, I got worried. I know you sometimes go walking to clear your head."

"I'm trying. But I'm not having much luck. I feel like I've got all this information, but none of it is the piece I actually need!

There's something wrong about the way we're looking at this case. Something is missing."

Lenore nodded. "And we can't even say what kind of thing it is. Tell you what, let's walk for a while longer, and then we'll see if anything shakes loose in the old skull. You can't force it, but your head is working on the problem. So put it aside and walk. Look at trees, not clues."

"Okay."

Vera and Lenore made their way through the autumn landscape, not speaking much as they went, other than to point out a direction or comment on a particularly striking aspect of the woods, such as a ring of red-capped mushrooms growing in a small clearing to the side of the track.

When Vera saw it, she paused, arrested by the colors in front of her. The grass growing in the clearing was a particularly dark green, and the blades were only about two inches in height. It was rather like a dense emerald carpet spread out specifically to invite one to step on it and admire the surrounding trees beginning their annual display of autumn colors. Though it was still early in the season, and more than half of the trees remained green, there were tinges of yellow around the edges of the birch leaves, and one branch of an oak had chosen to turn red in advance of its brethren. Here and there, peeps of orange emerged as a single leaf stood out among the population of leaves that remained a verdant summer green.

Vera wondered, not for the first time, how it all happened. Why should one particular leaf prepare to color and then fall before another? Was it the choice of each tree, to send an undeniable message to each leaf, commanding it to turn some beautiful, vibrant color, and enjoy an all-too-brief stage of glorious attention, before it inevitably dropped from its branch and was sent into the air all alone?

How alarming for a leaf (if indeed a leaf could feel alarm) to appear in spring and enjoy two seasons connected to a greater whole, always among its sister leaves, and surely presuming it would always remain so. What leaf could ever be ready for autumn? To learn that you would change your entire appearance over the course of a few short days, to catch the attention of every creature in the woods and know that the sight heralded some great change? Only to then experience a new kind of shocking coldness and be severed from the only home and family you have ever known? Vera always felt so sorry for the dried leaves on the forest floor, the ones turned brown by the cold, dry darkness of autumn night. Although it was a natural part of the yearly cycle of life in the north, it all felt a little unfair.

But standing in this little clearing now, Vera's heart lightened for a moment. Wind had swept the fallen leaves into piles around the edge of the clearing, pushed up against the undergrowth and the small shoots and saplings that occupied the understory. It was like a circular ridge surrounding the green grass, as if the leaves once again gathered together by choice in order to observe some natural event.

But there was no event to be seen, at least not at the moment. However, the ring of mushrooms in the middle of the clearing hinted of expectation. Rather like a stage carefully set with lights all around in advance of an actor appearing. Vera could imagine some fantastically dressed creature stepping into the middle of the circle, with the bright caps of the mushrooms acting like little lamps, indicating that something important was about to happen. Would they dance, or give a speech, recite a poem . . . who knew?

That moment, a little bit of darkness fluttered down from the opening between the trees above, and Lenore landed in the middle of the ring. Her wings spread wide for an instant before she tucked them back and looked at Vera.

"What are you doing just standing there?"

"I was daydreaming about what creature might magically appear in the mushroom ring," said Vera. "And as it turned out, it was you."

"Well, I *was* with you, so that makes sense. You didn't expect some other creature to pop up in a puff of smoke or a swirl of mist, did you?"

"Maybe," said Vera. "I do wish there were some creature with powers like that, because then I could ask them to explain exactly what's been happening with this mystery. I don't believe in magic, but I have to admit that I've been using logic these past several days, and I haven't gotten anywhere."

"Yes, we have," Lenore countered. "We had some luck in gathering information and learning some key facts from the witnesses involved. We just need to put everything together into a single picture, and that takes time, like I said."

"I know that. But every time I try to step out of my house in Shady Hollow, I feel like some new crisis unfolds or there's some terrible portent. Even inside my house, my mind is so taken up with worrying that I'll be arrested or something worse that I find it difficult to think."

"Then let's not go back to Shady Hollow right away. You're right that we need a quieter place where we won't be bothered while we work on this." Lenore looked to the left and right, her eyes bright with the reflected color of the sky. "Oh, I know. I have just the place. Follow me."

Lenore took off into the air once more, flapping her wings

until she caught an updraft. She circled once, and then flew off toward the southeast. Vera followed at a quick pace, keeping her friend in sight, beyond the branches above. Lenore's dark form would appear beyond a green branch, and then be obscured by another branch, becoming visible against the blue sky before being eclipsed once more by a sudden burst of orange as she flew over an oak tree.

Vera trotted along the track, no longer worried about fallen leaves, fully intent on allowing her friend to lead her to whatever haven she had selected.

Vera realized where they were headed before she saw their destination. There was only one location that fit their requirements: out of town, a comfortable haven, a trusted friend to host them, and the promising likelihood of snacks. As Vera passed beyond the dense part of the forest and into another clearing, her eyes were drawn to the single enormous tree growing in the middle. This elm was ancient and seemed as though it would endure many more generations. Huge limbs spread out dozens of feet horizontally, and here the leaves that covered the elm were just starting to turn, with little accents of gold among the green.

Lenore had arrived first and settled onto one of the main branches, the one leading to a doorway in the trunk. Lenore tapped politely with her beak and then called out, "Professor? Are you at home?"

An answering hoot confirmed that the owl was indeed home and awake, so Vera proceeded to the base of the trunk, where a long rope ladder dangled, providing access to land-bound creatures who wished to visit Heidegger in his tree. The fox swiftly climbed up the rope and clambered onto the wide branch next to her friend.

At that moment the door opened inward, and Heidegger leaned out, blinking in the light to see who had called on him. "Oh, hello, ladies. What can I do for you?"

"Hello, Professor. We find ourselves in need of a refuge," Vera began to explain. "It's so busy in town, and creatures keep interrupting us when we're trying to work."

"Oh, how well I relate!" the owl commiserated. He stepped backward, opening the door wider and ushering them both in with one wing. "My home is your home. Solitude is hard to come by and seems to be all the more rare when you most need it. If I had a coin for every time a student knocked on my office door just when I was getting into an article or book! Well, I would be able to afford a heavier door so that I didn't hear the knocking." He chuckled as he cleared stacks of papers and errant books off the plush seats in the middle of the main room.

Lenore sat on one squishy, round poof, shaping it rather like a nest. Vera sank down into another and looked around the comfortable, if somewhat cluttered, living room. The walls curved, mimicking the shape of the tree trunk around which the room was built. Small round windows on the outer walls allowed light in, giving the room an airy feel in keeping with its location in the treetop.

"What are you working on that requires such concentration?" the owl asked as he bustled toward the small kitchenette and put a kettle on the tiny hob.

"We're trying to solve a murder," Lenore said, with characteristic bluntness. "We have lots of information, but it's all in little scraps, and we don't know what order they go in or what is relevant because it's hiding under all the other less vital clues."

"Yes, you have the leaves, and now you need to build the tree.

Array them all out and draw the lines that will become your branches and your trunk, and if you do it right, the picture will emerge."

"That's the hope," said Vera. "And I really do have to get it right, or else the authorities will decide that I'm the murderer and take me away."

Chapter 20

"Nonsense!" said Heidegger. "But I suppose there are many creatures with no sense. So please make yourselves at home and use whatever you need that I have here. I will mind my own business, for I have so many papers to grade and correct that I am afraid I won't be able to lend much assistance. But I do have some ginger crème sandwich cookies and cinnamon tea. For it is no good thinking without having one's stomach fortified first. Will that help?"

Vera thought that would be very helpful indeed and said so.

"See? I knew this was the right place to come." Lenore looked quite pleased with herself. Then she got to work, opening her satchel and pulling out a small bundle of papers and a pencil to write.

Vera did the same, though she had more notebooks and a larger quantity of little papers. By the time the two friends put everything together in the middle, it did indeed look like a pile of leaves without a tree to hold them.

"All right," said Lenore. "I think the first thing we need to do is make each suspect their own branch. Who do we have? Vera. Darcy. Bradley. A random burglar. Otherwise unknown figure."

"Otherwise unknown figure?" Vera asked. "That's far too vague. It could be literally anyone in the city!"

"I'm just leaving the option open. Think of it as a small branch with only one leaf. But we don't want to limit ourselves in our thinking—cutting off a branch, as it were."

Vera nodded, recognizing the sensibility of the argument. The two of them spent a few minutes arranging the small scraps of paper into distinct groups, each one relevant to one of the suspects.

It was distressing to Vera to see how many notes accumulated on her branch. Known to the victim? Yes. Proven antagonism toward the victim? Yes. Opportunity to reach the location of the crime? Yes. Alibi for the time in question? Weak. Circumstantial evidence? Her notebook, within five feet of the body.

"It's this last item that disturbs me the most," said Vera, pointing to the scrap of paper on which was written *Vera's notebook*. "I was never in Bradley's apartment, so how did something I own end up there?"

"It is suspicious," agreed Lenore. "I don't mean that I'm suspicious of you. I mean that it's suspicious that the notebook is there at all. The police didn't say there was any blood on it, did they?"

Vera said no. "It's the mere existence of it that incriminates me."

"Well, then, that's just not very incriminating, is it? Any good attorney will poke a thousand holes in an argument that depends on the existence of a notebook. I'm sure Chloe has already said as much."

"Yes, she said almost exactly that. She said circumstantial evidence is the easiest to dismiss. But I think the fact that the police found it rather alarmed her. Not that she said anything. She's been extremely adamant about supporting my innocence. But the fact is that the notebook was there, and I don't have a good explanation for *why*. Well, I guess if it gets as far as a jury, a prosecutor could imply a lot, and it would be up to each jury member to decide which version of the story feels more truthful."

"That's the job of every jury," Heidegger interjected as he brought a small tray to where the two friends were working. "You can't guarantee what conclusions another comes to. All you can do is present the clearest, most concise, most well-supported argument you're capable of making. Whatever little scrap paper you have on each branch there, just make sure there's a citation on the back of each one listing how you know that thing to be true. And when you come to a fact, or what you think is a fact, and you find you can't cite the reason you believe it is a fact, *that* is a leaf of interest."

"That's a good way to think about it, Professor," Vera said. "I just wish most folks were as logical as you."

"We'll explain the logic to them," said Lenore. "Perhaps we should leave your branch alone for a little while, Vera. Let's look at Darcy's now."

Lenore bent over the grouping of papers related to Darcy. "What do we have here? First, we know that Darcy did have a motive to wish Rick ill. He was manipulating her into writing a book under Bradley's name, but only as a ghostwriter. She wasn't getting any credit or recognition, and she wasn't getting paid much. Looks like only the off-the-books payments that Rick was giving her every month."

"I don't know if that really is a motive for murder," said Vera. "In a way, Darcy would have been better served if Rick was still alive. And if anything, she might have meant to kill Marvel. After all, she was getting some extra money on a regular basis, and she could have made a public announcement about the fact that she was the author of the latest Percy Bannon novels, which would've created a stir that she might have benefited from . . . if she was strategic about it. If nothing else, she probably could have found a better job at a different publisher. With Rick dead, the only folks who know about Darcy's ghostwriting are Darcy and Bradley. And Darcy could've used Rick as a witness."

"That's assuming Rick would've told the truth in public." Lenore shook her head. "I don't think I would've bet on that. But as it happens, I agree with you that it doesn't seem like a brilliant decision on Darcy's part to kill him."

"I suppose we need to establish whether she could have, though," said Vera. "The police have verified that Bradley and Darcy were at the restaurant a few blocks away from Bradley's apartment beginning at 5:15 in the afternoon until the end of the dessert course at around 7 p.m. However, according to the interviews with the servers working that shift, Darcy excused herself to use the restroom, and she was gone for almost twenty minutes. None of the staff could say for certain if she was truly in the restroom that whole time, and in the hallway in which the restrooms are located, there is a door leading to the outside. It's possible for a creature to say they were going to the restroom, then leave through that door, run three blocks to Mockingbird Court, get up the stairs to the fifth-floor apartment, murder someone, and then leave again and return through that back door into the restaurant, stopping in the restroom to clean up and be seen walking out of the restroom at the end. It would be a tight timeline though."

"I'm exhausted just hearing about it." Lenore nodded. "Everything would have to go exactly like clockwork, not least of which is an incredibly compliant victim being in the exact location at the exact right time and not making a fuss while you killed them. Rick just doesn't seem like that helpful a creature."

"Too true," said Vera. "He was always out for himself, and he never would have done anything for anyone else unless he saw some benefit. I *still* don't understand why he was in Bradley's apartment in the first place, considering that Bradley was somewhere else."

"Well," said Lenore, "if we move over to Bradley's branch, there's a note on his alibi as well. True, he was in the restaurant along with Darcy for most of that time, but one of the servers said that Bradley also disappeared for a short amount of time: around fifteen minutes."

"Yes, according to Bradley, he saw someone he knew walk past, and he dashed out of the restaurant to chat with them. But Darcy remained behind, and indeed, it was during that time that she excused herself to the restroom. So, Darcy didn't see whoever he might have been talking with, and Bradley said that it took him almost half a block to catch up to them. No one from the restaurant saw that conversation happen either."

"Who was the creature?" Lenore asked, shuffling the small pieces of paper around in her quest to find the information.

"Christopher St. Pierre. An actor who Bradley apparently has been friends with for years. But the police haven't been able to contact them to confirm that the conversation took place. Apparently, the actor left the city the next morning for a tour. I'm sure the police have sent wingmails in the hope of getting the message to them. But with a traveling show, it will be incredibly difficult to get in touch with an individual amid the chaos of setting up and putting on the performance and breaking it back down again before traveling on. It will be a while before we know if Bradley is telling the truth about that encounter."

"Not to mention the fact that if they are Bradley's friend, they might lie in order to cover for him."

Vera shrugged. "Maybe. But for the moment, let's say that Bradley is lying. It means that he had exactly the same window of opportunity as Darcy. He would've had to run all the way back to his apartment building and get upstairs through the back since security would see him in the foyer and surely remember it. And then Bradley would have had to murder Rick quietly, clean himself up, and then return to the restaurant, again without being noticed, which would be particularly difficult for him, since he's something of a minor celebrity. And it doesn't make any sense that Bradley would follow Rick to his own apartment, kill him, and then leave him there with the door open so that the body would be found before Bradley returned."

"Yes, I agree that while Bradley certainly has some kind of motive, it makes no sense for Bradley to have chosen that location to commit the crime. Surely, he would have chosen Rick's apartment, or a simple city park with an out-of-the-way corner, or some other neutral location."

"So, we have both Darcy and Bradley with opportunity, but only Bradley with a motive strong enough to suggest murder was an option."

"If I may interject with an observation," said Heidegger. "It would only be possible for *one* of them to have opportunity.

Remember, we are talking about the *same* location in the *same* window of time. Either Darcy could've returned to the apartment and killed Rick and then run back to the restaurant, or Bradley could've done the same, but if *both* of them had tried that, they would have been seen by the other. The fact that both of them appeared to be convinced of the other's innocence, as evidenced by the fact that Darcy continues to aid Bradley and Bradley has not denounced Darcy, it strongly supports the theory that *neither* of them returned to the apartment during that twenty-minute window."

Vera couldn't argue with that logic.

But Lenore could.

"Unless they were working together," Lenore said in a speculative tone. "Is it possible that this is some elaborate ploy where both of them are lying to provide an alibi for the other, but in fact they planned it out to return to the apartment to get rid of Rick together, and then return in order to seem as though they weren't there at all?"

Vera shook her head slowly. "I don't think so. That would require a level of acting skill that I don't think either is capable of. And after all, if this was an elaborately planned murder, why was it done in such an unhelpful location as Bradley's own apartment? If Bradley was smart enough to engineer a situation in which he faked an alibi, and his assistant helped him do so, surely, he would be smart enough to not flee the city like an idiot at the first sign of danger."

"Yeah, that's probably true," Lenore admitted. "Plus, I'm pretty sure Darcy hates Bradley. She wouldn't cover for him, and she certainly wouldn't kill for him."

The two friends continued their work, now focusing on Bradley.

"We've established that the time frame is the same for him as for Darcy."

"Not quite," Lenore said. "Remember that it was his apartment, after all, and we've only got his word that it was corpse-free when he left it for dinner."

"True, but the detective said that according to the medical examiner's report, the murder was unlikely to have occurred before 5 p.m., and they were at that restaurant just after 5."

"Unlikely isn't the same as impossible." Lenore frowned. "But that still doesn't make much sense. If Bradley planned to kill Renard, he surely would have chosen a different location. And if it was an accident, he wouldn't have gone off to dinner, then come back with his own witness!"

"Darcy also said his behavior was completely normal all through dinner . . . as normal as Marvel gets, that is."

"Ugh. So that is yes to motive, and yes to opportunity. But no to . . . basic common sense." Lenore swept the little notes into a pile with her wing, sighing. "I'm not sure this is helping."

"Let's look at the tree, instead of the branches," Vera suggested. "Maybe if we pull back, we can see a pattern we missed before."

"Bird's-eye view! Of course." Lenore brightened up and moved back several paces to look at the whole arrangement on Heidegger's floor.

Vera said, "Let's start with the basic facts. Everything connects to Renard in some way."

"Speaking of that, where did you stay in the city when you were there?"

"I had a room at the Ambassador Hotel, which is right along the avenue by the park."

"And when you visited Chloe?" Lenore asked, looking at the map.

"She lives uptown in a neighborhood called Poplar Parish, which is where we had dinner, in a little corner bistro. But she works in the center of the city, so we also met there for lunch one day, too."

"And Darcy lives in the River District." Lenore marked all those spots on the map. "And Rick's home with his wife is here in Parkside West. Huh. All pretty scattered."

"But distance doesn't mean much in the city," Vera reminded her. "There's the tunnel system with the railcarts, and lots of ways to catch rides on any major street. Ferryboats cross every river and the bay. Truly, anyone can get anywhere in the city in less than an hour, sometimes much less."

"Good point," said Lenore. "Then let's start tracing movements. I'll take Darcy, you take Priscilla."

Vera nodded. She found and opened the folder on Priscilla, reading the notes Detective Knox had given her as thanks for the information she'd gleaned from Bradley and Darcy previously. She read through several short messages, all written on the thin, onion-skin paper used for express wingmail. They all had the mark of the metropolitan police force in the corner.

"What have you got?" Lenore asked.

"All the updates Detective Knox received from his department since he got up here. It must be nice to have a whole team to chase down leads and ask questions."

"Huh, what do you think we are?" Lenore reminded her with a sniff.

Vera smiled at her friend. "True enough. Here's the latest information they got about Priscilla Renard. She's still at large—that's a little scary, isn't it? But a sergeant interviewed the household staff and got her weekly schedule from them, so we know where she was supposed to be that evening. In some class . . . oh, no."

"What?"

Vera's breath caught as two very separate facts collided in her head. "It can't be!"

"What can't be?" Lenore pressed. Even Heidegger swiveled his head around to see what the excitement was.

"This is bad," Vera muttered.

Lenore hopped closer. "If you go all vague and mysterious on me now, so help me . . ."

Vera looked at her friend and felt her heart beating a little faster as she realized the import of what she had learned. "Lenore, I think I've figured something out! If I'm right, no innocent creature will be punished for Rick's murder."

"Great. What is it?"

"Well, I'm not totally sure yet, and I don't want to accidentally reveal something in case I'm wrong. Listen, I'm going to go search out one more piece of evidence, and then I swear I'll tell you everything."

"And where is the evidence?"

"If I'm right, it will be in the woods! Come on, Lenore. Professor, we've got to go, but will you do me one big favor?"

He bowed. "I am at your disposal, Miss Vixen."

"Fantastic. I'll need you to find Callie Standish—she'll have exactly what I'm looking for. Now listen closely because it may be a matter of life and death." After giving the owl precise instructions, she turned to her friend. "Let's go, Lenore."

"To where?"

"We're going to have a nice little chat with Bradley Marvel. And there's not much time left."

Chapter 21

The Harvest Festival was almost over. That night was the annual Sawmill Soiree, an open-air party that took place on the shore of the millpond with the huge sawmill as backdrop. It was a not-so-subtle reminder of the town's largest employer, but it was also a genuinely beloved event that creatures looked forward to all year. There was music and dancing, tons of food to eat, and endless opportunities for fun.

However, Vera Vixen was not at the Sawmill Soiree. Though dressed for a party in a full-skirted, emerald-green dress, she was standing on the other end of the millpond with her friend and attorney Chloe, gazing at the distant party across the way. She'd spent the last several hours trotting from place to place in her attempt to prove her new theory. Night seemed to fly in, the sky plunging into darkness long before Vera was prepared for it. She only had tonight—but at least she wasn't alone. She had her friends to help her.

"Why aren't we over there, again?" Chloe asked, extending her paw toward the glimmering party that looked like a mirage in the gentle ripples of the pond. Chloe was wearing a stunning black number that only a slinky cat could hope to pull off. "I packed this on a whim, but now that I know there's a party, it would be a real shame not to be seen in it."

"You look lovely. And we're not there because everyone else *is*," Vera explained patiently. "This is a unique opportunity to prove my innocence, Chloe. We have to seize it."

With nearly everyone attending the soiree, it meant the rest of the town was quiet, creating a strange sense of emptiness in the streets and the buildings. The streetlamps were still lit, casting a warm pool of light under each one. But most of the windows themselves were dark.

Chloe had not exactly been excited by the idea of walking into the woods outside town, but Vera pleaded with her until she agreed. "I need you, Chloe. We'll join the soiree as soon as we're finished. I can't do it alone, and you're my attorney, my last defense against injustice! Besides, Lenore won't come because she hates the place we're going."

"And *I'll* like it?" Chloe asked.

"More than her. You don't have claustrophobia. Lenore gets upset when she can't stretch her wings. And we're going to a cave."

"You've got to be joking. Is this some small-town gag?" The fastidious cat did not enjoy getting dirty.

"I'll explain on the way."

The North Track led out of town, narrowing as it wound further into the forest. For the first part of the journey, they could still see and hear the spectacle of the Sawmill Soiree at the other end of the millpond. Music floated across the water, startlingly loud and clear even from this distance. The amber glow of the bonfire reflected against the walls of the sawmill itself, making it appear even larger and more imposing than it usually did. Sparks from the fire drifted up into the windless night sky, until they could no longer be distinguished from the stars. Vera felt the instinctive desire to run that way and join the party. Yes, it would be fun, and carefree, which was exactly what she craved. But more than that, it would be safe. For at its core, the Harvest Festival existed to remind every creature of two things: first, cold and dark were on their way, in the form of winter; and second, no one had to face it alone. The silly contests and the soups and the soiree were all just saying, We're in this together. We have food and fuel, and we can make it till spring because we can rely on each other.

And so, to turn her back to the distant party, to head into the gloom of the forest . . . Vera reminded herself it was for a reason.

By the time the last light and music from the soiree vanished, the sky was an inky blue-black. Rags of thin clouds chased each other overhead, and the few winking stars provided no additional light. The moon wouldn't rise for a couple of hours.

Vera's thin green wrap flapped in the wind, which had picked up suddenly.

"What are we going to find out?" Chloe asked, looking a bit alarmed at the shadows of the massive oaks and the bulk of pine trees forming a wall. "And why do we have to go into the forest to do it?"

"It all comes down to the movements of Priscilla Renard on the day of the murder," Vera told her. "And afterward!"

"You really think she's guilty?" Chloe asked. "She's got gobs of money, so wouldn't she have paid someone else to do it?"

"No! That was the one thing she'd *never* do. Think about it, Chloe. Priscilla must have figured out Rick's blackmail schemes, and she knew about his cheating. She'd never trust another creature with something so very blackmailable as a hired killing. She'd want to do it herself."

"I guess. But where are we going? Are you suggesting she might be *in a cave*?"

"Detective Knox once revealed that he was using me as bait . . . well, sort of. He let everyone think I was a more likely suspect than he himself believed. He was hoping it would make the real killer more complacent, and maybe even make a mistake."

"Did Priscilla make a mistake then?"

"That's exactly what I'm going to test. I've set a trap for her!"

"You *what?*"

"Yup," said Vera, giving Chloe a conspiratorial grin. "I used Knox to get a message out to the metropolitan police because I've got a hunch that Priscilla has some connection there, someone passing on information."

"A mole?"

"I've no idea what creature, but I do believe that Priscilla Renard has been aware of every twist and turn in the investigation. And that's why I believe she'll show up here, to stop me from revealing the truth."

"I don't quite understand. Why would she appear in some forest cave and not in town?"

"Because I need to force her to admit her guilt, and she's not going to do that where there are witnesses. She will do it out here, though. Because she'll feel safe. And maybe she'll even try to silence me permanently. But I'm ready for that." From her bag, Vera pulled out a knife. "See? All set."

Chloe's eyes widened. "Yikes."

"It's quite easy to wield. Here, take it." Vera offered the blade to Chloe, who held it gingerly.

The cat gave a few swipes in the air, like a fencer. Then she said, "You really think you can fend a murderer off with this?"

"I don't have a choice," Vera said with a shrug. "This is a huge story, Chloe. And if I break the news, I'll scoop everyone. I'll be able to get a job at any newspaper I choose. Isn't it perfect?"

"You're using the murder of Rick Renard to . . . promote yourself?" Chloe asked, staring at Vera with an odd expression. "That's not what I . . ."

"What?"

"That's not what I thought would happen."

"Why not? I'm an ace reporter, and I'm innocent of the crime. But of course, the fact is that you always knew that. You knew that I was innocent for the simple reason that you also knew who was guilty. *You.*"

───────

Chloe's eyes widened, pupils almost round in the dimness. "Excuse me?"

"You heard me. I can't believe it took me so long to figure it all out. Once I had all the clues in order, it was obvious."

"Oh, do tell." Chloe now smiled, as if this were a play and she was enjoying it. She gripped the knife tighter in her paw.

Vera said, "There was something that you said when we were working through the initial suspects, and you mentioned how sorry you felt for Rick's wife for having to put up with his antics for so long. You said, *She's off to her knitting circle on Tuesdays and her playwriting class on Thursdays.* And I laughed, because that's something that always happens; folks filling up their evenings and weekends with the kinds of activities that you can only find in the city.

"But then Detective Knox was kind enough to provide me with some of the police reports he and his colleagues had put together regarding the murder. I read the account regarding Priscilla's movements around the time of the killing. Her household and business staff were asked about her whereabouts for the whole week, and it was revealed that she attended knitting circle on Tuesdays and a playwriting class on Thursdays. I didn't realize it then, but it swirled around in my brain just long enough. I remembered that you said *exactly* the same thing. Sure, a lot of creatures are into knitting and a lot of creatures are into playwriting. But to know both of her classes *and* the correct days that she went to them? You weren't making a general comment, as I first assumed. You were speaking from specific knowledge. You knew her schedule. But there was absolutely no reason why you should . . . unless you made it your business to know. Because you intended to kill Rick at Mockingbird Court, and to do so you needed to know not only his schedule, but that of those around him."

"Well, aren't you clever." Chloe sneered.

At this point, Vera realized that her old friend had given up pretending. She had killed Rick and framed Vera for it. And she didn't care that Vera knew. Vera felt a frisson of fear run through her, and her fur stood up on end. The fox had no idea why her former roommate could have hated her so much.

The cat started to circle around, preventing Vera from returning down the path they'd taken. "But I have to say, you were never as clever as you thought you were. Such a know-it-all, always thinking you had it all figured out. Acing all your classes, then getting the job at the paper, then having an affair with a boss to increase your influence . . ."

"That is not true!" said Vera. "I thought I was in love. My only crime was thinking that Rick was sincere."

"Oh, no. That wasn't your only crime," said Chloe. "You also kept the whole thing quiet, and that's because you knew it was wrong. You knew he had a wife. But when you left the city with no explanation, where do you think that left me? I was so worried about you! I went to your professors and to the other students in school trying to figure out what had happened. And yes, I went to the paper, and I found Rick, your boss. And he sounded so, so concerned. I agreed to meet him after work so that we might put our heads together and find out what happened, and that's when it all started to go wrong."

"What do you mean?"

"What do you think?" Chloe said. Her eyes were narrow slits, and she snarled as she moved closer to Vera. Her voice dropped. "If I had known what type of creature Renard really was, if you had *bothered* to tell me what was really happening between you two, then maybe I would've been aware of all his little tricks, and I would've been able to resist him! But the fact was, I was so concerned about you and the situation, and he was the only one who seemed to care. We kept meeting night after night. At first, we talked about you, but then we started to talk about other things.

And he was so charming, and it wasn't long before we started going out to dinner, or on other dates, and it seemed very exciting to be dating someone older and more experienced, instead of those idiots at school."

"Oh, Chloe. I had no idea," Vera said, horrified.

"It's not exactly as if it's out of character for him," Chloe snapped. "As I found out later, he did the same to any attractive young thing. We weren't together for long, a few months. Or maybe a little longer. He kept saying that he was going to leave his wife, and then we would be together all the time."

"He told me that too," Vera remembered.

Chloe made a snorting sound. "I'm sure that was his usual line, but of course he was married until the day he died. I wonder how many times he would've been divorced if he'd really meant it each time. A couple dozen? Closer to a hundred? We'll never know."

"Not anymore. Since you killed him. But I don't understand why. If you were angry over the affair, that happened years ago. Why wait till now?"

"It wasn't just the affair, Miss Know-It-All. While we were dating, Rick asked me to nip a few files from the city courthouse where I was working at the time. He said it was for background on some articles he was writing, and he didn't have time to go through all the bureaucratic rigmarole in order to get them. And it would be so easy if I just slipped a couple of folders into my briefcase when I left for the day.

"And I did it," Chloe said in a tone of disgust. "I think in those initial few months I would've done pretty much anything he asked. I was so stupid. When I asked him for the files later, he put me off, saying he wasn't done with them yet. And then he asked me to get a couple of others and said that he'd give everything back all at once. So . . . I went and I got the others, because I can't learn a lesson."

"What sort of files was he asking for?" asked Vera. The reporter instinct rose up in her. "If he didn't go through legal channels, he probably wouldn't have been able to cite them as sources anyway. So he didn't need them for articles, did he?"

Chloe shook her head. "They were cases that involved important city officials. They had a lot of information in them that never got into the public eye. There were notes from the district attorney about crimes they were pretty sure those officials committed, but they never put it into a formal complaint because they knew they didn't have enough evidence to convict. But the information was more than enough for Rick to blackmail those officials. He wrote one of them a note, and I happened to see it, which was what tipped me off to the whole scheme. The note was just a few words, but it was a phrase that I recognized from having read that file before I gave it over to Rick. Only someone aware of the crime would have known exactly what to say, and it probably seemed to the official that Rick would've known everything."

"What was the goal of the blackmail?" Vera asked.

"What do you think? Below the phrase was the amount of money required to buy Rick's silence. He must have been doing that to a number of folks in the city, every time he got a little scrap of information from his reporting or from sources like me. He funded his lifestyle with blackmail, which is why he didn't remain a lowly journalist for long. It's the same way he got every job he wanted, moving up the ranks despite not ever being qualified for what he was doing."

"But you couldn't tell anyone," Vera guessed. "Because you were complicit, and if you told anyone, you'd lose your right to practice law. And your reputation would be shattered."

"Exactly." Chloe sighed. "He knew precisely what he was doing the whole time. He went after me because I was an intern at the courthouse, not because he actually liked me. And he asked me to do the one thing that I would be unable to reveal later."

"Did he blackmail you, as well?"

"He didn't ask for money," Chloe said. "He just used me to get a little more information whenever he wanted it. And I had to do it, or he would expose my role in stealing the files and sharing them illegally in the first place."

"This went on for years?" Vera asked.

"He really encouraged my legal career," Chloe said with a wry grin. "It served him well to know a lot of folks who were able to access hidden information. For all I knew, there were a dozen folks just like me in similar positions around the city, all feeding him information to protect their own jobs and lives. If I'd waited a little longer, maybe one of them would've done the deed, and then I wouldn't be here now. But the fact was I was sick of waiting."

"But you did wait," said Vera. "Until I visited you again in the city."

Chloe smiled. "It was marvelous getting your letter. Like a gift from the past—a chance to finally end my nightmare and have a tidy suspect for the police to look for. I'd thought about killing Rick for ages, of course. I bet lots of creatures did; he was the sort to inspire dreams of murder. But when I knew you'd be in town, well, let's just say I was inspired."

"Inspired to murder. And to put the blame on me."

"Well, it was *your* fault that I met him in the first place," Chloe told her. "If you'd been a little more truthful in the beginning, you would've stopped a lot of this from happening."

"Yes, I made a mistake," Vera said. "But I'm not taking the blame for all the mistakes you made, or Rick made, or anyone else he was involved with made. You had a plan to kill him, and you did it all on your own."

"Yes, I did." Now Chloe looked a little bit smug. "It was a tidy scheme, and if I'd known how easy it would be to get rid of him, I would've done it a long time ago."

"And framed me."

"Yes, but I made sure to have a backup rube named Bradley Marvel," Chloe noted matter-of-factly, as if they were chatting about a mix-up for a grocery order. "Because I knew what was happening between him and Rick, and how often they fought. It seemed appropriate somehow to frame one incredibly annoying creature for the death of another. That's why I lured Rick to Bradley's apartment in Mockingbird Court when I knew that he and his little assistant would be out. Rick believed that I had managed to become Bradley's attorney and that Bradley was going to make an effort to buy his rights and take the series to a different publishing house."

"That would have gotten his attention," Vera murmured, looking toward the trees at the edge of the clearing. She could see no one. Of course, all sensible creatures would be at the soiree!

"Rick believed that I was willing to set up a meeting with Bradley where he could take the wind out of Bradley's sails once and for all, using the knowledge that I slipped him. Rick loves that sort of thing. You know, the dramatic meeting where he would reveal a secret that he wasn't supposed to know, lording it over everybody else." Chloe waved a paw disdainfully. "I let

Rick think that I was doing it to finally get free of the blackmail. I'm too smart to believe that was something Rick would've ever agreed to. Fortunately, *he* believed that I was dumb enough to think he'd keep his word. I manipulated him from the beginning of my whole plan."

"So how did you do it?" Vera wanted to keep Chloe talking. A cat who was talking wasn't a cat who was killing.

"I told him I would set up a meeting at Bradley's apartment and that Rick would be able to make a surprise arrival and catch Bradley off guard," Chloe told her. "I made a big deal about Rick needing to arrive at exactly seven minutes after the hour, and I told him he had to come in the back door that I would leave open for him so that the security in the lobby wouldn't be able to alert Marvel of another visitor coming up unexpectedly."

"He believed you?"

"Oh, yes, Rick bought it, of course. And he did exactly what I told him to do. At seven minutes past the hour, I was there at the door of Bradley's apartment. I had it cracked just enough to see Rick coming. I opened the door and pulled him inside before he could knock or say anything. Even then, he didn't suspect that anything was wrong. I told him that Bradley was getting something in the bedroom and that it would be especially shocking for Bradley to see Rick standing there in the middle of his living room when he returned."

Chloe chuckled at the memory. "I had Rick stand there facing the bedroom door while I slipped around behind him. I had the knife ready. It looked a lot like this one," she added, lifting up the knife that Vera had so generously offered her. "And I stabbed him in the back. He didn't make a single sound. He just crumpled down on the rug. The blood seeped out immediately. I have to say, it really did make a perfect crime scene. I arranged the last few details, including putting your notebook underneath the couch. I nipped it from your bag during our dinner—you obviously never noticed. But really, I assumed that they would focus on Bradley, and that was fine with me."

"Great that you had options," Vera said, backing up a few paces.

Chloe missed the sarcasm. She went on, "But I had *no* idea that Bradley would flee to Shady Hollow after he saw the body! That was . . . really rather wonderful. He looked so incredibly guilty. I couldn't have asked for more."

"So why did you start pushing me as a suspect? I know you were behind the anonymous tip."

"Well, I began to worry that the cops didn't really think Marvel was a likely murderer. But with your notebook and the knowledge of your connection to Rick, you made a very plausible killer."

"But you didn't set me up as well as you could have. You could've forged an incriminating note and left it with the notebook," said Vera.

"I was just being sensible. It's not smart to make things too obvious or to lock yourself into one path. I wanted enough suspicion so that the police would come to you as a suspect without feeling as if they were being steered that way. And if there was some reason that you could give yourself an unshakable alibi, then the police wouldn't immediately jump to the idea of the evidence being false. Clarity isn't always what you want when arguing a case. You want to nudge folks to come to whatever conclusion you've offered them."

"You must have been an extremely good attorney," Vera said.

"I would've liked to see you argue a case in front of a jury. But I suppose the only case you'll be arguing now is your own."

"Don't be silly, Vera. I have no intention of ever going to court or to jail. You're the only one who knows what happened, and if you can't *tell* anyone what happened, then the case dies here. With you."

Chapter 22

Vera stared at her one-time friend and couldn't imagine what must have been going on in Chloe's mind. A sudden gust of wind rustled the dying leaves in the treetops above and brought the sounds of music from very far way, the notes now dissonant and distorted. It would have been nice, she thought wistfully, if she'd just been able to enjoy the party.

"Chloe, let's be reasonable about this."

"I'm very reasonable. It doesn't have to be a dramatic show-down, you know," Chloe told her, still holding the long knife Vera had offered her earlier. She held it up menacingly and took a few steps to block Vera from dashing back to the main path. "I am not a violent creature by nature. And after all, we have a history. I don't want to be responsible for your death. Remember what I told you, Vera," Chloe said. "You could still run away. Leave now and you can start a new life somewhere else. Choose a new name, and you'll be able to do whatever you like. Go be a reporter somewhere out west, in a little town in a desert that doesn't care much about what happens beyond its borders. Or get passage on a ship crossing the sea. Explore a new land, one that surely has enough culture and beauty and interest that it will occupy you for the rest of your life. I won't say anything. I'll let you go, and I won't come after you."

"Even if I believed that, which I don't," Vera said, holding up her paws in a gesture of warning, "what makes you think I wouldn't come after *you*? I could easily write up all I knew and send it to interested parties in the city. The truth would eventually come out."

Chloe chuckled. "What truth? There is absolutely no evidence linking *me* to the crime. Just your wild suppositions. If you were foolish enough to share your theory with anyone, I would merely respond with the real artifacts and nasty stories of your youth, and the documented account *you* wrote about what transpired between you and Rick—the scandal he caught you in."

"But he didn't! He did it all, and I caught him. I just didn't understand the significance of it at the time."

"So you say, but the truth is what is most convenient. The city police need a murderer, and you make a lovely one. Whether you stay or go, your guilt will appear obvious. I am offering you a chance now, Vera, don't you see that? I'm doing it out of friendship."

"Some friendship," Vera said, now trying to shift to the side, a move Chloe halted with a meaningful slash of the knife in the air. "You framed me for murder. Was that an act of friendship?"

"Don't be tiresome," Chloe hissed. "It's all well and good to pretend that right always prevails. But that's just a dream. We have to deal with the world as it is, and this is your world now, Vera. A world in which evidence is stacking up against you, and there will be plenty of folks content to declare you the murderer. Can you imagine the headlines? The papers will love it. And there will be books written about the murder, and the trial, and the killer. My goodness, Fieldstone Books most likely already has one lined up, and Darcy will probably volunteer to write it."

"I'll tell them the truth," said Vera. "I'll tell them everything you did. Maybe you won't go to prison for the murder, but you'll face consequences. Do you think anyone will hire you as an attorney after hearing that you're a killer?"

Chloe smiled, her fangs flashing in the light. "I can't think of a better advertisement. Clients would come flocking, convinced I knew all the secrets of the justice system."

Vera took a step backward. "I'm sorry, Chloe. But I won't disappear just to suit you. The truth will get out, and if you want to stop me, you'll have to commit another murder to do it."

Chloe's eyes widened as she heard Vera's words. "You really would just toss aside our friendship entirely? You're not going to offer me the same courtesy I extended to you? You're not the only one who could leave, you know."

"You mean you would do the prudent thing and vanish into the woods, never to be seen again, at least not using your name?" Vera asked. She pointed to the forest, and the narrow path just visible between the trees.

"I believe in survival," Chloe said simply. "You can even tell the truth, as you're so fond of doing. Just give me a few days' head start; then you can tell the world that Chloe McKibben is a killer, and they can search for me as much as they like. I'll be gone. Consider it, Vera. It's an entirely reasonable option. You get to tell the truth, and I get to live free."

"I never wanted you to get hurt," said Vera, keeping her eyes on Chloe, watchful for any sudden moves. "I still don't want that." She shook her head slowly. "Would you promise me that you would never come back to Shady Hollow?"

"Of course," said Chloe. "You would never see me again."

"Okay, then. Go."

Chloe smiled triumphantly and took a few steps toward the path. But just as she stepped past Vera, she spun and lunged for the fox.

Vera instinctively threw up her forepaws to ward off the cat's advance. Chloe whipped the knife wildly, the blade flashing in the scant light.

"Chloe, stop! You can't possibly get away with killing me. Not here!"

"Of course I can. You're the fool who trusted me to come out here with you . . . but what are friends for?" The cat's eyes seemed to glow in the night, her malice no longer concealed.

"You can downgrade me to acquaintance!" Vera said, glancing around the woods as if help would suddenly materialize.

"Stop with your clever words, Vera. What happened to me wasn't a joke. It should always have been you!" Chloe hissed. She then plunged the blade downward at Vera's body, just where her heart was.

Vera gave a little grunt as she felt the pressure against her chest. Then she giggled. "Oof. Now I know what it's like to get into a real catfight. Yikes!"

"What the—" Chloe said, stunned by Vera's complete lack of reaction to being stabbed in the heart. She pulled back, raised the knife, and stabbed her again.

Vera looked down at her fur. "No blood. Which is good. This dress doesn't launder easily."

"You should be dying!" Chloe cried, withdrawing the knife. She stared at the pristine blade. "What is happening?"

The fox smiled at her former friend. "Prop knife. Used in the theater when a play calls for a fight scene. I borrowed this one from our local company. Callie, the director, lent it just for tonight. She didn't even ask why. But I guess that's what friends are for."

"You set me up!" cried Chloe.

"And you confessed."

"Too bad you're the only one who heard it. Fine. I don't need a weapon." Chloe flung the knife down and pounced toward Vera, who rolled to the side just in time.

Chloe was up on all fours, swiping at Vera with claws out, yowling.

The claws would be a problem. Backing up rapidly, Vera screamed at the top of her lungs, "If only Percy Bannon could save me!"

A second later, a massive shape burst out of the woods, trench coat flapping in the breeze. Bradley Marvel howled as he ran directly toward them. Chloe gaped at him as he ran straight past her and slammed *Vera* to the ground.

"Heroic, right?" Bradley whispered in her ear.

"Great job," Vera gasped back, her lungs being rather pressed at the moment.

While Bradley's mad dash distracted Chloe, Orville and Knox

rushed out of the tree line where they'd been in hiding. Lenore, too, swooped in from above, cawing loudly.

Orville never stopped running, and he bowled Chloe over in one swift motion. She was sent tumbling head over heels.

But the cat sprang up on all fours instantly, looking around wildly, searching for an escape route.

All she saw was a bear, a wolf, and a bison closing in on her, with a fox and raven circling. Vera retrieved the knife and was pressing the blade into the soft pad of her front paw, listening to the hidden mechanism as the blunted blade disappeared into the hilt and then popped back out.

"I really didn't think she'd fall for a prop knife," Lenore commented, landing. "Smart murderers always test their weapons."

Orville glanced at the raven. "You say that with such authority, Miss Lee."

"I read a lot." Lenore cackled.

"Hey, it worked, didn't it?" Vera said to them all. "I had to get Chloe to a location where she'd feel overconfident and in control. The prop knife was part of the psychology, as Detective Knox might say." Vera nodded to the bison.

"Indeed, Miss Vixen. And I also recall saying that sometimes it's helpful for someone to act as bait."

"You were all in on this?" Chloe hissed as the circle closed around her. Then Orville simply reached out and pulled her into a viselike grip.

Lenore said proudly, "Vera figured out that you were the only creature involved who could have known what the murderer knew. She gathered us together and laid out the plan."

"Against my better judgment," Orville added. "But I agreed because at least this plan didn't involve Vera running off into danger alone."

"Correct," Knox said. "We all ran together. Well, technically Miss Lee flew above and signaled the three of us as to your exact location. It made it easy enough to track you here and listen to the confession that Miss Vixen so skillfully extracted from you. First-class police work, for a journalist."

Vera curtsied to Knox. "Why thank you. I might even spell your name correctly in the article, Detective."

"We had a code phrase! I'm definitely using this in the next book," said Bradley excitedly.

Chloe spat on the ground, hissing, "I hate all of you."

"It's mutual," Lenore told her. "Congratulations, counselor. You just confessed your guilt—at length, I might add—to two police officers and two additional witnesses, one of whom is pretty famous! I don't think you've got much to look forward to in court, but there's always a chance for a gross miscarriage of justice." The raven gave a disgusted caw.

"Detective," Orville said, as he held the struggling cat, "the crime was in your jurisdiction. Would you like to do the honors?"

"Thank you, Chief." Detective Knox stepped up to the cat. "Chloe McKibben, you are under arrest for the murder of Richard Renard. You have the right to remain silent, though honestly that's a right you should have exercised a bit earlier. You will enjoy the hospitality of the Shady Hollow Police tonight, or until I see you escorted back to the city to face the consequences of your crime." He cuffed her, and then nodded to Orville.

The two gigantic creatures marched Chloe back down the track.

Vera watched them go. She took a deep breath, feeling the aftermath of the tension finally leaving her body. "Whew."

"I'll say," Lenore agreed. "Fake knife or not, that was terrifying to watch."

"That was so much fun!" Bradley beamed at them. "And great for research! Ooh, I can't wait to get back to my room at the inn to write some of this down. You ladies don't mind if I . . ." he gestured toward town.

"You go ahead," Vera told him. "We're locals. We'll be fine."

Bradley loped off, and Lenore gave her friend a long look. "Will you be fine? You went through a lot just now."

"Nothing a little dancing at the soiree won't cure!" Vera told her.

"You still want to go to a party? After nearly getting killed?"

"The band plays on, Lenore. And besides, it would be a shame to waste all the food. Joe made a special torte just for tonight."

"Oh, well in that case . . ."

The two friends returned to town, drawn to the cheerful din surrounding the sawmill. As they neared the party, Orville ambled up, announcing, "Prisoner is secure. Knox is staying there, just in case. Not that anything will happen. I've learned my lesson about easily unlocked jail cells."

Vera remembered the time when a certain beaver sprung a particular otter from jail, and she agreed that the new locks were better. She said, "Let's enjoy what's left of the soiree, shall we?"

They stopped by the long table where the Chitters family was serving drinks. Violet called out, "Sparkling water and soft cider on this side! Wine and beer and hard cider on the other side. For hot drinks, see the director himself!"

Howard Chitters, the director of the sawmill, waved his paw in a welcoming sweep. "Yes, I've got hot cider, tea, and cocoa over here!"

Vera felt chilled from her recent encounter, so she moved to Howard. "Hot tea, please."

"Sure thing," the mouse squeaked. "How about a cinnamon and clove oat milk chai?" He pointed to a gently steaming cast-iron cauldron behind him.

"Ooh, yes."

"Hot cider for me, please," Lenore added. "Cinnamon stick and honey? Why not?"

Orville procured a very large stein of beer, which Thad Chitters had nearly not been able to lift.

The friends found an empty table and sank down on the chairs, which were really just logs cut to varying heights to accommodate creatures of all sizes. Sipping her chai, Vera smiled as she took in the scene: dozens of creatures dancing to the lively music—fiddle and drum for now—and multicolored paper lanterns hanging from posts and strung along ropes over the large area cleared for dancing. At the center of their table, a candle burned in a punched tin cup, the pattern casting star shapes onto the wooden surface.

They heard from Barry Greenfield that the Harvest Queen contest revealed a surprise winner: Anneke Dutton, a mourning dove who'd joined the Shady Hollow Players just last year, while still a student herself.

A sheep approached carefully, burdened with a large tray filled with plates of something delicious and fragrant. "Dessert! Who's hungry for dessert?" the sheep bleated.

"What's that?" Vera asked as he got to their table.

"Joe's special. Pear pecan torte with brown butter icing. A slice for each of you, I assume?"

"You are correct!" Vera assured the sheep.

They tucked in and agreed that Joe had outdone himself. Orville asked Vera to dance, and they did. Then Vera asked Lenore to dance, and they did. Then Orville asked Joe to dance, and they did (others wisely cleared the floor for the two out-sized creatures). For the final number, everyone who could still muster the energy formed the traditional line—linking paws or wings or tails as required—and moved in a stately spiral until the whole dance floor was full. At the center, the Harvest Queen, wearing her crown of wheat, lifted her wings and wished a happy and peaceful autumn to all.

Everyone applauded, and the soiree was officially over.

"Oh, I'm so tired after all that. Plus, we caught a murderer!" Lenore sighed. "What a great night. I mean . . . not for you, I guess."

Vera shook her head. "I'm just glad it's over. But I can't think about what it all means until tomorrow. It is definitely time for bed." She chuckled, adding, "You'll have to come over and wake me up; otherwise I won't get up till lunch."

Lenore and Vera bid goodbye to several fellow partygoers nearby and joined the stream of creatures all heading back to home or den or nest. Lenore said, "You know, though, if you need any assistance with insomnia, I can recommend some truly bor-ing books. You'll be sure to drop off before you get through the first paragraph!"

"Oh, yeah?"

"Yup. There's this one written by a condor who's supposed to be a magnificent prose stylist, but I think that's just because no one managed to get through the book to review it. He talks about his feelings for four hundred pages."

"I'm getting drowsy just hearing about it."

"Oh, I've got more! In this other book, the author explains the evolution of the lute . . ."

The two friends headed down the narrower street that led toward Vera's den, laughing as they went. The deep autumn night folded gently in around them, peaceful and untroubled at last.

Chapter 23

The next morning, Vera managed to wake herself up, an accomplishment of which she was very proud. Both Lenore and Orville met her for breakfast at Joe's. Knox had been invited but chose to remain at the station to watch over their prisoner, now under lock and key in one of the two small cells, which normally held no one more dangerous than Lefty—on the rare occasions Orville kept him overnight on a charge.

After eating, they all headed to the police station. Vera had purchased a cranberry strudel and a "SawMillet" muffin for Detective Knox, along with a full mug of coffee. (Esme had kindly retracted her ban on serving Knox after learning about what had happened.) They met Darcy at the counter, buying her own breakfast, and the whole group walked out together.

When they got to the station, however, Knox wasn't alone. He was accompanied by a fox dressed in an exquisitely tailored outfit.

"And who's this?" Orville asked.

The glamorous fox turned around.

"Oh, hello. I'm Priscilla. You know, the horrible wife." She smiled sweetly, tipping her head in a coquettish gesture, holding the pose for a moment before bursting into laughter at her own expense. "I suppose I *was* pretty horrible to Rick off and on, though I can't say he didn't deserve it."

"Mrs. Renard!" said Darcy. "You came all this way? For what?"

"Detective Knox sent so many messages asking for information that it piqued my curiosity. And I wasn't doing much anyway. Society wives rarely do, besides commiserate with each other."

"You were aware of Rick's . . . er . . . activities?" Vera asked.

"Darling, how could I not be? Rick didn't know what the word *faithful* meant, whether in terms of marriage, or friendship, or in work relationships. I suppose it was just my luck that I was the one he married. My family comes from money, so I'm sure that played a role. But I always knew what he was up to. I can't tell you the number of times that he forgot to throw out the receipt for perfume or flowers that he bought for one of his flavors of the month."

"Wow."

Priscilla pulled out a small notebook, beautifully bound in red brocade. "After a while, I made it into a game to keep track of it all. I would make little bets with myself for how long this fox, or that cat, or that pretty little weasel would last. It was never very long though. I felt sorry for every single one of them. Rick only had one quality. He was a charmer. But the reason he did it was to get some benefit for himself. That's why I wouldn't give him a divorce. Soon after our wedding, I had already seen through his act, so nothing he did worked on me. And I didn't want some other innocent young thing to get snared by him, which is what would have happened eventually if he'd been free to marry again."

"But you didn't know about the blackmail and the bribery schemes?" asked Vera.

"Not until recently. I had my suspicions that he was up to something less than legal. I cut him off a long time ago, so he couldn't rely on my family's money anymore. But he was still living a much more expensive lifestyle than any of his jobs would've allowed him. I didn't know that it was blackmail until I started looking through his stuff. You see, I still have access to a lot of his papers and his accounts. And thanks to my family's financial status, the proprietor of nearly any bank is willing to do me a bit of a favor if I just wanted to take a peek, for example, at an account opened in my husband's name." She gave another smile, this one slyer. "He's not the only one who can be charming."

Vera said, "What made you come all the way to Shady Hollow? You could have just written back to Detective Knox."

"I came because I contacted the law firm where Chloe McKibben works, and they told me she was here. I was worried about what she might do."

"You suspected Chloe?"

"I knew she had an affair with Rick years ago and that they were still in regular contact. I had her name written down in my notebook. If I didn't do that, I probably wouldn't have remembered her. But as it happens, I added another name to that notebook not long ago, and I happened to flip through the names of some of his previous flames."

"But that couldn't be what alerted you."

"No. The thing that alerted me was Chloe McKibben contacting me two weeks before the murder, saying she needed to schedule an appointment with both Rick and me. She made up some nonsense about mediation, but she was very persistent about finding out both of our schedules, to such a degree that I found it a little bit intrusive."

"Wait," said Darcy. "Someone contacted me asking about Bradley's schedule. She didn't give her name, but it must have been Chloe!"

"They say curiosity killed the cat," said Vera.

"Or at least made folks suspicious of the cat," Priscilla agreed.

"So Chloe got both of your schedules?"

"Yes, I'm afraid so. You see, I didn't really connect her name to my little notebook until after the visit; it was just something that jogged my memory. And even then, I didn't really think it could be something as nefarious as murder. But that's exactly how she knew where Rick would be that day, and how she knew in advance that I would have a strong alibi. Though as it happened, I did have another reason to stop by Mockingbird Court that evening. I needed Marvel to sign a few forms for the publishing company. Brown likes all the *t*'s crossed and *i*'s dotted, and I didn't trust Rick to take care of things if I simply sent the forms along to the office. Unfortunately, Marvel was out at dinner at that point, which I didn't know until much later. So I simply left, with the intention of bringing it up the next time I saw Rick. Which turned out to be never." She gave a little shrug.

"I'm so sorry that you got involved with this," said Vera. "After all, he was your husband. You must have some conflicted emotions about his death."

Priscilla threw back her head and barked a laugh. "Oh, honey, there's no conflict at all. He treated everyone like trash. He'd be polite and kind if he thought you would be useful to him. But after he was done with you, or he didn't see your value anymore, he just ignored your whole existence."

"I suppose you wish you'd never met him."

"Oh, he could be charming too. And smart. And he wasn't so cynical when he was young." Priscilla paused, her eyes now distant, perhaps seeing the past, a different Rick. "I think he could have been a fine creature, if only he'd chosen to be. But he made every choice with his eyes open, and what are any of us, really, but the sum of our choices?"

"Some of us don't get to choose what happens," Vera said softly.

"No, but we can still choose what we do in response to what happens to us. Rick did, and every choice he made was calculated to serve him. So don't mourn what might have been. If it had been you who was killed, Vera, he wouldn't have spared a single thought for you."

Vera couldn't argue that point.

Priscilla brightened. "Anyway, now that he's dead, lots of folks will rest easier. What I should do now is reach out to every single name in my little notebook and invite them all to a party. I bet we would have a fantastic time celebrating. We could call it the Wannabe Widows Club."

"Oooh, that's a good name for a book," said Darcy.

"Do you want to write it?" Priscilla looked at the lynx. "You've been doing a lot of that lately. You'd be quite good at it. And you might enjoy writing something under your own name for once."

Darcy looked at her in surprise. "How did you know?"

"Rick was a talker. He told me because he assumed I wouldn't tell anyone, or he assumed I didn't care. But it's always good to pay attention. I knew what was happening at the publishing house because he would complain to me about it on those rare evenings that he actually came home. And as it happens, I have an interest in that publishing house, so I'll be taking over his position. At least for a while. I happen to know that you deserve a promotion. So . . . if you think you can write the *Wannabe Widows Club* while also working as a copy editor, that's fine by me."

"Oh wow," Darcy said. "Really? That would be . . . well, that's exactly what I've always dreamed of."

"Then I'll expect you to report to the office next week when you get back to the city. No sense waiting around, is there?" Priscilla stepped outside onto the porch of the station.

"No, ma'am!" Darcy smiled.

"Call me Priscilla."

Just then, someone spotted a bird in the sky, winging its way from the south—which could only mean news from the city.

"Oh, what now?" Vera groaned.

A massive golden eagle soared once in a circle high above, and then proceeded into its landing motions.

Priscilla shouted, "It's Maverick Brown! I can't believe he showed up all the way out here! He doesn't even like leaving uptown."

Vera watched as the massive bird descended in smaller circles, finally landing on the village green by the town hall. The crowd had made a large space in anticipation, and they all looked quite impressed by the majestic presence of this admittedly intimidating creature. Vera could understand why Maverick Brown—the wealthy financier and part-owner of Fieldstone Books—was successful in business, because it would be difficult to be in a boardroom without noticing him.

The eagle said nothing, and Vera observed that it was wearing a strange sort of vest that looked almost like it was made of straw, the golden hue blending in with its feathers.

No, it wasn't a vest at all, but rather some type of basket! Suddenly, a flap on the straw contraption popped open from the inside, and a small head appeared.

"Is that a . . . shrew?" asked Vera.

"Yes, of course," said Priscilla. "Maverick Brown is a true innovator. And so brave!"

Lenore said, "Wait, you mean the eagle is not Maverick Brown?"

Vera suddenly remembered none of the materials she'd read about him had revealed the famous creature's species.

The tiny shrew covered the short distance to the ground via a narrow rope. Then the creature looked up at the eagle and called out, "Clear! Go take a break. Be ready to fly in twenty!"

The eagle, evidently just a chauffeur, saluted with a single wing and strode off.

The shrew surveyed the crowd with the sort of calm that suggested he would stare down an army without blinking. Then he spied Priscilla and walked over.

"What are you doing here, sir?" Priscilla asked, obviously somewhat taken aback. "Did you follow me?"

"Wouldn't make much sense to follow anyone *else*, not when you're the one in the thick of things, what with it being your spouse and your family's publishing company in the spotlight.

I like a lot of things, including a good scandal. And I don't wait for problems to be solved; I solve them myself."

"Good philosophy, sir. One I like to follow as well." Already, Priscilla had regained her composure.

"Well, Renard, what have you got to report? It better be good because I don't want to think that I've wasted a trip."

"It's all sorted, Mr. Brown. Everything has been taken care of, and there is no tangible threat to the company. I dare say that there are some interesting new opportunities available to us, which may result in improved returns next quarter."

"So the business isn't going down in flames?" the shrew asked.

"Fieldstone Books will be just fine, because *I* am going to be in charge." Priscilla looked at the shrew defiantly, as if to say, *You got a problem with that?*

The shrew regarded Priscilla, then said, "One Renard for another, huh? Well, I'll take the bet that I'm trading up. I'm flying south for the winter soon, and I have no intention of fiddling around with a small-time company from a distance. You've got until the spring to impress me, Renard."

"Understood, sir. I have every confidence in myself," Priscilla said.

Vera decided that she liked this fox more and more.

Maverick Brown left with the same abruptness with which he arrived. The townsfolk chattered for a while about the incident (a large portion of the onlookers had no idea who he was, and wondered if it was another example of all the city folks who were flocking to Shady Hollow lately).

In the midst of this, Bradley had arrived. He'd foregone his usual trench coat and fedora, and paradoxically, his new look was even more incognito than the former. He approached Priscilla in a diffident way and said, "I hear that you're my new boss."

She nodded graciously and said, "I've already discussed Darcy's new role in the company, which means she won't be *assisting* you further. I trust you won't have a problem with that." The fox gave him a smile that was all teeth, and it was clear that she would not be putting up with any dramatics from the star author.

"Darcy knows what she's doing. More than I do most of the time," he added. "But here's the thing. Ever since I came up here and endured all this . . . chaos, I feel like whatever was blocking me is gone now. I've got all these new ideas for Percy Bannon! New plots, new characters, new places. I started writing all of them down, and I want to make them fresh and exciting, and I know everyone will love them if I get the chance to continue. Darcy covered for me very well, but I promise I'm back. I mean Percy's back. I mean, you know what I mean. I really believe the next Percy Bannon novel is going to be a hit."

Priscilla said, "Mr. Marvel, I am perfectly willing to read your next Percy manuscript, provided it is in fact *your* manuscript. I'll be in communication with you and Darcy throughout, and I expect results. You know, I read your very first novel again recently. *Weaver's Luck.* It's quite something."

"Well, that's something else I wanted to talk to you about. I know it's not my usual style anymore, but how would you feel if I made the next Percy Bannon novel actually . . . you know . . . good?"

Priscilla frowned. "You mean high-quality, sophisticated writing, with keen attention to the craft?"

Bradley scuffed a paw in the dirt. "Er, yeah. I know it's not exactly sought after, but . . ."

"Listen, Mr. Marvel. As long as the books sell, you can make them as good as you want." She offered a paw. "Deal?"

Bradley reached out and shook it. "Deal."

Epilogue

Vera sat at her own little table in her own little den, penning a letter to her mother. It was long—longer than any other communication she'd offered since leaving the city the very first time. This time, she wanted to give her parents the full story . . . her own story, and now it had a happy ending. Vera covered several sheets of paper by the time she was done, and she hoped it would all make sense to her family, who'd had to make do with scraps of information, hearsay, and guesses for too long. She signed it, then added a postscript, asking if they would care to visit Shady Hollow sometime to see the place Vera called home (she decided to save the mention of Orville for later).

As she was sealing the envelope, Orville walked through the

open front door, a bouquet of chrysanthemums in his paw. He offered them to Vera before taking a seat across from her. "They're on a boat heading downriver as we speak. Detective Knox put Chloe in cuffs and herded her to the brig himself. He didn't want any last-minute mistakes that might lead to her escape. I'm sure that once they reach the city, no effort will be spared to keep their newly notorious suspect safely behind bars."

"That's a relief," said Vera.

"The court case is going to be quite the show," he said, "I don't know if it'll be the crime of the century, but it's certainly the crime of the decade. And the fact that the murderer had not only a legal background, but connections to one of the most hated blackmailers in the city . . . well, there will be some interesting ramifications, whether important names get mentioned or not."

"Everyone likes a scandal," she noted wryly.

"You could go down to the city and tell them what happened—you know the details better than anyone."

"Maybe," she said. "But I think I'd rather not. I just wrote to my mother." She gestured to the letter. "It was so much easier to put it on paper than face my parents and speak the words, you know? I invited them to visit, but I think it will be a while before I can feel comfortable in my old city again."

"That's fair." The bear looked at her with concern in his eyes. "How are you really feeling? I imagine it will take you a long time to get past the shock of a betrayal like that."

Vera looked up at Orville, who had unexpectedly put the right word to all her feelings. *Betrayal.* Yes, that was the root of all her shock and sadness and anger. It wasn't even the fact that she had been framed for a murder. It was the fact that she had been framed by someone she thought she knew, and considered to be a friend, and who had not been content merely to frame Vera, but also had the audacity to march in and declare that she would save her from the trap that she had secretly set.

"It was a betrayal," Vera said. "I understand that in her own mind, she had reasons for doing what she did. And it's true that I didn't behave as well as I should have years ago. If I had been a little more clearheaded and hadn't panicked, then maybe I could've changed the way things shook out."

"But that doesn't justify what she did to you," said Orville. "She also made a choice. And she made it deliberately, and if she'd been successful, you would have suffered a lot worse than she did. I know it's easier said than done, but I think that the sooner you put all of this into the past where it belongs, the better chance you've got to feel differently about the future." He added, "I hope the flowers help too."

Vera gave him a wan smile. "Always."

"I've got to get to the station. There's a lot of paperwork, as you might imagine. But I thought tonight I might pick up dinner from the Bamboo Patch, and we can have a nice evening in?"

"That sounds perfect," said Vera. "I told BW I was taking the day off, but I also promised Barry I'd come in and help as he writes up the cover story on what happened. I don't think I've ever been the source for an article instead of a writer."

"First time for everything, I guess. Fortunately, Barry knows what he's doing."

"He does indeed. Barry was the first reporter to welcome me when I started at the *Herald*." Vera smiled at the recollection.

Orville excused himself, and Vera prepared to go to the bookstore. She'd promised to meet Lenore there to . . . well, to do nothing, which was a very appealing offer at the moment.

The bookstore wasn't officially open yet, so Vera was able to curl up in a chair in the history section and spend the next half hour or so in silence. She knew that Lenore was busy in the store because she could hear the raven flapping up and down as she moved from the top of the building down to the ground floor. Vera wasn't sure how much time had passed when Lenore appeared in the little alcove Vera had claimed, pushing a compact cart that was meant to hold books for shelving, but in this case, also held two mugs and matching plates each bearing a slice of cake.

"I thought you might need a little something. That cake is a new project by Joe and his son. Seven-layer spice cake with cranberry puree between the layers, which I thought sounded promising," Lenore said.

"Or did you think it sounded like breakfast?"

Lenore gave an amused cackle and offered Vera one of the mugs, which was filled with hot tea.

Vera took it and sipped. "Thank you."

"What are friends for?" Lenore took a sip from her own tea and then scarfed down a few nuts from the snack plate. She made herself comfortable on a bench near Vera's chair.

"I'm not too sure that I can correctly identify who a friend is anymore," Vera said. "I was so certain that Chloe was on my side, almost to the very end. How could I have been so deluded?"

"You trusted her. It would require a cynical or paranoid disposition to assume that everyone's intentions are antagonistic . . . until they actually give you a reason to think so. Then you know."

"I just feel like I should've realized much sooner. In retrospect, it all looks so obvious."

"Everything is obvious in retrospect," Lenore said. "When you're looking back, you only see the path that was traveled. When you move forward, you have endless options in front of you. It's impossible to know what will happen until it does. I'm just glad that Chloe's guilt was uncovered, and she's no longer a danger to you or anyone else."

Vera took another sip of the tea, which was strong and warmed her from the inside. "Did you have any inkling?"

"You mean did I guess right away that she was a vindictive murderer?" Lenore shook her head. "Nope. I will admit that I didn't feel especially warm and cuddly toward her, but that's true of most creatures I meet."

Vera laughed. "I've noticed."

"There were a few moments, I suppose, when I felt—not exactly suspicious, because that suggests I was aware of what I was feeling—but I felt just a bit wary of her," said Lenore. "Nothing too specific. Maybe it was something she said or just the way she looked at you when you didn't see her, or maybe what she *didn't* do in terms of building a defense."

"Maybe," Vera agreed.

"I think Mr. Fallow had some of the same ideas," Lenore went on. "Why else would he have made such an effort to verify her credentials? He would say that he was only carrying out his professional responsibilities, and I'm sure he certainly believed that at the time. But I think underneath all that, he was wary too. For him, it manifested as an urge to vet a colleague. At the core of it, something about Chloe's attitude worried him, and he wanted to do what he could to make sure you were safe."

"Yes, I remember I was a little surprised he'd bothered to inquire about her to the bar association. And he did warn me that it was perhaps not wise to be represented legally by someone who I considered a friend."

"I'll admit, I put most of *my* bad feelings down to jealousy."

"You? Jealous of Chloe?" Vera blinked in surprise.

"Well, I consider you one of my closest friends, but I only got to know you after you arrived in Shady Hollow, and your past was largely irrelevant. In fact, you usually made a point of not wanting to discuss it at all, which I respect. But then, suddenly, the moment you do get into a spot of trouble, this creature I've never met before arrives in town, proclaiming that she's here to make it all right and save you. And you were *so* happy to see her. After I learned how you'd been friends for years and had a bond that we didn't, well, I guess it ruffled my feathers."

"Well, the longevity of a friendship apparently is no measure of its strength," Vera said. "And for what it's worth, I do think of you as my best friend. Chloe was just my old friend. Emphasis on *was*."

Lenore held up her cup in a toast. "To friends."

Vera mirrored her gesture. "To *true* friends."

"Cheers to that!"

The End

Acknowledgments

This far into a series, it becomes tricky to express our gratitude to everyone in a fresh way. We've had such amazing support from friends and family, from our team at Vintage, and from the many booksellers across the world who have read Shady Hollow and then kindly hand-sold the books. Shady Hollow was born in a bookstore—Boswell Book Company in Milwaukee, Wisconsin, to be precise—and we are sure that the reason the books have found readers is because bookish folks in small towns and big cities alike recognized the voices of some kindred spirits. We remain forever indebted to everyone who told a potential reader, "I know what you're thinking, but *trust me.*" That trust is why real bookstores—on real streets with real trees, with real booksellers inside—remain vital to the culture of reading.

And this far into a series, it becomes tricky to say goodbye. But we must, for now, step away from writing about Shady Hollow, though it will always be there to read about. While our lives have both changed dramatically since that first wild idea, creating this world has been a pleasure and a privilege that we will never forget. We hope the books bring joy to those who find them. And we hope you, dear reader, will revisit Shady Hollow as often as you like. Perhaps we'll see you at Joe's (just up Main, by Walnut).

Always,
Jocelyn and Sharon,
writing as Juneau Black

P.S. It wouldn't be a mystery without a few cryptic notes, so . . .

Daniel: you know what you did

Jason: you earned your ladle

Caitlin: for jumping right in

Perry: pure dead magic

Brian: hail, the herder of cats

Nick: courage, milage, fromage

Mark: for driving us through the wilds of Minnesota and creating recipes for Joe's

Sarah Weinman: those reviews are something to cross off our bucket list

Read more from
Juneau Black

The Shady Hollow Mystery Series

"My new favorite comfort reads."
—Sarah Weinman, *The New York Times*